THE WOODLAND STRANGER

A FAIRY TALE WITH BENEFITS

The WOODLAND STRANGER

JANE BUEHLER

Published by Emily Jane Buehler
PO Box 1285, Hillsborough, NC 27278 USA
https://janebuehler.com

Publisher's Note: This is a work of fiction. Names, characters, businesses, places, events, locales, and incidents are either the products of the author's imagination or used in a fictitious manner. Any resemblance to actual persons, living or dead, or actual events is purely coincidental.

The Woodland Stranger (Sylvania Book 4) / Emily Jane Buehler
ISBN (print): 978-1-957350-08-0
ISBN (ebook): 978-1-957350-09-7

Library of Congress Control Number: 2023916371

*To everyone who didn't have
the words they needed to describe themself
when they were a teenager*

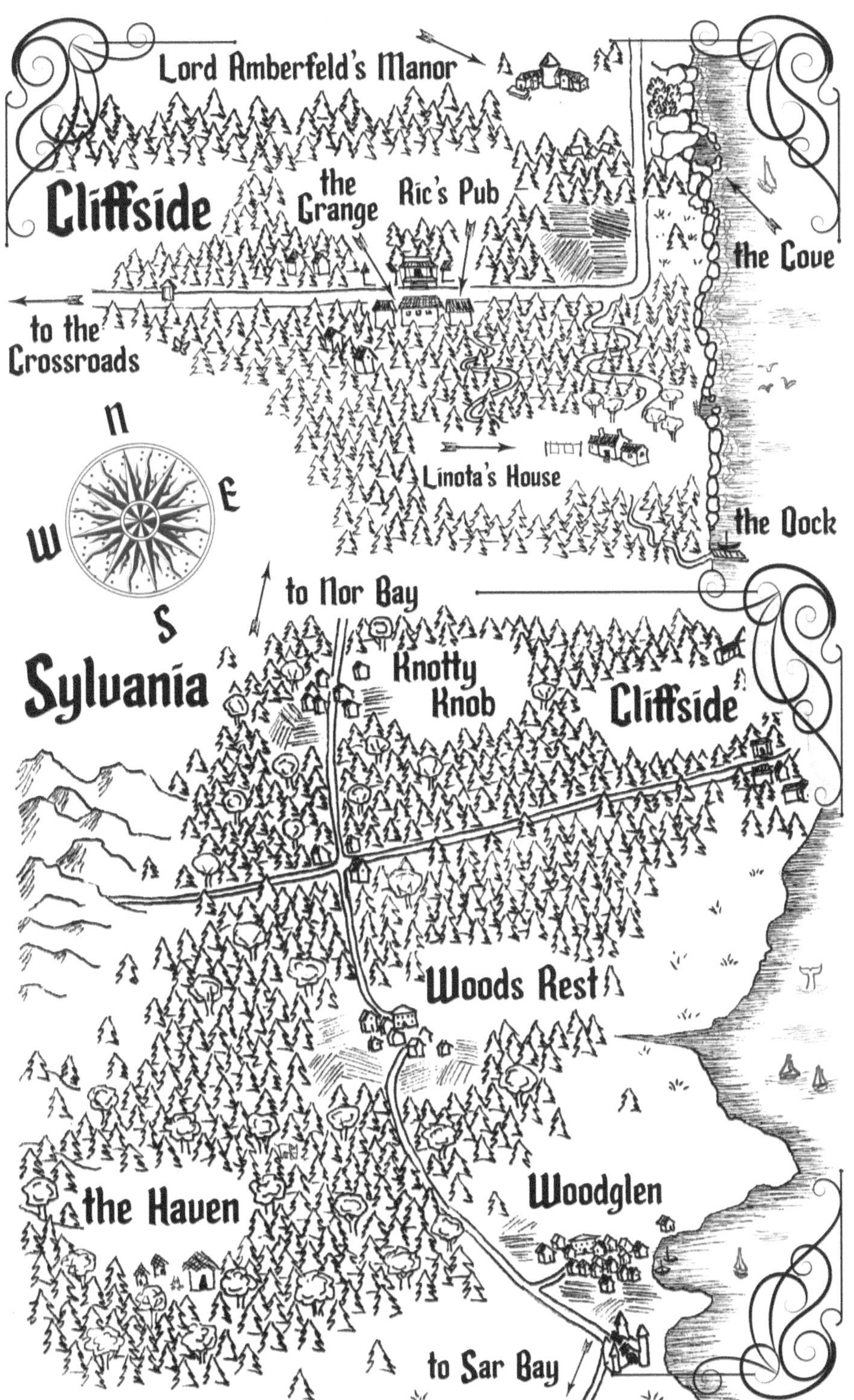

Lord Amberfeld's Manor
Cliffside
the Grange
Ric's Pub
the Cove
to the Crossroads
N
W
E
S
Linota's House
the Dock
to Nor Bay
Sylvania
Knotty Knob
Cliffside
Woods Rest
the Haven
Woodglen
to Sar Bay

Chapter 1

THE FOREST MIGHT BE THICK with trees, but they weren't full of the enemies Burne imagined.

He rubbed his hand over his mess of curls and took a deep breath, letting it out slowly. They were just trees, with birds singing from their tops and tiny green and yellow buds emerging from the branches. The forest air smelled sweet and earthy. He almost caught the feeling of hope Trillium kept saying was in the spring breeze.

The curtain rustled behind him and Trillium herself stepped out of the shelter. "Ready to go?" she asked with a smile.

Burne had been the tallest one in any room since he'd reached sixteen winters, and as an adult he was used to towering over anyone around him. But Trillium was tiny by any standard. She was many winters old, revealed only by the faint creases left after she laughed or the few wisps of gray in her dark hair or the carefulness she took in walking. Her green fairy eyes were as bright as ever.

"Ready? Is that a joke?"

"Oh Burne," she said.

"I don't want to fail again."

"I know you're trying your best," she said, taking his hand. "You just try again and if you come back tonight, it's no trouble."

"But I'm setting a bad example for the children."

"How is it a bad example to show them adults have fears and struggles and can fail at things?"

Trust Trillium to turn his cowardice into an uplifting lesson.

"You have some snacks?" She poked his backpack.

"And my shoes to wear when I reach the village." He'd gotten used to the fairy habit of walking barefoot since arriving here one turn of the seasons ago, but if he were returning to the village, he should dress like a human. "If I reach it," he added under his breath.

"And the present for your mother?" Trillium continued.

"Yes. Thank you."

When Burne had first arrived out here at the Haven, Trillium had helped him send his mother a message to let her know he was safe. He'd spent the time since living in the forest outpost with Trillium, her partner Woodbine, and the children they took care of, foraging for food among the undergrowth to supplement what they grew in the garden and maintaining the shelters the two fairies had built. Now he regularly scaled rock walls or tall trees, and he could walk through the forest barefoot. A turn of the seasons of living with a household of fairies and half fairies had given him more skills and confidence.

So why did the thought of returning to the village still make him shudder?

"Your mother will be glad," Trillium said, interrupting his thoughts. "I never knew a cook who didn't appreciate spring ramps."

"They're green onions, Trillium."

"They're ramps, young man! They're a forest delicacy."

He snorted.

"You see what your mother has to say about it."

Burne couldn't help smiling. His mother would probably *love* the weird onions Woodbine had packaged for him to bring her. He was eager to see her again. "I have them packed safely in my shoe."

"In your *shoe*?" Finally Trillium sounded disappointed in him.

"It's clean. I haven't worn my shoes since last spring."

But she was shaking her head. "When you do, your feet will smell like ramps."

"I hadn't thought of that."

Trillium tugged his bag off his shoulders and repacked the items.

The curtain rustled again and Alyss bounced out. At twelve winters, the top of her head reached Burne's elbows. She turned her big green eyes up to him.

"Want me to come with you, Burne?"

Did he? Maybe if Alyss were with him, he'd be braver. But what if they ran into Cap or Stone? What if the men knocked him to the ground with Alyss there to see it? What if they picked on *her*?

"No," he said. "You stay here and have your lessons. But thank you for offering."

Alyss frowned a moment, but then she squinted up at him, her lips curving. "You just don't want me watching you bumble through the trees."

Burne grinned. Alyss always teased him for this.

"Bumbling Burne!" she sang. "Cracking every twig and stuck in the brambles!"

"You've had seasons more practice than me," Burne said. "I'm much better than I used to be."

"You'll never be as quiet as I am."

She was probably right. Alyss and the other children were half fairy and had learned to walk silently from the start. The whole lot of them could hike through the forest without a single bird fluttering away. If they ever stopped talking, that is.

The children had been living out here in the woods since they were young. Before that . . . Burne didn't like to think about their lives before. They'd been taken from their human mothers by a tyrannical fairy queen and used as servants. The queen had been unpredictable and violent, and the fairies had been scared to cross her. But Trillium and Woodbine had smuggled the children out of the fairy caverns. They'd built the Haven, a sheltered spot deep in the woods where they could raise the children and keep them hidden from the queen. Their friend Thistle stayed behind and spread a rumor that the half-human children had grown sickly and died.

The queen, and most of the fairies, believed Trillium and Wood-bine were dead as well.

Trillium stood, lifting Burne's bag up toward his shoulders. He slipped it on. She glanced at Alyss and back to Burne.

"You know the King's Guard is gone," Trillium said.

"I know." Shortly after Burne had deserted his post, the villagers had overthrown the king, and the company he'd been a guard in had fallen apart. Cap was no longer his superior.

"Thistle says the new guards keep the peace—the humans call them peacekeepers now."

"I know." He shouldn't be scared to leave the woods. But knowing the Guard was gone wasn't enough to stop the fear.

"You'd better get going," she said, wrapping her arm around Alyss's shoulders. "The sun's climbing high." She reached out and gave his hand one last squeeze.

They were going to watch until he left. With another deep breath, Burne took the first step, then another. He followed the trail away from the Haven, nudging aside the thin branches that reached for him as he passed, and checked the sun for his direction east. He didn't really need to check, as he'd made this journey so many times now, but he grew more confident as his checks assured him he was heading the right direction.

His footsteps crushed softly on the thick layer of dead leaves as he cleared the bushes, walked out under the tall trees, and left the Haven behind. His pack was light and his muscles eager for the long walk. All around, new green leaves emerged from the branches, and a soft breeze whiffled through his curly brown hair as if the promise of spring was unfolding before him. When he reached the clearing where the stream tumbled down from the rocks, the dogwoods blossomed like snow and a stretch of clear sky opened above him.

So the dogwoods were blooming again . . . It was the exact time of spring when he'd begun his guard training a turn of the seasons ago. He'd been forced to join the King's Guard. Never mind that he'd never held a gun or even hit anyone—the idea he could pick up a gun and learn to shoot another person was preposterous. But what choice had he had? If he hadn't gone, they'd have come after him or his mother. Back then, the guardsmen caused all kinds of trouble for the villagers.

His mother had tried to keep him home by inventing ailments for him each time the Guard's recruiter came around. She'd said he wouldn't survive a season in the Guard. Her lying was embarrassing, but since he'd dreaded going, he'd let her do it. And it worked for a few moons, until the day when they would no longer believe her.

At the time, he'd decided to make the best of it. Maybe he'd grow stronger or tougher or faster during the training. Maybe he'd discover he could shoot a target a hundred paces away. Or maybe he'd be so awful at killing things that they'd let him work as a cook for the other guardsmen. He knew how to cook. He'd grown excited as morning dawned on the day when he had to report for training. Maybe he'd find a place where he belonged.

The shame of his first encounter with Cap still vexed him. An officer had pointed Burne and the other new recruits to a barracks and told them to claim an empty bunk. On the walk over, the men joked and smiled. Burne knew some of their faces from around the village. One man drifted to his side—Aaron, the son of fish-catchers. He was quiet like Burne, but he caught Burne's gaze and smiled just for him.

At the barracks, Burne found a bottom bunk in the corner near Aaron and quickly tucked the bed linen over the mattress. As the men dressed in their new uniforms, voices rang out in the hall and Cap came in with his arm around the shoulders of another new recruit, Stone. The badges on Cap's uniform showed seniority. They came straight toward Burne's corner.

"That bunk's taken," Cap said, shoving Stone forward. Stone grinned and handed Burne his bed linen. When Burne didn't move,

Cap added, "It was reserved. I reserved it." He bit his lip but failed to hide his own grin.

Burne had known Cap was full of it. The bunk had been empty and available. But his face heated and his mind grasped for a response and found none. Around the room, the other new recruits stayed quiet and averted their eyes. What if he fought back and it made things worse for him? And did it really matter if he had this bunk or a different one? Burne clutched the new sheet and his half-changed clothing and took his pack up. He shuffled to an empty bunk in the middle of the room. As he made up the new bed, Cap and Stone snickered behind him and the others continued to ignore him. Aaron didn't look his way again.

It turned out his mother had been right. He hadn't survived a season in the King's Guard. He hadn't even survived one moon. And now his guts were twisting into knots from remembering what had happened when he'd arrived and met the other recruits, and been assigned to Cap's squad, and how he'd tried to make friends and failed.

Burne inhaled slowly and let it out. Focus on the present, he reminded himself. That was what Trillium always said. The King's Guard was in the past and he could acknowledge what had happened and move on from it. The events of his past didn't have to define who he was now.

But somehow it seemed like they always did.

The moss pressed softly under his toes as he continued alongside the stream. The thick trees shaded the entire forest floor, blocking the bright sun glowing above, sparkling through chinks in the leaves and creating a diamond of light here and there as he crossed the woods. The breeze rustled in the branches above. The soft soughing mingled with the rush of the stream as it tumbled down from the distant mountains in its race to the ocean beyond the edge of the forest.

Just downstream of where they filled the jugs with drinking water, the ground leveled and he passed the pond that the stream flowed through. The pond was a speck compared to the ocean he'd grown up swimming in, but it was wide enough to swim short laps on the days when he needed some extra exercise. Around the edge of the pond, the water leaked out at a low spot and continued on.

Burne followed the stream down through the woods until it rounded a bend. He hitched his pack higher on his shoulders and turned away from the stream bank, heading due east in a straight line toward Woodglen. To keep his mind off the anxiety threatening to emerge, he listened for his steps as he walked and tried not to make a single sound. He made it ten steps in silence. He counted another ten. One, two, three—

A deer shot out of the bushes, leaping across his path.

Burne staggered backward, clutching the straps of his pack as the deer's white tail flashed. It had startled him just like the bear that time. His face heated, remembering . . .

Cap had rushed into the barracks begging for help, shouting about a bear that had Stone trapped up a tree. Burne had fallen for it like a rock dropped in a well. This was his chance to prove himself—to rescue Stone and be accepted by the men. He'd grabbed a long shovel and rushed out with Cap while the others trailed behind. Cap pointed him into the trees, where fierce growls rumbled behind a thick holly bush. But when Burne lifted the shovel and stepped toward the bush, the bear grabbed him from behind, its claws scraping his neck and belly as he screamed.

He wrenched himself free and fell into the holly as the men laughed. Stone appeared over him, grinning as he growled and brandished his fist. Long nails poked out—he'd gripped them to imitate claws and trick Burne into thinking he was a bear.

The deer had disappeared into the trees and the rush of its passing silenced. Burne's heart was pounding. Just a deer, he repeated, just a deer. He'd startled it, that was all. Maybe he shouldn't practice walking silently. Better to bumble along and let everything know he was coming.

Burne stared at his feet as he moved on. What would Cap and

Stone say if they saw him leaping in fright at a deer? He might've learned how to build shelters and survive by foraging in the past seasons, but he was still Yellow-Bellied Burne. A coward. No matter how much he wanted to be brave, he couldn't seem to change. Why did he always have to be scared of everything?

He continued toward the rising sun. After making this journey nine times, he was starting to recognize spots along the way—after the creek bend, the tall pine to the north marked the edge of the fairies' domain. He'd never been any closer to it than this, but Trillium and Woodbine had told him all about it. During Queen Oleander's reign, the fairies had lived underground. But last spring, as the humans had overthrown their tyrannical king, the fairies had ousted their queen. She was contained in the fairy caverns where she could harm no one. The fairies were free to live in the forest or even in the human village. Trillium and Woodbine could return home if they wished, and they no longer had to hide the children. They had talked with the children about if they wanted to find their mothers, but they didn't know how best to go about it.

Burne checked the sky and shifted his path. Even if he lost his way, as long as he continued walking east, he would come to the forest road. The road would take him to the village where his mother lived and where the former king had ruled from his castle. He walked on as the sun climbed higher before him and the shadows lessened. A squirrel leapt away from his path, skittered up a tree trunk, and clutched the branch. Its tail flicked angrily and it scolded him with a piercing little call.

Sunlight struck his eyes, a large patch of it beaming onto the carpet of leaves. The trees had opened up but more undergrowth thrived in the extra light, blocking his straight path. He wove between the trees and skirted a ditch where a massive tree had fallen, its dried ball of roots towering over him. The trunk had been neatly sawed off and taken away, probably by a villager to use as firewood. A trail began just beyond, taking him through the thickets and brambles. The chirping birds quieted as he passed, and a few times, a bird burst from the leaves along the trail and soared up to the high branches.

The air changed, losing the deep moistness of the forest shadows as sunlight warmed his face again. The sun had climbed to the top of the sky and beamed down on him through sparse branches. Wind whispered in through the trees, overtaking the rustling of the birds and other small creatures. Ahead through the trees was a wide-open space with waving fields of grain. Too open, not close and safe the way it felt under the canopy.

Don't, he told himself. Don't start to panic. He inhaled deeply and caught snatches of the ocean scent carried across the fields on the breeze. How he'd missed swimming in the ocean last summer!

His steps slowed and he swallowed. This was it.

He stopped two hundred paces from the edge of the forest and peered out. He'd angled himself through the trees perfectly—directly in front of him was the crossroad into the village. All he had to do was step onto the road and follow it between the cottages. He didn't even have to venture into the throng of shops. His mother's home was at the top of the town, close to the castle. Her wages as the castle cook and her frugality had enabled them to live in one of the nicer spots in the village, even after his father's injury and death. But how had his mother been getting by since the revolution? He should have been home long ago to find out.

The new village peacekeepers wouldn't know who he was. If they did recognize him, what would they care about someone who'd deserted from the King's Guard? They'd be more likely to detain him if he *hadn't* deserted.

But what if he ran into Cap or Stone? Had they left Woodglen when the Guard disbanded? Or were they in the new ranks of the peacekeepers? Or maybe they hadn't joined the peacekeepers but they lived in the village, getting drunk at the pubs as they used to. They were probably torturing puppies and kittens now that they didn't have him to pick on.

Ahead on Burne's left, something moved. He inhaled but caught himself before he jerked around, hearing Woodbine's lesson in his mind: Move quietly and carefully. Avoid startling the wildlife.

He turned his head slowly to peer through the trees.

A man knelt on the forest floor, inside the shelter of the woods. He was sitting back on his heels and staring off into the distance as if lost in a daydream.

Burne held his breath. Don't startle the wildlife, indeed. He'd expected a deer or a squirrel and instead he found a handsome stranger.

The man had a face like a statue in the castle garden, with his smooth jaw curved in sunlight and his neck in shadow. Where the buttons of his shirt opened, the rest of him looked hard as a statue as well. But his hair . . . Burne squinted. It was dark as Norlian coffee at the top, but as the strands fell away from his face, they shimmered like the morning sun on the ocean. Burne blinked hard, but he couldn't focus on the man's locks. In the filtered sunlight, they shifted from silver to green.

The man shook his head once as if returning from his daydream and dropped forward onto his hands. His hair fell across his face, blocking Burne's view. He crawled forward and reached out to take something. He was foraging, picking something as he crept across the leaves.

He was picking flowers.

Burne stepped behind the nearest tree trunk. His heart rate accelerated and his head started to get dizzy. He sucked in air and let it out, careful to be silent.

Why was he hiding? The man didn't seem dangerous—he was picking flowers, for skies' sake. And he wasn't anyone Burne knew. Burne could continue toward the road, and when the man noticed him, he'd wave and call good day and keep going on his journey. Villagers greeted each other all the time.

But his heart was racing already and besides, he didn't want to call good day and move on. He wanted to stop and talk. And if he stopped to talk to the stranger, he'd fail. Whenever this happened—whenever he met someone he found attractive—his words twisted in on themselves and refused to be spoken and his mind went blank. He'd say something foolish and embarrass himself, or stand silent like a dolt, gaping at the poor man.

He gasped in more air. He could do this. He peeked around the edge of the tree.

The stranger was gone.

Burne panted and sagged against the tree trunk. He scanned the woods all about but nothing moved. The space where the man had knelt was empty except for a few of the little flowers he'd been picking—the little purple hyacinths that bloomed first in the spring.

Chapter 2

BURNE LEANED ON THE TREE with his heart drumming like a charge of galloping horses. He waited to catch his breath but it wasn't happening. He kept seeing the handsome stranger and imagining what he should have done differently—he should have walked over and said hello like a normal person instead of hiding behind a tree trunk like a jittery squirrel—and the more he thought about it, the more disappointed he felt in himself.

Forget about the stranger, he told himself. He had a reason for coming here today—to visit his mother. His pulse wasn't slowing in spite of all the deep, calming breaths he was taking. He could hear Trillium's guidance: he closed his eyes, took another deep inhale and held it, slowly let it out, and focused on the sounds of the forest. Only he couldn't hear much of the forest over the buzzing in his head.

He opened his eyes and left the safety of the tree, marching through saplings toward the road. The panic welled up. It wasn't like the first time it had happened, back when he'd first escaped the King's Guard—the shaking and dizziness and the tingling all through his body, and his heart lurching about in his chest, leaving him numb and frozen for an hour. He didn't have attacks like that anymore. Only the dread came now. But as he neared the edge of the forest, the dread grew worse and worse, clawing its way out of his heart and across his chest toward his shoulders. What if he passed out again? What if he left the trees and passed out on the road, out in the open?

He gulped in more breaths but he couldn't manage to hold them, taking one quickly after another. He was halfway to the road from where he had first stopped, still among the trees. But now a deer was watching him from the grassy stretch alongside the road and it didn't seem afraid. It stood there, away from the safety of the forest and out in the open, watching him. Like the deer was mocking him, saying, Even *I* can step onto the grass to graze without getting all hysterical about it. Burne was more scared than a blasted deer, for skies' sake. And he was about to pass out, the dread all around him and his breathing fast like a panting dog's.

Maybe he should turn around and go back.

Burne stopped inside the edge of the forest and leaned his forehead on the scratchy bark of the nearest tree. The bark was rough under his fingertips. He caught his breath, trying once and again until he was able to take a deep one all the way down. His feet pressed into the spongy ground between the tree's roots, and the damp earth scent wafted up into his next deep inhale.

He could just go back. He didn't have to do this. It meant failing again but no one would say anything mean about it. They knew he was trying. He could try again, maybe even tomorrow.

But what if they *did* give up on him? He couldn't go on forever doing this. Even Trillium must have a limit where she'd lose patience with him. And if he couldn't do this, he'd never be able to do anything! What if he lost his chance—what if he gave up this time and another chance never came his way? Just like with the stranger: Burne hadn't approached and now the man was gone and Burne might never see him again.

Burne lifted his head from the tree trunk. His breathing was steady but the dark, heavy feeling still gripped him. If he continued out of the trees, the fear would take him and he'd be useless until it passed. So, he would turn around and go back to the Haven. Even just thinking about turning back made the tightness in his chest ease.

He slowly inhaled the fresh air from outside the forest, trying to catch the salty tang, and exhaled it all the way out. The deer hadn't budged, staring at him with its big brown eyes. He tried to scowl at it, but it was just an innocent deer, who was probably wishing he'd get on with things and leave so it could resume eating the spring grass. The deer blinked. Burne shook his head and turned back.

Burne kicked at a low branch as he retreated into the woods. The birds and other small creatures moved around him but he was apart from them, all alone walking through the trees. Trillium would say something flowery, like he was never alone because her well-wishes accompanied him, and he might have believed it when he set out this morning, but whatever positive thoughts had accompanied him had worn out somewhere along the trail.

What had gone wrong? He hadn't even been too nervous this time, which had made him hopeful he'd be able to avoid the fear that welled up each time he tried to leave the trees. Maybe if he hadn't been startled by the man picking flowers, he'd have succeeded today.

A few minutes passed as he walked. Already he felt back to normal inside. Should he turn around and try again?

He kept heading back to the Haven. He couldn't handle going through all those emotions and nerves a second time in one day.

He retraced his steps as the sun moved over his head until he was again following the sun, this time as it headed down the western sky. His pace dragged as he postponed his arrival. Trillium would say his failure was no big thing. But what would he tell Alyss and the other children?

As he walked, the stranger he'd seen kept returning to his mind. Who was he? He hadn't resembled any of the villagers Burne remembered. He'd have noticed if any of the shopkeepers or fish-catchers had been so handsome. Had the stranger arrived in the village during the past seasons while Burne was living in the forest? The revolution must have brought changes to the village, and probably lots of new people lived there and traveled through.

But something was different about the man—Burne couldn't

picture him raising chickens or tending fields or heading onto the bay in a fishing boat. Farming and fishing were the two occupations most villagers practiced to make a living in Woodglen. The stranger had been picking wildflowers. Was he some kind of herbalist? Or did he just like flowers?

"Next time," Burne whispered, "I'll ask him."

What would he say? He tried to imagine the scene. It was another trick Trillium had taught him, this one to stop himself from getting overwhelmed and tongue-tied. He could think through a situation he might face and practice what he'd say.

He didn't know how to flirt. But he'd watched the footmen in the castle flirt with each other or with the maids—it always started with smiling and banal talking, and sometimes the other person ignored it but sometimes they didn't. The risk of being rebuffed wasn't unique to him.

And sometimes it worked out. How many moons had he watched Jim make inane conversation with the man who delivered vegetables to the castle (while Burne did all the heavy lifting, carrying the overloaded crates into the kitchen) and those two had ended up bonded. And Trillium had met Woodbine while gathering herbs in the forest when they were young, and their friendship had blossomed into a romance as they grew up. Anything was possible.

Next time he saw a man he wanted to talk to, he would come out from behind the tree trunk—or no, wait, he wouldn't even be hiding in the first place. He'd be walking through the forest and he'd spot the man gathering flowers or whatever else he'd be doing that day, and Burne would simply call out, "Hello." That was all he needed to say. Hello. It was one word. He could get one word out without flubbing things.

And maybe the man would frown and wave him on, or narrow his eyes in derision. And if he did, Burne would flush hot with embarrassment and stumble away. But maybe the man wouldn't— maybe he'd be friendly. And it was better to try, right?

"Next time I see him," Burne said aloud, "I promise I'll talk to him." He stared up at the sky, all pale blue and hopeful, at least according to Trillium. He didn't feel any of that hope at the moment, but still he said, "Give me another chance."

He should focus on his first task of leaving the forest. Do that first and then worry about talking to handsome men. But if he had talked to the man, he'd never have turned back today. One success would have helped the other. Anyway, it was out of his hands.

Burne trudged through the woods, his mood immune to the chirping birds and the soft sunlight. A branch snapped behind him and he whirled about to find another deer. It stood frozen in the path where he'd walked and stared at him. Cap and Stone came into his head again, throwing stones and shouting. Burne turned away and left the deer alone.

After that, each time he heard a crackle of leaves or the rustle of a bush, he expected a deer, and they no longer startled him. He'd never seen so many deer as on this walk—it must be the springtime and the promise of tender shoots drawing them out to forage in the middle of the afternoon. He spotted one drinking at the creek as he climbed up alongside it and another by the pond. With all the swimming he'd done, you'd think he'd have seen a deer at the pond before now. Another deer was rubbing its antlers against the rough bark of a tree in the clearing where the creek first emerged over the rocks.

The land rose more steeply. The sun dipped toward the tops of the mountains, which Burne glimpsed through the trees. And finally tiny trillium flowers bloomed up through the leaf litter. His steps slowed.

The forest floor hardened into the path to the Haven and the leaves under his feet no longer swished as he walked—because the leaves weren't real. Trillium and Woodbine had hidden the path with one of their fairy illusion spells. The path resembled the rest of the forest floor, covered with dead leaves and clogged with bushes, but Burne knew the path was there. The trillium flowers were real, though, along with the woodbine climbing up the slender trunks he passed. As Trillium's and Woodbine's name plants, these plants gave their spells more power. The spells hiding the Haven from humans were remarkable.

Burne followed the path to where it ended at a wall of boulders, right where he had stood beside Trillium that morning.

He closed his eyes. Not looking at where he was going was the easiest way for him to get inside the shelter because if he looked, he would see the illusions. Some of the boulders were real, but others were mirages hiding the entrance. Seeing them made it harder to convince his mind they were not there, and he'd feel the rock if he reached out and touched it. But if he closed his eyes, he wouldn't see the false boulders and become confused.

He patted his hands along the biggest boulder, following the shape with his steps. Walking this path with his eyes closed was easy now because he had done it hundreds of times. The rock curved away from him and he walked down the cool, narrow space between the shady boulders. The first curtain brushed his face. He pushed it aside and smelled the scent of baking bread and the smoke of a candle as warm air touched his cheeks. He passed under the other curtains.

Burne opened his eyes.

The front room was nearly empty, with only a rough, low wooden table surrounded by cushions on a woven rug, and a pair of chairs in the corner. Half the walls were rock, the backs of the boulders shielding the entrance, and a curtain covered the opening between them. At the edges of the rocks, wooden walls completed the room, and the thatched roof blocked out the light. This room was always dark. At the far side, late afternoon light spilled from the doorway to the kitchen.

Trillium came through the doorway. She must have seen the disappointment on his face because she came to him and took his hand, peering up at him with concerned eyes. Glancing down into her kind face, Burne knew she'd forgive him for having no courage. She wouldn't even see it that way—she'd find a way to make today's failure into another step on what she called his "journey."

"I'm sorry I wasted the ramps," he said.

She laughed. "It's no matter. We'll pickle them and you can give them to your mother in a jar. What happened?"

"Same thing as always."

She held his hand and waited.

"I tried everything, deep breaths and all that. But it happened again—this feeling in my chest like I was going to pass out. I was too scared it would get worse if I kept going."

"You know if it did get worse, it wouldn't kill you."

"I know." Back when he'd had full-blown attacks of anxiety, Trillium had explained how they would pass if he waited. She'd also muttered a lot about humans and their abominable practices. Trillium said the trauma of his time in the King's Guard might be the cause of the attacks. But it hadn't caused him to be a coward—he'd always been one.

"Are you sure you don't want one of us to go with you?" she asked.

Burne shook his head. He didn't want her trekking across the forest all morning only to watch him fail. "Something else happened," he mumbled. He wasn't sure why he was telling her. But she'd been like a second mother the past seasons and he needed to tell someone.

Trillium waited, focused on him.

"There was a man in the forest."

"Here?" Her eyes widened and she gripped his hand.

"No, no, nothing like that."

Her hand relaxed on his.

"He was near Woodglen at the edge of the forest. He was . . . I think he was picking flowers."

"Did you talk to him?"

"No."

Now her brow furrowed.

"But I wanted to," Burne whispered.

A smile played at the corners of Trillium's lips. "So he was handsome, I take it?"

Burne nodded.

"Oh, Burne," she said with a sigh, pressing his hand. "I know it's hard but you need to believe in yourself. Someday you will."

"I wish I had talked to him."

"Next time you will. He didn't see you?"

Burne shook his head. "He disappeared."

"Disappeared?" A note of tension crept into her voice.

"I mean, he must have moved off. I hid behind a tree when I first saw him and when I looked back, he was gone."

"Are you sure? You're sure you weren't followed?"

"No, I didn't see him again. Just a lot of deer."

"A lot of deer?" Her eyebrows lifted.

"You know. Grazing and drinking and . . ."

"And what, Burne?"

Burne swallowed. "Uh, watching me?"

"Did any of these deer run away?"

Something was wrong but he couldn't figure out what. "No?"

Trillium dropped his hand and strode to the curtain. She whipped it aside. The stranger from the forest was standing outside.

Chapter 3

THE STRANGER STOOD IN THE doorway. A grin spread across his face. "I knew you weren't dead," he said to Trillium.

"Grape Hyacinth."

The grin faded. "It's Gray now."

Trillium slowly shook her head, her face serious. "You're not to tell anyone."

"That you're living in a boulder castle in the woods? Why would I? Is Woodbine here with you?" The man—Gray—peered over her head into the dark room but he didn't appear to notice Burne, who'd frozen like one of the deer he'd seen earlier. Gray held a bunch of the purple hyacinths he'd been picking. The little ones—grape hyacinths. And fairies were named after plants. Trillium had called him Grape Hyacinth. Was that his real name?

Trillium reached for Gray's arm, drawing his attention back. "Promise."

"What?"

"Swear you won't tell."

"Fine. I swear. Ow!"

Trillium's fingers had tightened on his arm. She tilted her head.

Gray huffed. "I swear on every flower in the forest I will not tell anyone you and Woodbine are living in a love nest in the western woods—"

She gripped him harder.

"—or anything I see."

"Good," Trillium said, dropping his arm. "Since you're here, you might as well be useful. Go make dinner with Burne."

And then Gray noticed him.

And smiled.

He had the same green eyes as Trillium, Woodbine, and the children. He was definitely a fairy.

Well of course he must be a fairy if he knew Trillium already, and his words indicated he did. Close up, Gray looked every bit as beautiful as he had that morning, and his hair was just as strange. But now, inside close quarters, he seemed to suck all the air from the room and leave Burne struggling to breathe. As Gray's lips curved higher, Burne's insides twisted along with them. He pulled in another breath.

Burne was staring. And his face was hot and his mouth was sagging open. He shut it and swallowed as Gray stepped toward him. Gray was barefoot. Burne hadn't noticed that this morning.

"Dinner, Gray," Trillium repeated, watching them. "Not . . . dessert. Burne, make sure he helps you—"

Gray's smile faded. He frowned down at Trillium. "I'll help. I'm different now."

"Then prove it," Trillium hissed, and he scowled. But only for a moment. He swiveled back to Burne.

Burne lurched to the doorway, his ears hot. He swore he could feel Gray's gaze on the back of his neck. He entered the kitchen with Gray behind him.

Next time, I'll talk to him.

He'd promised himself.

Burne turned to Gray inside the doorway, and his heart clogged his throat.

"Hello," Burne said.

"Hello yourself," Gray replied, smiling again. "You're Burne?"

Burne nodded.

"And you live out here with Trillium and Woodbine?" Gray surveyed the kitchen and Burne followed his gaze. Afternoon light poured in the large window onto the sturdy table that filled the center of the room, and the buckets of water Burne had carried from the stream lined one wall. Twists of drying onions hung from the rafters.

"For now," Burne said, watching the light catch on Gray's face. Gray was a little shorter than he was, and his chest filled his shirt better. His hair looked even stranger close up. It was shaggy and dark but it really did have silvery tips like he had seen earlier, although they no longer shifted to green—the color must have been a trick of the light in the trees. His shirt was dyed a pale blue color that Burne had never seen in clothing. The bunch of hyacinths in his hand was starting to sag.

"Here," Burne said, taking down a clay cup. He reached for the dipper in the nearest water bucket, filled the cup, and held out his hand to Gray.

Gray glanced down at the flowers. He passed them to Burne, and their fingers touched for a moment. Burne ignored the spark of the touch and found a knife, which he used to slice off the bottoms of the stems. He stood the flowers in the cup and pushed it to the center of the table.

"Thank you," Gray said. "That should help them . . . stiffen up."

Burne blushed.

"I have to say, you did that exactly right. My sister has a flower shop in Woodglen so she's always nipping the ends off flower stems and dipping them in water."

Somehow, everything he said sounded vaguely suggestive. He was talking about his sister, for skies' sake, not trying to suggest anything. But his voice rolled over Burne in a way that felt like a seduction.

"Woodbine showed me," Burne said. "She teaches nature lessons."

"I'll bet she does." Gray's smile faded and his green eyes widened. "You're not their love toy, are you?"

"Their *what*?"

"Their— Never mind. I'm dying to hear how you ended up here."

The memories washed over Burne—joining the King's Guard, the mocking and abuse, running into the forest . . . He couldn't tell Gray all that.

But Gray was waiting.

He'd promised himself he'd talk to Gray. He had begged for another opportunity, and he'd been granted one. He had to talk.

"I was lost in the woods?"

"You lived in Woodglen."

Burne wet his lips. "Yes."

"And you got lost in the woods."

Burne swallowed and nodded.

"And Trillium found you."

He nodded again.

"And she forced you to come live here and use those big muscles of yours to carry water for her and Woodbine, and she hasn't let you go home since."

"No!"

"You tried today. You finally escaped their clutches and made it all the way to the edge of the forest. You gazed out at the road to the village, desperate to return."

Burne's face flushed again. "You saw me?"

"And then their spell kicked in, trapping you in the forest, compelling you to return."

"Fairy spells don't work that way," Burne said. "You—"

"Some of them do," Gray said, and smirked.

"You saw me?"

Now it was Gray who merely nodded. His smirk faded into the slightest smile.

"You followed me back here? But I didn't see you."

"Yes you did. You just didn't realize it."

"What do you mean?"

"I can tell you, but I'd rather show you."

Show him what? "Okay . . ."

"Are you ready?"

"For what?"

Gray turned into a deer.

Burne staggered back into the table and caught himself. He blinked and Gray was back, grinning again.

"You can turn into a deer!"

Gray shook his head. "That's impossible. It's just an illusion. Look."

Gray held out his hand and as Burne watched, it shimmered and turned into a furry deer leg ending in a pointed hoof.

"It's still my hand," Gray said. "It just looks like a deer hoof to you. Feel it." He held his hoof-arm toward Burne.

Burne reached out. His fingers hovered over the hoof. He touched it. At first, he felt the smooth hard surface, but it wasn't quite right. He was touching fingers, warm fingers that closed around his. The hoof faded and Gray was holding his hand.

Burne gazed at their hands as Gray's fingers twined into his. They were rough from work, like his, but Gray held him gently. He shivered as Gray's touch seemed to run all through him, and his mind must have shut off and all he could do was stare at their hands. What would Gray do if he looked up? Nerves shot through him as he wondered it.

"Dinner, Gray!" shouted Trillium from the front room.

Gray slowly pulled his hand away from Burne's. "Come on. We'd better get to work or she'll get out her fairy whip."

Burne's head snapped up, his eyes widening.

Gray was smiling again. "Burne, I'm just teasing." He pursed his lips and regarded Burne. "I'm always teasing. I can't help it. You'd better get used to it." He lifted his eyebrows once and turned to the table. "So," Gray said, placing his hands on the wide boards. "Dinner."

Burne jerked into action. He turned and pulled items off the shelves—onions and barley and a pan and a knife. This was familiar at least. When he'd arrived last season, and Trillium and Woodbine had found out that his mother, Kate, had run the castle kitchen, they'd put him in charge of preparing the Haven's meals. Cooking out here was a lot different than helping his mother in the large kitchen at the castle. Here they had only what they gathered and grew, supplemented by a few supplies sent by Trillium and Woodbine's accomplices at the fairies' village. But he must have learned something from helping his mother all those seasons because he managed to make meals everyone ate.

Of course, they ate soup a lot, but no one ever complained.

Gray was waiting on him. Talk, Burne commanded himself.

"Why did you follow me?" he asked as he continued to gather supplies.

Gray shrugged. "I was curious." Gray waited only a moment before continuing. "I thought you'd be living in a compound out here with lots of guns and animal skins."

"Me? I hate guns."

"Well, now I can see that. But at first glance, with your hair all tangled, coming in from the wild—you seemed like a brute."

"I did?"

Gray was smiling. He was teasing again. Burne liked how comfortably Gray filled in the spaces, even if he was speaking nonsense.

"How come Trillium and Woodbine never turn into deer?" Burne asked, pushing his hair back from his face. It *had* gotten unruly in the past season. "Or pretend to?"

"They probably could if they practiced."

"What made you practice *that*?"

"It was different for me. I've always been talented with illusions."

"They used illusions to hide this place."

"That's different," Gray said. "They used spells and plants to help—plenty of trillium and woodbine flowers, I'm guessing. Without those things and using our own magic, we can change only ourselves."

"So *you* can change into anything you want?"

Gray shrugged. "Pretty much."

"But you couldn't change something else the way they've done with the boulders out front."

"I can change anything if I'm touching it," he said, "but I'm not so good at casting illusion spells that last when I'm gone." His brow furrowed. "That might be a metaphor for my life."

Burne didn't follow Gray's thinking. Should he ask what Gray meant? It might be too pushy. He stoked the fire in the hearth before turning to the shelf with the jars of herbs and selecting his favorite soup mix, mulling over everything he'd learned about fairies in the past season. Could Gray communicate with animals? Could he turn invisible?

Gray was staring at the growing pile of ingredients. "Apparently you all work up quite an appetite out here," he said.

Burne shook his head. "There are ten of us."

"Wait, those two have *ten* love—"

"No! Whatever you're going to say, no." Burne rolled the onions across the table and handed Gray a knife. "Cut these. They make me cry."

"Yes, sir," Gray said.

Burne would never stop blushing today. "I'm sorry. I should have asked. I don't—"

"I don't mind," Gray said, peeling the skin off an onion with capable fingers. "I like taking orders. Well, from you, anyway."

Skies above.

"So, who's going to eat all these onions I'm being ordered to cut?" Gray asked.

"There are seven children."

"Chil—" Gray went still, all joking gone from his face. His wide eyes met Burne's across the table. He must have guessed who the children were.

"Are all of them here? All of them survived?"

"Yes."

On cue, voices sounded through the windows—lots of voices all chattering at once. The wooden door swung open and Woodbine entered with the youngsters spilling in around her. Their cheeks were rosy from the cool spring evening, except for Alyss with her darker skin. Nem came in last and closed the door.

Silence fell. The whole crowd focused on Gray.

He'd paused with the knife midway through an onion. He inhaled slowly, his nostrils flaring. "Hello," he said. "I'm Gray. I met Burne in the woods and invited myself home with him. Trillium said I could help make dinner."

The younger children relaxed but the older ones kept studying him and no one moved. Woodbine also stayed quiet although she leaned back on the wall. If Trillium had known who Gray was, Woodbine might, too.

Nem stepped forward. She was the oldest at sixteen winters. "How do we know you're not from the old queen?" she said.

Gray put his hands flat on the table, leaving the knife wedged in the onion. "Because I think she's a beast and I'm glad she's locked up underground, and if she ever showed up here, I'd help Trillium and Woodbine hide you."

Nem squinted at him.

"I swear it on every flower in the forest."

"What's your name again?" Nem asked. Woodbine smiled.

"Grape Hyacinth."

Nem's gaze darted to the flowers on the table, now standing erect. "He's fine," she said quietly.

Her words released the children. The younger ones swarmed Gray as he resumed chopping the onion, and they were all talking at once.

"Whoa, everyone, stop," Burne said. He had a lot of practice making dinner amid this crowd. "One at a time. What did you do today?"

"Woodbine took us to the waterfall," Alyss said, peering up at Gray. Gray peered back, wielding the knife without watching what he was chopping. Hopefully he had some magic fairy sense protecting his fingers from being sliced off. "I'm Alyssum," she added, "but you can call me Alyss."

"We learned about the weather," Chrys chimed in, and everyone turned to him except for Gray. Gray pursed his lips as his eyes turned from Alyss up to Burne. He was wondering about something.

"And we talked about chopping down trees," Alyss said.

Gray's eyebrows lifted.

"We talked about forest management," Chrys said, "and how to use trees without hurting them, and how to pick which ones to cut down when you do need wood."

Nem touched Burne's shoulder. "How long till supper?" She spoke coldly but Burne was used to her personality. She took care of the others even if she didn't do it with smiles and hugs.

"About an hour."

She nodded and herded some of the children back to the door and out. Woodbine followed them.

"Where do you live?" Alyss was asking Gray. She had stayed behind with Chrys.

"In the human village at Woodglen. I have a sister there."

"Did you live underground like us?"

Burne flinched every time one of them mentioned their past, but Trillium said it was healthy for them to talk about it when they wanted to. She must have done a lot of talking with the children over the many winters they'd been at the Haven, because the children understood how they had been taken from their mothers involuntarily and hidden away from them.

"I did live underground," Gray said. "I didn't like it much."

"Me neither. Do you have a mother?"

Gray pushed the chopped onion to the side with the knife and reached for the next one. "Everyone has parents."

"But does she live with you?"

"No. I don't know where she is now."

"You don't?"

Gray only shook his head.

"I'd like to find mine," Alyss said. Burne had heard this before. Some of the children were quiet about their thoughts but Alyss always blurted hers right out. "Woodbine says we can try to find her but I shouldn't get my hopes up because it's been so long. And I shouldn't expect her to be a certain way but I just need to wait and see what she's like."

Gray had talked so much when it was the two of them, but now he was letting Alyss do all the talking.

"I want to meet her and see what she's like. Maybe she won't want me but at least I'd know. Trillium and Woodbine won't let me go with her if she's not going to take good care of me."

"That's good."

"Do you think your mama misses you?" Alyss asked.

"No," Gray said carelessly, but then he stiffened. He stopped chopping to contemplate Alyss. "But she's a fairy. We're different that way. We live in one big group and it's like everyone's your mother. It's not like the small families humans have. Your mother's a human. She'd want you with her."

Burne turned to the fire in the hearth as Alyss resumed her questions. She chattered with Gray as Burne added wood to the fire and poured water into the large soup pot to heat. He set Chrys to stirring the bowl of sunflower seed butter they'd have on their bread.

Gray finished the second onion and reached for the next. Burne took up the iron pan heating near the fire and held it steady over the table using both arms. Gray left the knife, scooped up the chopped onions with both his hands, and spilled them into the pan. They sizzled and the pungent smell of frying onions hit Burne as he tossed them. Gray's gaze lifted to Burne's flexed biceps and he bit his lip suggestively. Gray gathered the remaining bits of onion.

This time as he dropped them into the pan, he met Burne's gaze. Somehow the fairy could make even onions sexy. And he knew it. He broke into a grin as he returned to chopping, with Alyss gabbing away at his elbow.

The daylight faded from the windows, and Chrys moved to light the lanterns around the room. Burne stepped out the door to collect potatoes and turnips from the shed outside the back gate of the courtyard, where they'd been stored from last season's harvest. He should've done this first but he'd been too distracted by having Gray with him in the kitchen. He'd have to cut the root vegetables into extra thin slices so they could catch up with the rest of the soup ingredients.

The smooth stones that paved the courtyard glimmered—if Burne looked closely, he could find the fairy lamps tucked under the eaves. They came on as evening fell and magically illuminated the space all night. Burne found them comforting—it was nice knowing this space was always bathed in their warm glow.

The wall of the hut where the children slept took up one side of the courtyard, and a railing made of woven branches fenced in the rest. Over the railing, the dark trees blocked the view east. Burne circled around the empty fire pit in the center of the courtyard—he needed to get a fire going—and made for the gate.

Burne stepped out into the shadowy clearing beside the trees. The tangy scent of new plants pushing up through the soil wafted in from the forest, and the chilly air held the distant rush of the stream passing a short way off in the woods. Light shone in the window of the children's hut, but the usual cacophony of voices was absent. Nem must have asked them all to practice quiet time before supper. As he passed Trillium and Woodbine's hut, the view to the west opened. A gap in the trees revealed the mountains that the sun had disappeared behind, leaving the sky pink as the first stars appeared. Soon it would be black under the trees, in spite of the half moon high in the sky. It would probably be too dark for Gray to find his way back to the village on his own.

He'd be spending the night at the Haven.

Burne's blood raced at the thought. Where would Gray sleep? Where did Burne *want* him to sleep? When their hands had touched the second time, when Gray was showing Burne the deer illusion, Gray had held his hand as if he wanted to keep holding it—as if he might want more than one touch. Now, alone in the dark, outside the courtyard wall, Burne allowed himself to imagine things. He remembered Gray's fingers in his and imagined touching Gray's face. Gray was talkative but he had a sensitivity about him. Burne imagined Gray going silent and waiting on Burne to act. Burne wanted to pull him in and kiss him.

He caught himself dreaming and shoved the thought away. He couldn't go imagining things like that, not with Gray standing a few paces away in the kitchen. He'd never be able to talk to him coherently if he imagined kissing him. Besides, Burne had never kissed anyone, much less tumbled them, not even when the maids in the castle had tried cornering him in the pantry and putting his hand on them and wheedling him to kiss them. Of course, he hadn't wanted to kiss the maids. But he *had* wanted to kiss men before, and he'd missed all his chances. When his friends had started pairing off in a never-ending swap of courting, Walter had suggested they kiss—just to see what it was like. But Burne had been too nervous. And the times he'd felt another man notice him or when someone had approached him and tried to flirt, he'd floundered and escaped as soon as he could. He had no idea how any of this worked.

Had Gray kissed people before? Probably. Probably kissed and a lot more. He was so confident. Probably nothing frightened him.

Burne hefted the basket of vegetables into his arms and walked back through the courtyard and to the kitchen door. As he nudged it open with his knee, he paused on the threshold. Gray had finished with the onions and stood leaning on the table with his sleeves rolled up to reveal solid forearms. His hair screened his face the way it had when Burne first spotted him in the forest. Gray had seen Burne in the forest, too. What had Gray thought when he saw him?

The lantern light shone on Gray's arm. His shaggy hair covered the back of his neck and his trousers were too long and dragged on the floor over his heels. His arm was all Burne could see of his skin. Gray was silent as Alyss rambled on, something about trees.

Alyss finished her speech and spotted Burne in the doorway. Gray turned. His lips parted slightly and he watched Burne in silence, and again the air wooshed from the room, leaving Burne breathless. He came inside and pulled the door closed behind him.

Chapter 4

WHEN BURNE HAD THE SOUP ready, the whole crew gathered to eat in the courtyard. As long as the weather held, the courtyard was the best spot—otherwise they had to crowd inside and sit on the floor cushions. The courtyard's fire pit kept the space warm—so warm that Burne suspected magic was involved, although he'd never figured out how. Even when he was the person who built the fire, it gave off heat that filled the courtyard to the edges and never drifted away into the forest.

But tonight, Gray had built the fire. Trillium had entered the kitchen as the soup simmered and sent Gray out to do it. Gray responded by lifting his brow in a challenge and sauntering out the door. A moment later, the ring of the axe sounded, joined soon after by Gray singing something about the trees growing high and meeting his love in the forest by and by. Trillium huffed and left the kitchen, but later, when they'd gathered outside with bowls of steaming soup, she'd complimented Gray on the fire and thanked him.

They finished eating and the children washed the bowls and utensils. Their stream of chatter diminished as they grew sleepy. After a day hike with Woodbine, getting them to bed was usually fairly straightforward. They took the rinsed kitchenware inside to drip-dry overnight. Then Trillium and Nem herded them through the doorway to their sleeping quarters. Woodbine slipped out as well, leaving Burne and Gray alone by the dying fire.

The embers glowed red, emitting only a single crackle every

few minutes. Gray lounged on his side on the ground, poking a twig into the glowing crevices and studying the flame that burst up before blowing it out and poking the fire again. Burne leaned forward on the stump he'd used as a chair.

"Does anyone else know about this place?" Gray asked quietly.

"Trillium and Woodbine have friends who send supplies—their names are Thistle and Larkspur. I'm not sure who else knows. It was truly a secret?"

"Yes. Thistle told the fairies Trillium and Woodbine were dead. Not everyone believed it—we thought they'd run away to live in the forest and not be trapped in the caverns and ruled by Queen Oleander—but no one said anything because the queen seemed to believe it. Soon after, the children who waited on the queen started falling ill, but I never connected it with Trillium and Woodbine's disappearance. Thistle is a healer and she told the queen the children couldn't survive without sunlight because they were half human. But nothing moved Oleander to free them. One by one, as they grew older, they disappeared and Thistle said they had passed on. But Thistle must've been smuggling them out and getting them here."

"But Oleander's locked up now, right? They said she was contained somehow, after the revolution."

"Yes."

"So it would be safe for the children to leave here. Trillium and Woodbine talk about it all the time. They want to do what's best for them but they're not sure how. They've spoken with the children about what they want, and all of them have said they'd like to try to find their mothers. I think also . . . they haven't said this, but I think it's getting harder on Trillium and Woodbine to live out here with limited supplies, even with me to help fix things and get wood and all. This past winter it felt like we were always running low on everything."

Gray dropped his twig into the fire and sat up. He stared Burne straight in the face, and nothing about him was teasing.

"I think I know Alyss's mother."

Burne sat up. "How do you know?"

"Her name's Ladi. She's Norlian and she lost her child to a fairy. The child would be about Alyss's age, and Alyss's mother must be from the north for her to have skin so dark. Ladi lived with the women in Woods Rest who took in the little ones rescued by your Princess Rose last spring, but none of those children were old enough to be hers."

Even living at the Haven, Burne had heard the story about what happened last spring: The human king's daughter, Rose, had escaped his plans for her life-bond with a visiting prince and disappeared into the forest with her fairy lover. She had discovered her birth father was not the king but a fairy. Being half fairy, she'd been able to learn to see past fairy illusions and used her half-fairy sight to infiltrate Oleander's caverns and steal back all the children who remained there, taking them to a home where some of their mothers lived in Woods Rest.

And after that, Rose had helped the human villagers overthrow the king and was chosen by the fairies as their new queen. Because of her, Burne was safe from the King's Guard. As a child in the castle kitchen, he'd seen her a few times when her mother had come to visit Kate and brought her along. He'd always been too shy to speak to her. Of course she wouldn't remember him, but someday he hoped to thank her.

"Where's Ladi now?" Burne asked.

"She lives in Woodglen. She's apprenticed to the herbalist and she hangs out with my sister all the time."

"Your sister with the flower shop."

"Yes. Hyacinth."

"Your sister's name is Hyacinth?"

Gray groaned. "Don't."

But Burne couldn't resist a chance to tease Gray, after all the teasing Gray had done earlier that day. "Hyacinth and Grape Hyacinth. Did your parents adore hyacinths?"

Gray closed his eyes and shook his head. "We're twins. She popped out first. I was a surprise."

"I'll say," Burne said without thinking.

Gray's eyes flew open and Burne blushed. Where had that come from?

"Just don't start talking about how 'cute' grape hyacinths are," Gray said.

"But they are—" Burne began, to see what would happen.

"They are not *cute*. Just because they are little does not make them *cute*. If you examine them closely, they have thick clusters of leaves and a strong stalk topped with swollen florets, and they produce a multitude of seeds that spread across the ground in addition to creating new bulbs below the ground. They are hearty and reliable."

"But when you hold them in your hand for too long, they wilt and you need someone to help you revive them."

Gray gaped at him. "Skies, Burne. You'll be putting me in my place in no time." Gray tried to hold in his smile but was beaming all the same.

Burne ducked his head. Where had this bold side of him come from?

Gray's half smile faded. "What should we do about Alyss?"

"She wants to find her mother. We have to bring them together."

"But how do we do it? How do we tell her?"

"Let's ask Trillium and Woodbine," Burne said. "They have to be better at understanding children than we are."

Burne left Gray by the fire and found Woodbine in the hut she shared with Trillium out behind the children's sleeping quarters. A few other huts were scattered out here under the trees. They'd been used for storage until Burne had taken over one last season and, after seeing that, Nem had moved into another, citing a need for "adult space." As Woodbine opened the door, Trillium arrived from helping get the children to bed. They followed Burne back to the courtyard, where Gray repeated everything he'd told Burne.

"Would Ladi want Alyss?" Woodbine asked. Beside her, Trillium reached for her hand and gave it a squeeze.

"She never talks about her child," Gray said, "but she thinks she's dead. When Princess Rose brought the children to Woods Rest, they were all too young to be hers and everyone thought the others didn't survive. Maybe she tries not to speak of her."

Woodbine's brow was creased with worry. Trillium put an arm around her waist. "We wanted to find their mothers. Now it's happening. We just have to figure out what's best for Alyssum. And for Ladi."

"We could invite Ladi to come here to meet Alyss first," Woodbine said. "Once they meet, Alyss could go on living here for a while if she needs time to get used to her new situation."

"We should talk to Ladi at the very least," Trillium said, "before we tell Alyss."

"Tell me what?"

They all jumped. Alyss stood in the doorway to the sleeping quarters. She hugged a blanket around her.

"What are you doing out of bed?" Trillium said, going to her, but Alyss pulled away and came out into the courtyard.

"You were talking about me. I heard you."

Woodbine and Trillium glanced at each other over her head. Trillium knelt down beside Alyss.

"Alyss, we think we know where your mother is. Gray knows her."

Alyss's eyes widened.

"Do you still want to meet her? We can take our time and let you—"

"I want to go," Alyss said.

"Trillium and I will talk to her first—"

"No," Alyss said. She blinked back tears. "If she doesn't want me, she'll leave. I'll never get to see her. You can't tell her first. I want to see her. I want to go to the village."

Trillium's lips pursed in concern. "Are you sure?"

Alyss jerked her head up and down vehemently. She crossed to where Burne sat and reached for his hand. "Burne," she said, gazing up at him, "will you go with me?"

Burne stared down into Alyss's wide eyes and swallowed. "Yes."

He said it quickly before he could think about it too much. Already his heart was beating faster but he held Alyss's gaze until Trillium ushered her back to bed, saying they would make a plan in the morning. Woodbine and Gray were talking but all Burne could hear was his pulse pounding. He would have to succeed now no matter what happened. If he had Alyss with him, he would have to leave the safety of the trees and walk into the village even if it made him feel like he was dying. He couldn't let her down.

If the panic rose up inside him, he'd keep walking until he got Alyss to where she needed to go, and once she was safe, he could collapse in a puddle in the nearest alleyway behind a shop in Woodglen. The panic would pass—it always passed.

"What's wrong?" Gray asked.

But what if his tormentors were there—Cap and Stone and all their cronies? They didn't command him anymore. They wouldn't have any power over him. And yet, they would. He'd be the same cowardly person he'd been last spring.

Burne watched the glowing embers of the dying fire. Gray nudged him with an elbow. "What's wrong?" Gray had taken the seat on the stump beside Burne's, and Woodbine was gone.

"I'm scared to leave the forest," Burne said. Admitting it was embarrassing, but saying it to Gray eased the pressure in his chest.

"How come?"

Burne swallowed and wet his lips. "I don't know. I get to the edge of the forest and this feeling comes in my chest. This . . . this heavy dread like my heart's going to stop if I leave the trees."

"Is that the only time it happens—when you try to leave the forest?"

"Now it is."

Gray kept silent for a moment. "When did it start?"

Burne sighed. "It's been a full season. Last spring I was in the King's Guard and I left to hide in the forest. I mean, I deserted my post." Now Gray would know what a coward he was. He hung his head.

"I wouldn't have even joined the Guard," Gray said.

"They made me join."

"I mean I would've deserted before I even started."

"I was too cowardly to do that."

Gray didn't reply.

"Anyway, I hid in the woods and I didn't know what I was doing. I couldn't kill anything and I didn't know which berries were safe to eat, and it was spring so there were no nuts to scavenge. I pretty much ate onions for a quarter-moon and then Trillium found me. Just in time, too. I'd been about to risk eating some unfamiliar mushrooms."

"Why did you hide in the woods?"

"I knew no one would follow me into the woods. Back then, before the revolution, the villagers all said the woods were dangerous."

"Ah, right," Gray said. "Filled with evil fairies."

Burne blushed. "My mother never said it but enough people did that it seemed true."

"So you hid in the woods even though everyone said they were dangerous. Doesn't sound cowardly."

Burne frowned. Somehow Gray twisted everything around to make it less bad.

"And Trillium found you and decided to keep you?"

"She told me if I gave away her secrets, my tongue would fall out."

Gray barked with laughter. "That's not how fairy spells work!"

"I know that *now*."

"Bad Trillium."

"I kind of knew she was making it up. She didn't seem dangerous. But I was so grateful to have shelter I would've stayed regardless. She fed me and let me sleep in one of the huts. The first night was when it started."

Burne paused, remembering. "I was lying on the cot and I started to feel strange, like my heart was beating funny. I thought, I'm safe now. I have food and a place to hide. But the feeling got worse and my arms and legs started going numb. I stood and I was shaking so hard I could barely walk but I felt such dread, I couldn't lie down. I went out into the night air and must've passed out. I woke with Trillium there and she wrapped a blanket around me and helped me back to bed. It happened again and again for a while. But now it only happens when I try to leave the forest."

"You feel safe here. It makes sense you'd be anxious over leaving."

"I'm just a wimp."

"Burne, you went into the forest when you thought it was full of dangerous monsters. That doesn't sound like a wimp."

"I only went because I was running away from something worse."

"Being a guard was that bad? Worse than being some fairy's love slave?"

Skies. "That doesn't sound so bad anymore," Burne muttered.

"What was that?"

"I'm a wimp."

Gray sighed dramatically. "You keep telling yourself that over and over. It's making you believe it. Here—" Gray touched Burne's elbow and turned to face him. Burne sat up. "Repeat after me: I am brave."

"What? No."

"Just say it, Burne. I. Am. Brave."

"I can't."

But Gray was starting to smile at him and it was hard not to smile back.

"Just try," Gray wheedled.

"Mm brv," Burne mumbled, staring at the ground at his feet.

"What?" Gray squeezed his arm.

"Fine, I'm brave, okay?" Burne pulled his elbow out of Gray's fingers. He felt embarrassed saying those words, like a fraud, no matter what Gray said.

"You are brave. I agree."

"What about you? What are you scared of?"

Gray sat back. "Never doing anything meaningful with my life. Being the lazy twit everyone thinks I am."

"Why do they think that?"

"Because I was."

"How do you mean?"

"I never helped with anything. The fairies have all these posts you can take up—like being a gardener or forester or making baskets or kitchen duty. And you get to do the things you're gifted at or whatever, but you have to do something to pitch in. Only I never would. When I grew old enough to help, I was always goofing off instead, or flirting or sneaking elderberry wine or tumbling the person who was supposed to be training me, and if someone made me work, I'd do a mediocre job so they wouldn't ask again. No one *wanted* my help after a while."

"But you're different now."

"Not really. I help Hyacinth with her flower business and I don't cause trouble the way I did. But I'm still not doing anything useful."

"You're helping your sister."

"Sometimes I think she's only tolerating me to make me feel useful. And I don't have my own goals or an occupation that's truly mine."

"I'm the same way. I've never had a role where I was doing things I'm skilled at. When they called me to join the King's Guard,

I was scared but a tiny bit of me thought, I'll make the best of it. I got excited that maybe I'd find something I could do well. But I was terrible at it. I don't know what I'd do if I left here. At least here I can help with the cooking and gardening and taking care of the buildings. Back in the village, I'll be a disappointment again."

Gray's eyes were shining in the dim light. "I worry about letting Hyacinth down. She's making her dream happen. What if I *did* find something I wanted to do? I couldn't leave her."

"What kinds of things do you do for her?"

"I do all the deliveries and I go in the forest to gather things for her spells," Gray said. "She's really talented at using plants in spells. And at talking to animals. And most things. And she always loved flowers so when we were able to leave the caverns, she knew exactly what she wanted to do. She's planted things all over Woodglen and she practically runs the team at the castle gardens."

"The castle gardens?"

"The gardens are open to the public. Volunteers do all the gardening."

"That's a big change."

"Everyone around me has taken advantage of new opportunities, and I've just been stuck."

How could he help Gray feel better about himself? "Trillium says we're not defined by our vocation. She says we should just try to help each other out and be happy each day."

"I don't think I accomplish that."

"You help Hyacinth."

"Not that part."

"You're not happy?"

Gray considered a moment. "When I followed Hyacinth to the village, I thought it would be . . . different. Fun. Free. But it's noisy. I don't think I realized how noisy humans are. And everyone works all day, then goes out for ale and passes out asleep. Like the sun rises and sets and rises and sets and it's the same, over and over."

"Do you have friends?"

Gray shook his head. "Not in the village. I met someone new recently but she fell in love."

"With you?"

Gray smiled. "No. With a fish-catcher. She's always off with him, which is *fine*, of course. She's a mermaid."

By now, Burne knew better than to believe Gray when he said things so outlandish.

The fire was practically out, and the chill night air was seeping into the courtyard. Whatever spell had trapped the heat must be wearing off.

"Are you going back to Woodglen tomorrow?" Burne asked.

"I could walk with you and Alyss. Unless you'd rather not—"

"No, I'd like that. And Alyss will, too."

"You can do this, Burne."

"I have to. Alyss needs me to be strong and do this with her. I want to be there to hold her hand if she needs me."

"Well, I'll be there to hold yours," Gray said.

Burne met Gray's gaze. In the dim light, Gray's eyes were a deeper green. They hadn't even known each other a full day but it felt like they'd been friends for a dozen seasons. Friends, or whatever. Was it possible to know each other so fast? Nothing about Gray seemed insincere, as if he, too, liked whatever was happening between them.

"I hope I don't mess it up," Burne said. "I wish I could practice leaving the woods before I actually have to."

"Maybe you could practice with something else. What else scares you?"

"I don't know. Everything?"

"I bet you're scared of kissing."

Burne's stomach dropped.

"See, just talking about it terrifies you."

"I've never done it," Burne said. But he'd been imagining it a few hours earlier.

"You've never kissed anyone?"

"I won't know how."

"Nobody knows how the first time. That's why you get someone to show you."

"You've done it."

"Some. Here and there."

Burne fixed Gray with a stare. "You've done it a lot, Gray."

"Yeah."

"With who?"

"With everyone."

"How about now. In the village. Do you have . . . anyone?"

Gray rolled his eyes. "Hardly. I think I must not understand
humans. They have dances each moon, and I went to the first one
and it was so different from the fairy dances. I kept trying to talk
and flirt and everyone gawked at me like I was a three-headed pirate. I was tempted to turn into one just to see what happened."

Burne lifted his brow.

"I didn't. And anyway, I was thinking maybe I should take a
break from romance and try to figure myself out, so I let it go. I
flirt with the ladies at the grange home and with Old Billy down at
the docks, and I hang out with Hyacinth and go to bed at sunset.
Anyway, the point is, I haven't kissed anyone since before I left the
fairy village with Hy and went to live in Woodglen. I'm totally out
of practice. I'll be as awkward as you."

"You don't have to help me."

"Silly Burne." Gray bit his lip to stop a smile. "You think I'm
doing it for you."

"Why would you want to kiss me?"

"Why wouldn't I? And don't say because you're a wimp."

"I'm awkward—"

"You're authentic."

"And gawky—"

"Tall and strong."

"And I let myself be bullied—"

"A peacemaker who refuses to fight even when provoked."

"I'll be bad at it."

Gray humph-ed. "I'm not going to force you."

Burne's heart sank.

"Disappointed?" Gray watched him through slitted eyes.

The cool night air pressed around Burne and he shivered. Gray's eyes made him shiver too. He reached up to touch Gray's face the way he'd imagined doing it. Only starlight shone in the courtyard, illuminating a silver curve along Gray's cheekbone and tinting the ends of his lashes.

Burne leaned forward and kissed him.

Gray was warm. His face was warm, and his lips and his hair where Burne's fingers slid into it were warm, and when Gray shifted, pulling Burne closer, his arms around Burne made it feel like the fire was again crackling beside them. Burne didn't know what he was doing but Gray's lips moved under his, kissing him back, and it felt too good for it to be the wrong way.

They broke apart, but Gray held him close, his breathing heavy.

"You've never done this?" Gray said.

"No."

"Are you scared now?"

"No."

"You don't need to practice."

"But I want to practice more," Burne said, and kissed Gray again.

He was practically in Gray's lap the next time they stopped to breathe. Heat radiated from Gray, and his own skin was flushed hot. If only they weren't sitting on stumps but on cushions or the forest floor or—

They could go to his hut.

At the thought, Burne's insides clenched up, panic swirling through him.

"We should sleep," Gray said. "Tomorrow's a big day."

Burne didn't stop to think. "Do you want to come to my hut?"

Gray didn't reply. His hand smoothed over Burne's chest. "Somehow I don't think I'll get much sleep if I go with you."

"I don't think I'll get much sleep either way."

Gray laughed softly. He took Burne's face in his hands and tilted it down to his own.

"Let's try to sleep tonight. I'll make sure you get another chance to spend the night with me." And he kissed Burne one last time.

Chapter 5

BURNE LED ALYSS AND GRAY through the trees, following the path he'd memorized over the last few moons. Beside him ambled a bear—or rather, Gray disguised as a bear. Up close, Burne could tell the bear's movements were jerky. Gray could use his illusions to imitate only things he had seen or could imagine, and he'd admitted to never having seen a bear in real life.

Walking to the village was a lot more fun with Gray as company.

"How about a squirrel?" Alyss said. She'd been trying to find something Gray *couldn't* imitate.

The bear shimmered into Gray for a moment. He winked at Burne and shimmered away, leaving a squirrel on the ground, leaping along beside them. Gray made a pretty believable squirrel, with barely a flicker in the air where his body actually stood. He'd explained he had to hide the parts of him that weren't the animal, but he could do it with invisibility, or by imitating the background, or a mix of both. He was much better at illusions than invisibility, though, and invisibility tended to make *all* of a fairy disappear. So he used a background illusion while also trying to use his invisibility skills and do a mix of both, but this was tricky. So sometimes the background he was imitating appeared to shimmer. But no one would notice unless they inspected things closely, especially with a mottled backdrop like a forest. Burne reached over to poke Gray, to make sure he was there.

"Stop that," the squirrel said, and Alyss peeled in laughter.

They'd gotten an early start. Burne had dragged himself from his warm blankets, having spent the past seven hours replaying his kisses with Gray and imagining where they might have gone—or might go—and pretending his own hand on his erection was Gray's. Back when he'd lived in Woodglen, he'd always imagined touching and tumbling with men he invented—dashing strangers from other lands who rode into Woodglen and swept him onto their horses. But somehow Burne was sure Gray would like being the center of his nighttime fantasies, if he knew about them.

Had Gray lain awake all night? Had he imagined Burne stroking his shaft until he came in his hand?

Gray had probably imagined Burne doing something Burne didn't even know was a thing people did together.

Alyss had been ready to go at dawn, but Burne had insisted she eat a slice of toast and wait for Trillium and Woodbine to wake up and help them pack a few things and make a plan. And for the sun to rise high enough that they could see their way through the forest.

Gray had dragged himself into the kitchen from the front room shortly after Burne set the water to boil. Even with sleep-encrusted eyes and his hair at all angles, he was handsome. He'd slumped onto a seat near the hearth and been uncharacteristically quiet. "Need some tea," he'd mumbled when Burne had asked if he was all right.

As he walked in the forest, Burne smiled at the memory of Gray's disheveled state that morning. The sunlight was brightening. They must be in the last stretch of trees before the forest road and Woodglen, where the forest thinned out. But the fallen tree with the massive roots wasn't in sight. They must have come a different way than he had yesterday. He'd been watching Gray as they walked instead of keeping track of the path. But it didn't matter. They could easily find their way back to the village along the road, wherever they came out.

"Almost there," Burne said.

The squirrel started growing until it was as tall as Alyss. Its beady eye peered sideways at them, and its huge front teeth snapped.

"Ugh," Alyss said.

"That's really terrifying," Burne said.

The squirrel turned into Gray. He'd woken fully after a cup of tea, but his hair was still a mess. An adorable mess, Burne thought, wishing he could smooth it down. Now that he'd seen Gray using his magic so easily, Burne suspected the silver streaks in Gray's hair were an illusion.

"What?" Gray asked, narrowing his eyes.

"Nothing." Burne couldn't stop himself from smiling.

Gray shook his head and turned to Alyss. "Want to see a new one? I just learned this."

She clapped in excitement.

Gray's shirt melted away and Burne ogled his muscular chest.

"A naked person?" Alyss said.

Gray grinned. His trousers started to fade.

"Eww, stop!" Alyss said.

But where his legs should have been was a shimmering fish tail. The fins at the bottom were walking like thin little paws under the massive tail, in a way that defied the laws of nature.

"A fish man?" Alyss asked.

"I'm a merman!" Gray said. "I saw a real merperson for the first time last moon—my friend I was telling you about," he added to Burne. "My merman illusion is a thousand times more authentic now."

"I thought you were teasing," Burne said, scanning up the tail until his gaze caught at Gray's middle, where the scales ended below his navel and hips, dipping provocatively.

"You can meet her," Gray said.

Burne forced his eyes the rest of the way up. "I would like that."

The trees dwindled and a hint of the ocean reached them on a gentle breeze. And Burne remembered what was coming. Through the thinning branches was an open, sunny expanse with the dirt track of the forest road running down the middle. At the sight of the road, his body reacted as if by habit, seizing up with dread, and his steps faltered. Nothing was out there—even the squirrels were hiding after the noise his group had made walking through the forest. He'd simply made this approach so many times he reacted automatically, but today would be different because it had to be. He halted facing the road. Alyss slid her small hand into his.

"We're a little too far north, I think," Burne said, checking the sun. It was so high he couldn't tell the direction from it. They'd been slower today with Alyss along, or maybe all of them had been rambling more slowly and enjoying the walk. Gray certainly hadn't seemed in a hurry, showing off his illusions. As if he liked the company.

"Do you want to walk on the road," Gray asked, "or stay in the trees?" His appearance had returned to normal. He asked the question as if it were no big deal that they would step out and onto the road in a moment. And it wasn't. Burne could do this.

He should get it over with. If the panic overwhelmed him as he left the trees and he passed out, at least they'd be outside the village where no one else would see. And Gray would be with Alyss if it happened. But it would be awful to have Gray see him like that. "Let's—"

Someone shouted. Something moved on the road through the trees to the south—someone was coming from the village.

Burne's fear spiked and he drew Alyss back into the shadows. It was probably a farmer with his pigs or a craftsperson heading to sell in Woods Rest. They didn't have to hide. But just in case . . .

"Here," Gray said, holding out his hand. "Hang on to Alyss's hand."

Burne took Gray's hand so the three of them stood linked. The air shimmered around them.

"Are we squirrels?" Alyss whispered, and Burne realized what Gray was up to. He could hide them all if they were touching.

"We're trees."

They waited in silence.

More voices shouted and talked as a group of men neared on the road, and Burne's pulse sped up. The men wore packs and strode along jauntily, startling the birds into hiding. They were loud but Burne couldn't make out their words. But he didn't need to hear their words to recognize the men. Those were the voices that had yelled at him during his guard training: Cap, Stone, and three of their lackeys sauntered along the road, heading north. Tremors skated down his spine. Why were they here?

Thank the skies the men were so loud. Another moment and Burne would have been on the road and encountered them face-to-face. Maybe confronting them directly would be better. If they saw people hiding in the trees, they'd come investigate, and being caught hiding would be much worse. But regardless of how the men came across Burne, that would be it: They'd laugh at his cowardice and push him around the way they had last spring. The dirt smell of the hard ground beneath his feet filled his nostrils, as if his face were even now pressed into it, with Stone's boot on his jaw.

He slowed his inhales to quiet his breathing, and clutched Gray and Alyss as the figures came abreast of where they hid in the trees. The men couldn't see him. Gray was hiding them with an illusion, keeping them safe.

Maybe Gray couldn't tell how badly Burne was reacting, how the voices alone had made him quake in fear. Was Gray afraid? Or Alyss? Did the men actually sound scary to other people, or was he the only one who reacted this way? He shouldn't have left the Haven. It was too much of a risk. Once the men saw him, he'd never get away again. He should have stayed hidden, should not have ventured out into this border near the edge of the trees where the shelter thinned and someone could spot him. The forest had been safe and he'd come too close to the edge.

But he'd had to. Alyss needed him to be here. And he wanted to be here with Gray.

A breeze stole through the trees and found Burne, riffling his hair. The space was too open. The men would see him. He had to stay motionless. But his pulse raced and all his instincts told him to run. If one of the men glanced their way, he might lose control and pull away and break the illusion.

The men passed without turning toward the trees, and the raucous voices faded into the distance. They'd been dressed as villagers. They were no longer guards, and they hadn't carried any weapons as far as Burne could see. Although they'd never needed weapons to damage him before.

Burne kept breathing—in, out—hanging on to Gray's rough, warm hand. Gray had seen. Gray had seen what Burne was like and now he would leave. As soon as they reached the village, he would politely excuse himself and Burne would never see him again.

"Friends of yours?" Gray asked gently.

Alyss pulled her sweaty hand out of Burne's grip. His other hand, clammy and shaking, was pulverizing Gray's fingers. He was the one sweating. He let go of Gray.

Gray shook out his fingers. "Remind me never to challenge you to a thumb war."

"A what?"

"Nothing." Gray turned to Alyss. "That's not what most humans are like," he said, "all noisy and shouty."

Alyss swallowed. "Okay."

"I mean, they are noisy, but usually in a friendly way."

"Okay . . ."

"Let's stay in the trees," Gray said and stepped away.

The three of them picked their way southward alongside the road, and Burne's body eased back to its regular state. No one else passed on the road. Birds resumed their morning songs, and squirrels hunted under the leaves for nuts hidden last fall. Within a few minutes, the junction to Woodglen appeared. This was it. The moment Burne had dreaded. There was no way to postpone it any longer. At least Cap and Stone wouldn't be in the village.

"Ready?" Burne asked Alyss, offering his hand.

But Alyss was facing forward and didn't see it. "What if she's . . . different?"

"We talked about this, remember?" Burne said gently. He knelt down beside her. "You've thought about her so much, and she might be different than what you've imagined. It might feel awkward when you meet her. But you can take it slow as you get to know her. I'll be there and you can tell me if you want to leave or if you feel scared. You can take as much time as you need to talk to her, and we can go home tonight if you're not ready to stay here."

Alyss took a step.

Burne swallowed and stood. His chest was tight but the feeling wasn't unbearable.

And then Gray's hand slipped into his.

"Come on," Gray whispered, and nudged Burne forward.

They stepped out from the trees onto sunny grass still damp with dew. Burne squinted in the light. He took a deep breath and the panic stayed down. He had to keep moving, if only to keep up with Alyss, who was padding toward the roadway. Gray stayed beside him, holding his hand.

The foraging squirrels paused to watch them pass. Burne's mind was calm enough to wonder how the squirrels would react if Gray turned into one of them. Did animals see fairy illusions? He almost laughed, imagining the squirrels' reaction to a giant squirrel creeping out of the forest. They were halfway across the grass and he'd stayed calm.

The deserted road stretched away in three directions. Alyss gasped suddenly and stopped, but no one was in sight. She gaped up at the turrets of the castle—seeing it for the first time, Burne realized. He was so used to the sight he'd barely noticed it towering over the fields to the right. If they took the right-hand road, they'd pass beside the castle wall.

Burne touched Alyss's shoulder. "Maybe you could visit the castle gardens with your mother."

Alyss pulled her gaze away and smiled at him. She continued walking toward the road. Far down the stretch ahead of them, the first of the village's cottages shone with the bright sun on their smooth thatched roofs. They reached the edge of the grass and Burne stepped onto the packed dirt.

He'd done it. He was doing it. He was walking home to see his mother, and he wasn't shaking or fainting. He wasn't even too nervous now that he was doing it. He wanted to let Gray know he was okay so he squeezed his hand and let go of it and smiled at him. His hand felt empty though and he wanted to take Gray's back. He tried to forget the feel of Gray's fingers in his and focus as they started toward the village.

They walked slowly. As they neared the first cottages, a farmer trundled toward them pushing a wheelbarrow and tipped her head as she passed. A villager with a stack of baskets in their arms hurried from a cottage, and more people milled ahead as the village square came into view. A young boy pinned laundry on a line outside one home. Some of the faces were familiar but he'd been gone long enough and changed so much they might think him a stranger. No one called his name or stopped him.

"It's this way," he said, leading the others into a side lane. His mother's cottage was third in the row. It appeared the same as in his memory with its thatched roof and his mother's favorite flower—hollyhocks—curling up from the dirt in front of the windows as they'd been when he'd last been here, a full turn of the seasons ago. A side window was open with a pie cooling on the ledge. Skies, if he'd remembered there'd be pie, he'd have been out of the woods three moons ago.

Burne stopped beside the cottage.

"I'll go find her," Gray said. They'd agreed on a plan before setting out that morning. Burne and Alyss would wait at Burne's mother's house while Gray found Ladi. And Woodbine and Trillium had agreed they no longer had to keep the Haven a secret, so Gray could tell Ladi the whole story.

"Promise you'll bring her," Alyss said. "No matter what."

"If I have to carry her over my shoulder, I'll make sure you see your mother."

A new fear grew in Burne's chest, but this time it had nothing to do with his own safety. What if things didn't work out for Alyss?

Gray strode back to the main road and turned toward the village, walking out of sight. Burne exhaled slowly and faced the cottage door. Beside him, Alyss peered up at him. "Remember what you told me," she said. "Your mother will always be glad to see you."

He swallowed and knocked.

When his mother opened the door, she shrieked. The next moment he was engulfed in her arms. All the warmth of his childhood rushed back with her firm embrace and the smell of her clothes. "Burne Burne Burne," she was saying as she pressed him against her. Finally, she stepped away to inspect him.

His mother hadn't changed except for the deeper wrinkles at the corners of her eyes. She was stout—his father had been the source of Burne's beanpole shape—and pale with bright blue eyes from her southern ancestors. She beamed at him. "I wondered when you'd be home."

"I'm sorry for staying away."

"No need to be. Come in. You shouldn't even be knocking—it's still your home." As his mother pulled him in the doorway, her arm moved out to include Alyss. "And who's this?" she asked nonchalantly.

Alyss held out her hand the way they'd practiced. "Alyssum."

His mother took Alyss's hand. "I'm Kate," she said, and she closed the door.

She led them down the hallway to the kitchen. "Are you hungry?"

"Can we have the pie?" Burne asked.

Kate laughed. "It's not sweet. It was for supper but I suppose we're celebrating. We'll eat it and you'll tell me all about where you've been this past winter."

"You got my message?"

"Yes, written on tree bark." She smiled. "I knew you'd be fed and sheltered if you were with the fairies. How did you find them?"

"They found me. I deserted my guard post and fled into the forest." Saying it to his mother made Burne drop his gaze to the cottage floor.

"Pshh, no matter," his mother said, taking the pie from the window. The scent of the baked crust wafted into the room and Burne's stomach responded with a rumble. He sank into a chair at the kitchen table, dropping his pack on the floor. Alyss took the chair beside him.

"The king didn't deserve you as a guard," Kate continued. "And from the stories in the pubs, no one would blame you for leaving. Thank the skies the king is de—" She stopped herself as her gaze flickered to Alyss. "Thank the skies he's gone," she finished. She turned away from Alyss before muttering, "The rotten bastard."

"I wanted to come home sooner," Burne said. "I knew it was safe to return but I . . ." He didn't know what he could say to explain how he felt and why he hadn't.

"He was helping us," Alyss said.

Kate cut into the pie, releasing the aroma of caramelized onions. "You have brothers and sisters?" she asked casually. She was holding back her curiosity until she figured out what was going on. Watching the way Kate interacted with Alyss and listening to how she asked questions to draw out Alyss's thoughts, Burne recognized his own tactics over the past season. Maybe he'd learned how to talk to the children from growing up with Kate as a mother.

Alyss launched into a description of the Haven and how she'd lived there after escaping from the old fairy queen. She hesitated a few times at first but talked more easily as she ate her first piece of pie. Burne wasn't sure what Kate knew about the fairies but he guessed she'd have heard Princess Rose's story and knew some children had been rescued. He could tell when something clicked together in her mind because her lips parted and her focus drifted for a moment. But she brought her eyes back to Alyss and kept listening. Kate slid a second piece of pie onto Alyss's plate.

Where was Gray? Had he found Alyss's mother? How had she reacted when he told her the news?

And what would happen next? Now that Burne was here, sitting in his mother's house, he didn't feel settled or like he was meant to *stay* here. He knew his mother would love for him to stay, but he hadn't meant to return to the village for good and abandon everyone at the Haven. He'd meant only to visit. With how much effort it had taken to get here, he hadn't thought past this moment. If Alyss needed to return to the Haven tonight, he'd go with her. And if not, he'd still go back into the woods to continue helping Trillium and Woodbine.

Would Gray go with him?

He shouldn't even think about it. Gray had a life in the village. His sister needed his help. Burne couldn't expect him to uproot himself to live in the woods with a bunch of children.

But if Gray stayed here and Burne returned to the woods, when would they see each other again? When would he get to kiss Gray again? Or to follow up on Gray's promise—Burne shivered thinking of it—to spend the night together?

And now that Burne had reappeared in the village, people would start to talk. Soon enough, Gray would hear stories about him. Perhaps he already had—what stories were they telling in the pubs? Did Gray frequent the village pubs? He'd said he didn't go out much but maybe he'd crossed paths with former guards and heard them talk about a man called Yell, and now Gray would learn the cowardly Yell from all their stories was Burne.

Yell. That was the nickname they'd given him. Short for Yellow-Bellied.

But Burne had a chance to help with something bigger than

himself. Maybe more of the children could find their mothers. And if not, they could have a safe home in the village where they'd be warm all winter and eat pie for dinner instead of soup every night. He could help provide that. He could do something meaningful to counteract the stories Gray was sure to hear about all the ways the other guardsmen had tormented him, all the pranks they'd played, and how cowardly he'd been.

"Gray came with you?" Kate asked Alyss. Burne startled at the name.

"Burne brought him home yesterday."

Kate threw her hands up in mock surrender. "Well now you've completely lost me. Gray from the flower shop?"

"You know him?" Burne asked, his nerves tensing.

"Oh, the whole village knows Gray. He makes deliveries for his sister. The flower shop is flourishing since she took it over. I think she uses spells on her flowers. They make you feel lighter just seeing them."

"Do you like Gray?" Burne asked, not quite meeting his mother's gaze.

Kate's eyes narrowed a smidge. "He's a good lad. Do *you* like Gray?"

Alyss tittered.

A knock sounded at the front door.

Alyss clung to Burne's hand as they stood and followed Kate into the front room. Kate opened the door. The woman outside— Alyss's mother, Ladi—looked kind. That was the first thought in Burne's head and he wanted to cry with relief. She had large dark eyes that found Alyss immediately and she blinked a few times and bit her lip but didn't cry. Her skin was the dark brown of a Norlian and her hair was pulled back but it curled like Alyss's did. She had to be Alyss's mother.

She stepped inside and Gray came in behind her. He'd told her why she had to come to Kate's, but she'd had only a scant moment to adjust to the idea Alyss was alive. Ladi knelt in front of Alyss, started to reach for her, and stopped herself.

"Hello," Ladi said, and her voice was warm and welcoming.

"Hello," Alyss whispered. Burne recalled saying that one word to Gray last night and how Gray had filled the conversation for him.

"I'm so glad to meet you," Ladi said. After a heartbeat, she slowly lifted her palm, offering her hand. Alyss extended her free hand and took Ladi's.

Alyss's grip on Burne loosened and dropped. Burne had never seen her lost for words. Beside them, Kate reached for Gray and dragged him back to the kitchen, and Alyss glanced after them, distracted, and let go of Ladi's hand. Ladi kept her hand out, all her focus on Alyss as she blinked back tears.

Burne knelt beside Alyss. "Alyss, do you want me to stay here with you?"

"It's okay," she said, peeking at Ladi and turning back to Burne. "You can go with Gray."

"Why don't you take Ladi to sit on the bench?" He pointed her toward his mother's seating area, where sunlight shone in. "I'll be in the kitchen down the hall. If you need anything—like a glass of water or anything—you can come there, okay?"

Alyss nodded. She reached for Ladi's hand again and Ladi stood shakily and followed Alyss to the cushioned bench by the window. Alyss was quiet but moved calmly. Burne watched another moment before slipping out to the kitchen.

His mother and Gray were sitting like statues at the table.

"Are they okay?" Gray whispered.

"I think so."

"Should I bring them drinks?" his mother asked.

"Let's give them a few minutes . . . Maybe we should talk normally so we don't seem like we're eavesdropping," he whispered.

"Okay," Gray whispered back. "You first."

Burne cleared his throat. He couldn't think of anything to say.

Gray grinned and turned to Kate. "Is that mushroom pie?" he asked loudly.

"Oh! Why yes, it is. Would you like a piece?"

As his mother served pie to Gray, Burne slipped into his seat and gobbled up the last few bites of his own slice. He remembered the new bunch of ramps Trillium had wrapped for him and took them from his pack.

"I brought you some—"

"Ramps!" his mother said, reaching for the cloth with the flat green leaves poking out the top. "I haven't seen ramps in ages. We used to hike into the hills to gather them each spring before the king started patrolling the forest for poachers. Oh, aren't they wonderful?"

"They're onions," Burne said, but his mother continued to exclaim over them as she tucked them back into the cloth napkin and stashed them on the counter.

As his mother quieted, Alyss's voice drifted down the hallway, alternating with Ladi's. Kate put the kettle on and Gray was engrossed with eating his pie. Alyss was gathering momentum. Hopefully she'd be back to talking nonstop soon and Burne would know she was truly okay.

"So," his mother said, turning from the stove. She had her hands on her hips in a way that said "You have done something wrong."

Gray's eyebrows lifted but his mouth was full of pie.

Burne swallowed and bit his lip.

"Let's talk about your hair."

"My hair?" Burne automatically ran a hand through it and several pine needles fell out.

His mother was shaking her head. "Looks like a squirrel built its nest on your head, Burne."

"I didn't have any scissors," Burne said.

She frowned. "You managed to shave, didn't you?"

"Only because Woodbine had a lot of very sharp knives. You

wouldn't have wanted me to cut my hair with a knife, would you? You always told me to be careful around them."

"When you were *twelve*," his mother said, and she pulled a pair of shears out of the cupboard and came around the table behind him. Burne didn't dare argue. He didn't exactly want to have hair like a squirrel nest, which was a fair comparison, but he'd liked the idea of not being recognized in the village.

Burne backed his chair away from the table and his mother draped a towel over his shoulders to catch the clippings.

Gray was grinning. He finished his pie, then scooted his chair away from the table and leaned back on two legs, smiling across at Burne. Kate darted a frown his way and he sobered up and dropped back onto all four chair legs. And grinned again.

Burne's face heated. Kate came around him and pulled his chin to face her and produced a comb from her pocket. She drove it into the mess on his head and hit a knot. Burne winced as she tried to work it out.

"You might as well cut the knots off," Gray suggested.

"I think you're right," Kate said.

"I'm right here!" Burne tried to see Gray but the comb held his head in place.

"Just leave him those nice curls on top," Gray continued.

"Skies' sake," muttered Burne.

Kate brandished the shears. "You watch it, Mister Hyacinth, or you'll be next."

"Me?" Gray's voice was incredulous.

"Yes, you. Your hair may be smooth and shiny but it's falling in your face as much as Burne's is."

"It's elegant," Gray protested. "Besides, I can make it short anytime I want."

At that, Burne tried again to see him. The comb yanked against him.

"What good's an illusion if you can't see through your hair in your face?" his mother chided. "You'll still trip over anything in your way."

"Fairies don't *trip*," Gray muttered. But he must have worried she'd go after him with the shears because he stayed silent as Kate began snipping the past few seasons off Burne's head.

Chapter 6

AFTER BURNE'S HAIRCUT, HIS MOTHER brought drinks in to Ladi and Alyss, and when she didn't return, Burne and Gray followed her to the front room. Alyss sat beside her mother with her mother's arm around her.

Kate and Ladi were eager to hear all about the Haven. Burne had gotten so used to the idea of the Haven being a secret, it was a little strange to talk about it. But the fairy queen was no longer a threat, and if any humans managed to find their way to the Haven, they wouldn't be able to see the way in because of the illusions.

First Kate and Ladi had questions for Burne about the Haven and the other children living there. Then Alyss asked questions about Ladi's life, followed by Ladi's stories about the children Princess Rose had rescued and brought to Woods Rest. Finally Kate told stories about the day Princess Rose climbed a fairy ladder into her castle tower to rescue the kitchen staff and ultimately defeat the king. It was nonstop talking all afternoon. Burne's head swam with the chatter. He'd grown used to the relative silence of the forest. Gray was right: humans were noisy.

Burne sat quietly on one side of the parlor and tried to focus on the voices swirling about him. And he tried not to notice Gray. Gray sat across the room on a wooden chair with a caned seat. He faced Burne and each time Burne did peek at him—since his gaze was constantly drawn to Gray—Gray would return his gaze and a smile would hover about his lips, and Burne's face would heat and he'd check to see if his mother had noticed him noticing Gray.

So far, she hadn't reacted to their cross-parlor glances.

He was behaving like a juvenile. He shifted on his own caned chair, trying to find a comfortable position. How did Gray sit on his chair for so long, slumped to one side with his leg crossed over his knee and one arm dangling over the back, without moving?

Gray raised his eyebrows and pursed his lips to hide his latest smile. He silently mouthed words.

What was he saying? Burne's brow furrowed and he shook his head.

Gray tugged on a lock of his hair and said it again. "I like your haircut."

Oh. Burne tried to hide his smile.

Gray tucked his own hair behind his ear.

Skies, it *was* smooth and shiny. Burne stopped staring at Gray's hair. "Thank you," Burne mouthed back.

The sun was setting outside the parlor window. Alyss was asleep on the cushioned bench, her head on Ladi's lap. Ladi had been staring at her with her fingers in the child's hair since Alyss drifted off.

"Tell us again, Burne," Kate said. "What are the children's ages?"

Burne jerked his attention back to his mother. She sat beside Ladi and she'd asked him something. Children. The children at the Haven.

Kate continued. "Ladi's friend Kitty in Woods Rest also lost her child many winters ago. She may be one of the children in the woods."

At the words, Ladi's arm curled protectively around Alyss where she slept.

"Anemone is the oldest," Burne said. "We call her Nem. She's sixteen winters. She's tall and slim with straight brown hair."

"Like Kitty," Ladi murmured.

"And the next oldest is Chrysanthemum. He's fifteen."

"Kitty had a little girl."

"Freesia is fourteen, but she's not tall. And Gladiolus is thirteen. He has freckles and his hair curls."

Ladi shook her head. "Too young to be Kitty's."

"The other two are younger."

"Is Kitty still in Woods Rest?" Kate asked.

"Last I heard. But she talked about traveling away." Ladi continued in her soft Norlian accent. "'Tis hard on her, being there. Not just losing hope—course that was hard. But seeing the others find their babes and knowing she never would. She wants to help but being there makes her sad, I think."

A silence stretched out after her words.

Gray sat up. "When did you come to Woodglen?" he asked Ladi.

"Day before the revolution."

"Ladi traveled with Princess Rose," Kate said proudly, "right before she climbed the tower to save us all."

"Wasn't here a moon before you and Hy showed up," Ladi told Gray.

"How do you think Kitty would react if she found out about her daughter?" Gray asked.

"Oh, Kitty's the toughest of all of us. She'd take to it in a snap."

Burne cleared his throat. "Nem's who I'm worried about."

"What's she like?"

"She's quiet. She takes care of the others. She . . . she doesn't express herself much. Like she keeps it all inside. I often can't tell how she truly feels."

"Mm-hm. Jus' like her mama." Ladi smiled.

"We'll have to talk to Nem about what she'd like to do. Trillium could do it. All the children talk to her the most." All the children *and* himself. "She's so much better at knowing the right things to say."

"You don't seem so bad at it," Ladi said, and she focused on Alyss again. "Alyss said what a help you've been to her."

Burne blushed and avoided looking at Gray. Gray would give him an I-told-you-so look.

"I'd like to help reunite Kitty with her daughter," Ladi said, "but with Alyss here—" She ran her fingers lightly over the sleeping child's arm.

"You're needed here, Ladi," Kate said. "Burne can take care of things."

Burne raised his eyebrows.

"But he jus' got back," Ladi replied. "What about the peacekeepers? Malota or Berta could go. They both raised children."

Kate was shaking her head. "They're both ill. Apparently, someone had a bug and the peacekeepers had a meeting last night and now they're all laid up with it. Can't keep anything down, I heard. Besides, the children are hidden, remember? None of us would be able to find their fairy hideout."

"I'll go," Burne said. He couldn't resist glancing at Gray, who sat up. "I can go back to the Haven and talk to Trillium and Woodbine about it."

"Well it's too late to go now," Kate said, peering out the window, where the sun had disappeared and a purple twilight lit the cottage across the lane. "You'll have to go in the morning. I could make a space in—"

Gray cleared his throat, and Kate's sentence cut off abruptly. And suddenly Burne knew his mother had noticed him stealing glances at Gray all afternoon. She smiled sweetly at Gray and waited.

"Burne can stay at my place," Gray mumbled. Burne had never seen him less eloquent. "I'd like him to meet Hyacinth. If he wants."

His mother's gaze swiveled to him and she lifted her eyebrows.

"Thank you," Burne mumbled back, staring at the floorboards with his face hot. "I'd like that."

"Let me wake Alyss," Ladi said, touching the child's hair.

"Make sure she's wanting to stay with me right off. I don't want her to wake and find you gone."

When Alyss sat up, rubbing her eyes, Ladi and Kate went to the kitchen and Burne crouched beside her. She blinked at him.

"Hey sleepyhead," Burne said.

"Hi Bumbling Burne," Alyss replied.

"What do you think of her?" He didn't need to specify who.

"She's nice," Alyss said.

"Do you want to go home with her? We could all stay here if you want." Burne crossed his fingers against the floor. He *really* didn't want to stay at his mother's instead of Gray's.

"It's okay. I'd like to go. Only . . ."

"What?"

"What if she doesn't know any bedtime stories?"

"I'm sure she knows some," Burne said. He'd have to tell Ladi how Alyss needed a story at bedtime.

"What if she doesn't know the right ones?"

"What if you told her the story the first time? And then the next time she'd be able to tell it to you instead. Would that work?"

Alyss pressed her lips together. "I could do that."

"You've got your ragdoll?"

"She's in my bag."

"I'll come by in the morning and see how you're doing."

"Gray can come, too," Alyss said.

Before Burne could make excuses for Gray, Gray was standing beside him. "I'll be there."

Gray extended a hand and pulled Burne to his feet as Ladi and Kate returned from the kitchen. Ladi carried Alyss's pack. Burne spoke with her for a moment. As Alyss joined her, Ladi turned to Gray.

"Be sure and let your poor sister know you're okay. Said she got a cryptic message last evening about a fox in the woods and you not coming home."

Gray's body went stiff and he gazed at the floor. "It wasn't meant to be cryptic. I'm not skilled at communicating that way."

"I thought it was easy, you being twins and all."

"That twin thing only works in the village," Gray said. "I was in the forest. I tried to send the message with a bird but the silly thing was all hopped up on earthworms and couldn't form a coherent thought."

"But your sister never has trouble . . . ?"

"She never has trouble with anything," Gray said. He smiled at everyone and said goodnight, but his voice was tense. "Come on," he said to Burne and stalked out of the room.

Burne looked to his mother. She jerked her head after Gray.

As Burne followed Gray out of the parlor, his nerves tingled. Being with Gray had been easy all afternoon when they hadn't had a chance to be alone, or earlier when they'd been walking through the forest with Alyss as a chaperone. Now it would be just the two of them.

A thrill shot through him but also dread. What if he messed things up? What if Gray wanted to kiss him? Well of course he'd want to kiss, when he'd offered Burne to stay the night with him—but what if Burne couldn't do it right? They'd kissed last night and it had been fine. More than fine—it had been amazing. But the moment Burne imagined them lying together his stomach went sick with fear. But hadn't kissing felt that way before he'd done it? And kissing had turned out all right.

If only, just once, he could try something new feeling excitement instead of dread and certainty he'd fail.

Gray waited by the front door with his hand on the knob, already opening it. The moment Burne stepped into the hallway, Gray slipped out.

Scant daylight remained and the lane bustled with villagers heading home. Gray waited for Burne to come beside him before he started off toward the village square. He hooked his thumbs in the top of his trousers and didn't speak.

Something was wrong, and Burne hadn't the faintest idea what it was.

"You don't have to take me home," he ventured.

"I want to."

"What's wrong then?"

Gray shook his head so his hair fell across his face. "Hy would say I'm being a baby."

"You're way too good-looking to be a baby."

Gray's head bent forward, a smile showing. He tossed his hair back and sighed. "I'm a bad fairy."

Burne raised his eyebrows and grinned. "Yeah?"

He chuckled. "No, I mean I'm bad at *being* a fairy. All the stuff that comes easily to the others—I can't do it."

"You can turn into a human-sized squirrel."

"But that's one thing I can do. I can do *one thing* well."

"So you couldn't send a telepathic message to your sister from a quarter-league away. That seems really difficult."

"I'm bad with spells, I'm bad with making potions, I don't know my plants and herbs . . ."

"Nobody's good at everything."

"I guess I'm kind of sensitive about it. I've just been a joke for so long."

"You're not."

"I am to the fairies." Gray seemed determined to stay grouchy, and Burne had a flash of himself when Gray had tried to convince him he was brave and he'd been determined to see himself as a coward. Was this how he had acted? And was this how Gray had felt, trying to convince him?

They entered the village square and circled the green to the right. The village was different than how Burne remembered—it was lively and noisy with happy voices and music drifting on the air. The shops had fresh paint on the walls and flowers bloomed on the green. People walked to and fro as shopkeepers locked up for the night.

They neared a shop Burne didn't remember. Flowers filled the windows—colorful bouquets in vases and blossoms on plants growing inside the glass. Vines trailed up the bricks of the storefront, curling over the door with moonflower blossoms and some sort of evening primrose opening as night fell. How had Gray's sister coaxed moonflower and primrose to grow so early in the season? Maybe she *did* use spells.

There *had* been a flower shop here, now Burne thought about it, and they'd sold hats and ribbons and stockings and things, but no one he'd known had ever frequented it. The prices had been better suited to merchants and courtiers than the average village worker.

A painted wooden sign swung over the shop's door proclaiming The Fairweather Florist in swirling pink and green lettering. A bluebird sat atop the sign. It twitched suddenly—it was a real bird. It let out a series of complicated trills as they approached.

"Stars," Gray muttered. He turned to Burne, rolling his eyes. "My sister has a legion of birds and butterflies that do anything she asks. That one"—he pointed at the bluebird—"never shuts up. She says he's her ambassador, charming customers into entering. I say he's going to poop on someone's head someday."

"He seems—"

"Oh, can it, Featherstone," Gray called up at the bird as it launched into a new round of chirping.

"See?" Burne said. "You can talk to birds just fine."

"Sod off." But Gray couldn't stop himself from smiling.

The shop door was locked but from under his shirt, Gray brought out a key on a chain around his neck. The key hadn't been there earlier when Gray had been a bare-chested merman, or maybe it had been hidden by the illusion.

"Hy must be out," Gray said. "I hope she didn't need me. I found Ladi at the herbalist's so I haven't been home since yesterday." He swung the door open and led Burne into the dark shop.

A hundred flower scents bombarded Burne at once. Smells of

earth and spring and rain drifted beneath the heady perfume of the blossoms in the damp air. The streetlamps cast shadows into the room and silhouetted the flowers growing in the windows as Burne shut the door and cut off the breeze following him inside.

Gray fumbled with a lamp on a counter running across the back of the shop and golden light illuminated his features. Burne turned away before Gray caught him staring. Gold-tinted colors bloomed all around. He had never seen so many flowers in one place. The ones in the windows grew in container gardens and more plants hung in pots from the ceiling.

"Your sister must love flowers," he said.

Gray snorted but he was smiling. He left the lamp on the counter and stepped through the doorway into the back room. Burne followed with his pulse accelerating.

He entered a windowless room with a few simple chairs and a low table where Gray lit another lamp. A narrow staircase climbed up one wall. The room was close and silent.

"Hy will probably be home soon. She's not a late-night person. Her room is down here with the kitchen." He indicated a doorway at the back. "We both hate this room," he added.

The seats were cozy but Burne felt a strange claustrophobia. "It's hard not having windows," he said. "I must be used to living outside."

"That's it exactly. After all those winters living underground, I never want to not have a window again."

A silence stretched out. Gray hooked his thumbs into his trousers again.

"So, um, do you want to see my room?"

Burne's face heated. Was Gray nervous, too? He wasn't talking the way he had at the Haven—full of nonsense and teasing. He *seemed* nervous. But he'd done all this a thousand times before.

Burne swallowed. "Okay," he managed to rasp out.

Gray moved to the steps and started up. He tapped the edge of the ceiling as he passed underneath it. "Don't bang your head."

Surely Burne was missing a chance to make an off-color joke with those words but his brain wasn't functioning clearly. He ducked under the rafter and followed Gray up.

Through a door at the top, he entered the attic room. Faint light shone in two dormer windows overlooking the square. A cool breeze twisted in through the one slightly ajar. The ceiling sloped down almost to the floor, with its full height only along the center of the room. A chest and a low bed stood at the far side. Burne closed the door behind him.

Gray stood in the center of the room, staring at the floorboards. Seeing him without his usual self-possession tugged at Burne's sympathy.

"Hey," Burne said, and Gray glanced up. "Earlier, when you turned into a merman . . ."

"What about it?"

"Was that your real chest?"

Gray broke into a smile. He looked at the floor again, sliding one hand into his trouser pocket and grinning, and when he peeked up to regard Burne, his eyes glinted in the faded light. "Maybe."

"Come here," Burne said softly, and he leaned back against the wooden door. He pressed one hand flat against the boards, steadying himself.

Gray came before him and stopped, leaving a sliver of space.

Burne slid his free hand into Gray's hair, cupping the back of his head, and pulled him forward to kiss him.

This time they weren't sitting on stumps. As their lips met, Gray's body moved closer and nudged against him. "Is this okay?" he murmured between kisses, and Burne whispered back. Gray pressed into him, trapping him against the door. The crush of Gray's body made Burne hard at once but he didn't have time to worry if Gray noticed. Gray's lips demanded kiss after kiss. And Gray's hands caressed his lower back and moved to his hips, holding him in place.

Gray ground his own hips against him.

He broke their kiss to let Burne gasp.

It felt so pleasurable, shivers running down to his toes and warming his center. And yet, Burne's heart thudded as if it might break and he felt dizzy and feared he might faint. It felt . . .

It felt like it did when the panic overwhelmed him.

"Stars, I want you," Gray whispered.

Burne tried to ignore his panicky feelings. He wrapped his arms around Gray and started forward, backing him along straight toward his bed. He didn't know what he was doing but if he kept moving, maybe the panic wouldn't rise any further. Burne bent for another kiss and stumbled, knocking into Gray. He caught them both, started moving again, and walked them both sideways into the sloping ceiling.

Gray cursed and let go of him. Burne's forehead smarted where it had smacked the ceiling. He rubbed the spot.

"Did I hurt you?" he asked, horror filling him. Had he bashed Gray's head against the ceiling as hard as he had his own?

"I'm fine. Here. Sit before you hurt yourself." Gray took his hand and tugged him across the dark room to the bed.

Burne sat, rubbing away the soreness on his head. What had he been thinking? At least the panic had receded—along with his erection.

Gray sat beside him.

"I don't know how to do this," Burne said.

"How to kiss me?"

"All of it."

"You were doing fine." Gray's voice sounded kind.

"I didn't feel fine, though. I was all in my head trying to figure out what I should be doing."

"There's no *should* here," Gray said. "Just do what you feel."

"I feel like running down the stairs and out of the shop to hide."

"Okay, well don't do that."

"Tell me what to do."

Gray settled back. "Let's see. It's not complicated. Some people like you to kiss them a bunch and touch everything and whisper about how beautiful they are. Women usually like that. And sometimes men do, too. But with other men, you can pretty much grab their penis and get started."

"Is that what you like?"

Gray grinned. "I like anything."

"But is that what you want me to do?"

Gray took his hand. "You can do whatever you want." He kissed Burne's fingers and then kissed each of his knuckles before lowering their intertwined hands to rest between them.

"What was it like your first time doing . . . this?" Burne asked.

Gray laughed softly. "Someday I'll recreate my first time for your amusement," he said. "It was a mess." Gray rubbed Burne's fingers. "You inquired about the state of my chest?" He unbuttoned his top button with his free hand.

Burne's sight had adjusted to the dim lighting. He gazed into Gray's eyes. They'd met just a day ago but Gray's features were as familiar as his own. He wanted to kiss this man, to do everything with him. And most of all, he wanted to not disappoint him. Everything scared him the first time. He could do this.

Burne nodded. He swallowed as Gray's fingers moved down against his chest, popping open the next button. His shirt parted, revealing the top of a curling tattoo on his skin. Pop, pop, pop and Gray's shirt fell open.

The tattoo was a giant bluebird. Burne blinked, and the bird moved, winked at him, and vanished.

Burne screwed his eyes shut as laughter bubbled inside him, releasing his tension. "I thought that was real."

Gray laughed, too.

When Burne opened his eyes, Gray's chest was tattoo-free and the key to the shop hung against his skin. From what Burne could see in the darkness, Gray looked as splendid as he had in the woods that morning. Burne leaned across their clasped hands and kissed

Gray once to try it out. Gray kissed him back but when Burne stopped, Gray let him go.

"Can I take your shirt off?" Burne whispered. Where had that come from? But skies, he wanted to see Gray without it. Gray smiled and bit his lip. Burne kissed him again, untangling his hand so he could push Gray's shirt off his shoulders and down his back. Gray shook it the rest of the way off.

Burne pulled away to better see Gray and Gray watched him back with no hint of embarrassment. His hair had fallen into his eyes and his hands rested on the quilt as if he never worried about what to do with them the way Burne always worried about his own. Burne wanted to touch Gray's chest but he remembered what Gray had said. He reached out to the buttons on Gray's trousers instead.

When he darted a look at Gray for permission, Gray nodded.

What was he going to do? Touch Gray the way he touched himself? But what if it wasn't right?

His chest tightened and he pushed the feeling away. It would be fine.

He leaned in to kiss Gray again as he undid the buttons. Gray held his face, brushing his thumbs over Burne's cheeks. Gray's erection pressed against his underclothes beneath Burne's fingers and Burne couldn't find his way through so he found the top hem and pushed all the clothing down but it might not have been far enough. Gray took hold of Burne's collar and tugged on his shirt, asking to take it off, and suddenly Burne remembered standing naked in the Guard's training yard, in the middle of the rows and rows of his peers. Cap had tricked him, telling him he needed to change his uniform minutes before he needed to report for training. He'd taken his uniform off and handed it over, trusting Cap to give him the new one. But Cap had taken his uniform and left the barracks, leaving Burne nothing to wear.

He'd been flustered and stuck, with no idea what to do. He couldn't risk being late to training—he knew the punishment for tardiness. Could the punishment for arriving in his underpants be any worse? Maybe the superiors would know he'd been pranked by his comrades and overlook it. So he'd gone to the training field practically naked.

He still felt the shame when he remembered the snickers of the men around him, his face flaming as he took his place, the vulnerability of standing exposed on the hard ground. And the comments afterward in the barracks about how scrawny he was.

The colonel hadn't punished him but he also hadn't let him leave to find his uniform. Burne had had to perform the entire day's training almost naked, getting scraped and bruised as he ran and climbed, and with the others taunting and poking at him, and shoving when the colonel wasn't watching. No one would partner with him and by the end of the day, everyone followed Cap and Stone's lead of ridiculing him. He hadn't reported them as the ones who'd played the prank but they'd nonetheless despised him. What had they wanted him to do?

Yellow-Bellied Burne, they said. A coward. Because he hadn't fought back? Did they want him to fight them? They knew they could beat him. What was the point?

He was breathing too fast. He slumped on Gray's bed in the dim light from the streetlamps and tried to calm himself, but his pulse raced and his chest was tight, the tightness spreading across his shoulders and through to his back and down his arms. "I'm not dying," he mouthed silently. His fingers tingled and his heartbeat skipped but it didn't mean anything. His heart wasn't going to stop. It always felt this way when he had an attack.

The dread had gripped him, though, like a metal glove around his heart. It would go away—it always went away. But sometimes it took hours.

Gray sat beside him, watching him. Shame welled up in Burne's chest. He'd led Gray on with his kisses and taking off Gray's clothes and then he'd failed and all the romance had fizzled out. Gray must be disappointed. Burne's hand rested on Gray's arm and it shook as he withdrew it and dropped it to his lap.

He couldn't do this. He should've known better than to kiss someone as beautiful and confident as Gray. Burne couldn't even look at him.

A door creaked below them and someone came into the sitting room.

"Gray?" a woman's voice called up the stairs.

Chapter 7

"GRAY? ARE YOU HERE?" THE woman's voice called.

"Come on," Gray said quietly, touching Burne's elbow. "Come meet Hyacinth."

Gray called down to her as he stood and pulled his clothes back on. He ran his fingers through his hair. Burne didn't move.

"Come on," Gray said again and went to the door.

The shaking in Burne's hands had stopped. His feet were numb as he stood and his shoulders were stiff with the awful feeling filling him, but it couldn't hurt him. He just had to wait it out. He forced his legs to move, imitating a normal gait across the room. He kept a hand on the wall to steady himself as he navigated the staircase down to the ground floor. Each step was careful and he made it down without stumbling.

Gray's sister stood in the center of the parlor in a flowered dress. She smiled at Burne as soon as he saw her. She had Gray's perfect cheekbones and thin lips and his smooth dark hair, but hers was darker even than Gray's and fell down her back.

Her eyes darted to Gray. "Your message makes a little more sense now."

"Sorry about that. I tried." Gray rubbed the back of his neck and his cheeks looked rosy in the lamplight. "Um, this is Burne. He's Kate's son."

Hyacinth lit up. "Kate's mentioned you. I'm so glad you're home."

"There's a bit more," Gray said, "and you're going to be overcome with happiness so why don't you sit first."

Burne furrowed his brow at the way Gray spoke to his sister but Hyacinth only rolled her eyes. "He thinks I'm too ebullient," she said to Burne. She crossed the room with a slight limp and sat on a cushioned bench.

"I didn't say 'ebullient,'" Gray replied. "I don't even know what that means."

"Maybe it was 'exuberant.'"

"I said you're *always* in a cheerful mood even when you have a bad day." He plopped down next to her on the bench. Burne slowly sat across from them. His breathing was steady and his heartbeat slowing, but the tightness across his chest was excruciating. He should ask to leave—he could go outside and lie on a bench in the park until it passed. But Hyacinth was smiling at him. No one would understand if he left suddenly. He tried to focus his attention on Gray and Hyacinth.

He'd been at the Haven for a full season but otherwise he'd never seen a fairy, and seeing Hyacinth and Gray together struck him. Hyacinth's skin shone with the shimmer all fairies had and he guessed she wasn't using any illusions the way Gray did. Her hair was black. Was Gray's hair naturally as dark as hers without his illusions?

"Whatever's wrong with being cheerful?" Hyacinth asked Gray.

"Nothing," Gray muttered. "Prepare yourself to be euphoric." He slouched sideways and put one foot up on the footstool in front of his sister. "I meant for the bird to tell you I was following a . . . mysterious and beautiful man into the forest and might not be home as usual."

Had Gray truly thought he was mysterious and beautiful or was he just saying so?

"Well *that* would have put my mind at ease," Hyacinth said. "What were you thinking, following a stranger into the forest?"

"That he was mysterious and beautiful?"

"It was just me," Burne said, "so he wasn't in any danger."

"And he thought I was a deer," Gray added.

Hyacinth shook her head. "Stars help me."

"But it worked out because he was living in a fortress made of boulders with—can you guess?"

Hyacinth lifted her brow in response.

"Trillium and Woodbine!"

Delight flooded Hyacinth's face as she gasped and covered her mouth with both hands. "I knew they weren't dead!"

"It gets even better," Gray said, and he told Hyacinth about the Haven and the rescued children, and how he'd known Alyss must be Ladi's missing daughter. Burne half-listened. The dread that had gripped him so firmly finally ebbed, little by little. He yawned. Hyacinth was rapt and tears coated her cheeks. Burne yawned again. At last, Gray finished the story.

Hyacinth wiped her tears. "So they—"

Gray took her arm to cut her off. "It's been a long day and Burne needs to return to the Haven tomorrow. Let me get him settled upstairs and then I'll answer all your questions, dear sister."

They stood and Hyacinth clasped Burne's hands. She smiled a dazzling smile through her tears and pressed her lips tight without speaking. Her hands squeezed his and let go and he suspected she wanted to hug him.

Gray led Burne back up to the attic room. Burne could walk easily again, and his breathing was calm and deep. Gray shut the door behind them. "Look," Gray said, coming to stand by him, "about before, I'm sorry I misunderstood what you—"

"No, don't. I mean, you didn't. I'm sorry. I wanted to . . ." Burne didn't know how to explain what had gone wrong.

"It's okay," Gray said. He went to the bed and folded back the quilt and blankets. "Get in bed and get some sleep." When Burne approached, he asked, "Are you okay now?"

"I think so." Most of him felt back to normal, and the tightness in his chest was definitely receding.

"We'll figure it out in the morning, okay?" Gray said.

Burne dipped his head once. And Gray moved past him and shut the door behind him.

Burne exhaled in relief at being alone. What had happened earlier . . . it was just a panic attack like it had been every other time, and it was passing like it always did, and his heart was beating steadily and he wasn't going to die. He sank onto the bed. The morning—he'd see Gray again in the morning.

Burne slowly unbuttoned his shirt—the way Gray had unbuttoned his own, and tried to unbutton Burne's. Skies, how had he messed up so badly earlier? He tugged his trousers off before lying down on the sheets—comforting sheets that smelled like Gray. He still felt mortified about leading Gray on and disappointing him.

But their talk with Hyacinth had reminded him about everything else that had happened that day. Had Ladi tucked Alyss into bed? Probably she'd done it hours ago. Alyss was probably fast asleep, with Ladi sitting beside her. And if Ladi's friend in Woods Rest was Nem's mother, maybe Nem would want to meet her and maybe Burne could help. He wanted to help all he could, however he could.

He stared at the ceiling in the darkness. He'd have to figure it out in the morning. If he ever fell asleep . . .

Burne blinked a few times. The pale light of a sunrise shone in the dormer windows. One window was slightly open and a breeze stole through the room. He stretched in the warm blankets.

Where was he? He'd come to the village to see his mother but he had slept . . . at the flower shop. In Gray's room. He was in Gray's bed, alone.

Burne groaned as he remembered. He'd wanted to be with Gray so badly and Gray had brought him home and he'd messed everything up. If Hyacinth hadn't arrived when she had, what would Burne have done? Gray must be so disappointed after how he'd responded to Burne's kisses. He'd sent Burne to bed like he was a child. Burne covered his face and lay quietly, letting his mortification sink in.

The house was quiet. Burne sighed and slowly sat up, scanning the room. Now that light illuminated the space, he noticed how plain it was. The bed was tucked under the eaves and small, not what he had expected for someone as experienced with romantic encounters as Gray seemed to be . . . but Gray had said he hadn't had any partners since coming to the village. The quilt on top of the bed was worn. On the dresser was a comb and a small glass bottle of black seeds. A pair of shoes poked out from under the dresser. Maybe Gray wore them to blend in around the village.

From his season at the Haven, Burne was used to how simply the fairies lived. But somehow, he had expected Gray to have more things. He looked so sharp and together—how did he achieve it with only a comb?

Burne ran his hand over the back of his head where his mother had cut the hair short. At least she had cleaned him up somewhat. And anyway, Gray hadn't minded when his hair had been snarled and shaggy. Would Gray give him another chance? And if he did, would things between them go any better than they had last night? Thinking about curling up beside Gray in this bed and holding him filled Burne's chest with warm desire. He liked Gray so, so much. Why did thinking about touching him feel so perfect, but when it had been happening, he'd been terrified?

Gray had said they would figure it out but their time together was running out. Burne wanted to return to the Haven to help Trillium and Woodbine with the remaining children, and he should bring the news about Nem's mother. Especially because she might be leaving Woods Rest—if Nem wanted to visit her, they should leave right away. Gray would need to stay here in the village and resume his duties at the flower shop. And he probably wouldn't want to spend more time with Burne, when Burne couldn't even kiss him properly.

Slowly, Burne pulled his clothes on and went to the door.

When he opened it, voices drifted up from below. They were faint—they were coming from the front of the shop.

"I promised to help you," Gray said.

"And you have," Hyacinth replied. "But this is more important. I can make the deliveries too, you know. They'll just be a little slower."

"I don't want to let you down. You know everyone thinks I will."

"Gray, you need to find where you belong. You're not letting me down if you're doing that."

Burne didn't want to interrupt but he didn't want to eavesdrop either. He moved to shut the door and the voices stopped. So instead of backing into the room, he went down the steps.

Hyacinth and Gray leaned on the counter in the flower shop, one on each side, watching for him as he entered. A wave of sweet flower scents rolled over him. In the daylight, the flowers filling the room were even more stunning. Hyacinth stood and came to him.

"Sorry for bombarding you with questions last night," she said. "I was so happy to meet you."

"I was too," Burne said, keeping his gaze on her though he itched to peek at Gray.

"You'll have tea and biscuits, won't you, before you head out?"

"Hyacinth's biscuits are something else," Gray said.

"Don't," she warned, glaring at him.

"One bite," Gray continued, "and you'll want to smear them with butter and jam and—"

"Ugh, I'm your sister, Gray! Stop." She headed into the sitting room, and they followed.

"It's just Burne," Gray said. "He doesn't care."

Hyacinth turned back to Burne. "He does this when we take tea at the grange home with the residents. He does it to embarrass me. Only Gray could make biscuits sound titillating."

"I've noticed that about him," Burne said. Having the facetious Gray back was a relief.

"Those ladies love talking dirty," Gray said.

"Well my biscuits don't appreciate it. They just want to be eaten."

"Mm-hm."

Hyacinth shook her head and moved into the back room. "I walked right into that one."

Standing in the silent room, Burne finally glanced at Gray. Gray smiled at him as if last night had never happened. Burne smiled back and exhaled the tension from his shoulders.

Hyacinth returned with a tray of biscuits and jam. "The tea is brewing," she said. Gray lurched into motion and went to retrieve it.

"What kind of jam is it?" Burne asked as they settled down. Hyacinth spread the dark blue-purple jam onto a biscuit.

"Blueberry. From the bushes at the castle last summer."

"She has quite a garden out back," Gray said, "and she's taken over the village green and the castle gardens and filled them with all her bushes and trees."

"Honestly, Gray, you make it sound like I'm an invader. I haven't heard anyone complain about having more blueberries to harvest."

"She's petitioning the village council to plant fruit trees all along the road to the castle."

"There's such excellent sunlight out there. It's a waste not to. Besides"—Hyacinth's eyes narrowed, and a mischievous smile curled her lips—"if we had more fruit trees, we could be having plum jam on our biscuits this morning. Plum jam is your favorite, isn't that right Gray?"

Gray blushed—actually blushed. Burne had begun to wonder if maybe fairies didn't. Gray glared at Hyacinth as if daring her to continue. Why would plum jam make him blush?

"So Burne," Hyacinth said, "tell me about Trillium and Woodbine. I'm so glad to know they're well. Woodbine taught me all about growing things, which is saying something since we lived underground."

Between bites, Burne told her about the past seasons at the Haven and everything he'd seen. It still felt odd to talk about the Haven. But it wasn't like Hyacinth was going to cause trouble for the children.

"Woodbine always led us on nature walks too," Hyacinth said. "Not often, but the queen needed herbs and flowers for her spells so she couldn't keep us entirely trapped."

"Did the fairies have a school in the caverns?" Burne asked. "We used to have a small one here but it ended during the last king's reign."

"It might be returning," Hyacinth said. "The village printer has been teaching the children to read and his partner started teaching them numbers, and the grange has talked about turning their efforts into a proper school. But we didn't have anything like that. Everything with the fairies is very informal. Elders share the stories of the past around the bonfire or the hearth, and somehow we all learn to read and write. Everyone finds what they like or what they're drawn to, and someone who knows about it takes them on and teaches them."

Gray shifted in his seat.

"And some people just figure it out later," Hyacinth added.

"That's Hy's polite way of saying, *Gray never figured it out*," Gray said.

Hyacinth frowned at him and exhaled. "Gray might not have trained for anything but he has skills."

"Like what?" he said.

She kept her eyes on her brother even though her voice addressed Burne. "He's the most charming person in Sylvania. He could win over anyone."

"That's not useful for anything besides tumbling lots of people."

"That's not true. He could be a diplomat to another continent or he could work with people who've lost loved ones. Gray has an innate sense of empathy. He always puts others at ease. Remember when Astilbe's partner passed on and she wouldn't leave her rooms for three moons and she stopped eating? Who got her to come around? She was out in the passages calling for you."

"Because she wanted me to— Never mind."

Hyacinth frowned. "You'll never admit you have talents aside from being a talented lover."

Gray stood. "Thank you for the biscuits, dear sister. Now I'm taking Burne out of here before you embarrass me further."

"Let me pack biscuits to take back with you," Hyacinth said, rising. "And this time, take a jacket. It's chilly at night. And don't forget your grape hyacinth seeds—you never know when you might need them." She went into the back room.

"You're coming?" Burne said.

"We should talk, don't you think?"

Burne blinked to clear his gaze. Maybe Gray hadn't given up on him. "Thank you."

Gray reached to take his hand and squeezed it.

The village square was coming alive as they stepped out of the flower shop a few minutes later. The moment they did, something fluttered overhead. Featherstone swooped in to land on the shop's sign. He lifted a wing and itched around his feathers with his beak, fluffed himself up, and settled down.

He burst into song.

Gray shook his head, rolling his eyes, and walked away.

They stopped in at Kate's to tell her they were off. And they visited Ladi's apartment behind the herbalist's shop to check on Alyss. Her steady chatter drifted through the window as they neared, and when Ladi let them in, Alyss beamed at them from her seat at the table. She had a stack of pancakes in front of her.

"I've been wondering," Burne said as they walked away from Ladi's door. "What happened to the children's fathers?"

"Some of them were known," Gray said, "but others kept it secret when they brought Oleander a child."

"Why? Were they embarrassed?"

Gray pressed his lips together. "No one my age thought it was wrong cause we'd never seen a human. We had no idea they were like us. We'd grown up thinking they were like cats with kittens—once the child was weaned, they'd never think of it again." He paused, frowning, before he continued.

"I guess the men didn't want anyone knowing they were doing the queen's bidding. No one liked her much. Anyway, as we learned the truth about humans, that they weren't dim-witted animals, some of those men tried to refute the truth. But it was hard to deny with Rose right there, cause obviously she's as clever as anyone. And then they'd say, but she's half fairy. But more and more fairies were visiting Woodglen and meeting humans and seeing what they were like. Some of the men left the forest. Oleander would know who they all are, but I don't think *anyone* wants to ask her."

Maybe those men disappearing was better. If they cared about their children, wouldn't they have come forward by now? And Ladi hadn't mentioned her former lover or his betrayal. Maybe she'd found a way to move on from it.

They retraced their steps from the day before, down the road away from the village until they came to the place where Burne had first seen Gray. As they stepped under the branches, Burne scanned the forest floor for the patch of grape hyacinths Gray had been picking. More of the little purple flowers were blooming.

"How do you use them?" Burne asked, gesturing at the flowers. "You said you're no good with plants."

"Mostly I'm not. I've had a little success with grape hyacinths though. Hy's been trying to teach me things and that was the easiest place for me to start."

"Since they're your name plant." They passed the patch of

flowers and entered deeper into the woods. Burne automatically led the way.

"Yes. The seeds are the most potent part so I gather those when they're ready. Well, the bulb is most potent but I don't like to kill the plant. I'd only dig one up in an emergency."

"But you were picking the flowers . . . ?"

"You can stew them and get out a mildly useful essence. And they're pretty." Burne turned back, waiting for Gray to come up beside him. Gray bowed his head and his hair hid his face. "Hy likes to see them growing," he added quickly. Burne kept watching until Gray peeked up and smiled. "I do, too."

The undergrowth diminished and they continued side by side. "You seem to know how the plant magic works," Burne said. "I bet you could work with other plants too. Maybe you just weren't ready to learn before."

"Maybe."

"Gray, if you're not good at anything, neither am I. All I ever did was errands for my mother, and when I had my first chance at a real post in the King's Guard, I utterly failed."

"From what I've heard about the King's Guard, I'd be alarmed if you'd succeeded."

"It's not like I wanted to be a guard. I guess I just wanted not to be scared of it. I'm scared of *everything*. Every new place I go or thing I do, I'm scared. And no matter how many times I get through doing new things, the fear never gets better. It's always there."

"Is that what happened last night?"

Burne watched his feet as he walked. "I'm so embarrassed."

"Why? Because you didn't want to tumble some guy you hadn't even known a day?"

"I wanted to."

"But you weren't ready. It's okay."

"I disappointed you."

"No, don't think that. Even if we don't ever go there, I'd still want to get to know you."

Burne rolled that thought around in his mind. Being friends with Gray? He'd probably continue to be attracted to him. But if he couldn't handle any more than kissing him . . . ?

The sun was rising behind them, casting a fresh glow under the trees. With his hair short again, the breeze tickled the back of Burne's neck. Burne stole a glimpse at Gray. He never got over how handsome Gray was and how much he wanted to be near him. He didn't want to give up on something more for them.

"I want to be better," he said. "I want to be braver."

"Remember what we were doing this time yesterday?"

"Walking the other direction."

"And remember how you felt?"

Burne ducked his head. "Yes."

"Like it was impossible to leave the forest. And you did it, just like that."

"But I dreaded it. I put it off for three moons. And I panicked when we saw those guards I recognized. I want to be excited about challenges and not panic the minute something goes wrong. That's what I can never achieve no matter how many times I make myself do something."

"Maybe the excitement doesn't come just by doing the things. Or maybe different people feel different ways when they have a challenge."

They walked a few paces in silence as Burne remembered the past night.

"I wasn't just scared," he said at last. "Last night, I mean."

Gray waited for him to continue.

"It was like the start of one of my attacks of anxiety, like I used to have when I first got to the Haven. I was trying to keep it back and keep kissing you but I couldn't stop it." He regarded Gray beside him. Behind Gray a patch of dogwoods stood in a clearing, their snowy blossoms open to the sky. Framed by the blossoms,

Gray could've been the prince in one of Burne's mother's long-ago bedtime stories.

"I want to kiss you," Burne said, "but I'm scared of what will happen."

"Take your time," Gray said. "I can wait."

"You're sure?"

"Mm-hm. But in the meantime, how would you feel if I used you in all my fantasies?"

Burne tripped over a root.

"Don't worry," Gray said smoothly as he kept walking. "I won't imagine anything *too* smutty. I'll imagine what you'll do to me when you find your confidence."

Burne got his legs working again and watched Gray walk ahead of him. Gray wanted him to be confident. And Burne wanted himself to be confident. He just had to figure out how.

Chapter 8

BURNE AND GRAY CROSSED THE forest quietly this time. Burne was getting tired of all the walking. But the previous day had involved interacting with a lot of people and all that talking—at least walking in silence was peaceful.

When they arrived at the Haven around midday, they shared the news they'd learned about Kitty who lived in Woods Rest and who'd had a daughter Nem's age. Trillium went to speak with Nem, and Nem said she'd like to go to Woods Rest. Whether or not Kitty was her mother—although it did seem likely when Burne checked with Trillium about Nem's exact age—Nem wanted to meet her. And if they didn't get on, she said matter-of-factly, she'd come back home.

Once Nem had decided, a sense of urgency filled the Haven. It would be awful for Nem to make the trip only to find Kitty gone from Woods Rest.

"Are you sure you want to take her, Burne?" Trillium said. They sat on the two chairs in the dim front room as Woodbine helped Nem pack for the trip. Gray lay on his front on the floor cushions, propped up with his arms around a pillow.

Trillium had congratulated Burne on succeeding at leaving the forest and visiting his mother but she kept fussing over the idea of him traveling even farther from the Haven, as if she worried he wouldn't be able to do it. Maybe she worried because she sensed he wasn't entirely fine with the idea. What would happen if they met the group of men whom they'd seen on the forest road yesterday morning? Or if something else happened that Burne couldn't handle? He'd have Nem to take care of this time.

But he'd gotten through the incident yesterday, although it was largely thanks to Gray. And there would always be a chance something difficult could happen. He didn't want to hide forever just in case something went wrong. He'd left the forest once. How different could it be to walk to Woods Rest instead of Woodglen?

The hem of Gray's shirt pulled up as he shifted his arms around his pillow, exposing a patch of skin. Burne swallowed. Walking to Woods Rest? No problem. He'd left the forest once and he could do it again. His feelings for Gray were the thing making him helpless and terrified.

He swallowed again and turned to Trillium. "I'm sure. I want to help and someone has to go with Nem."

"It's her first time traveling anywhere," Trillium said, wringing her hands, "and she's right at that age . . ." Trillium bit her lip.

"Where men will notice her?" Gray supplied.

Trillium exhaled. "Yes. Unfortunately."

Burne hadn't been able to protect himself from bullies. Did he really think he could protect Nem? Would he fight if it came to that?

"She'll have me to help defend her," Gray said.

Burne melted inside. Gray had walked all the way back to the Haven with him and folded himself down onto the cushions with no appearance of leaving anytime soon, but Burne hadn't dared to hope he was planning to stick around beyond today.

"You're not terribly menacing," Trillium said. But her manner toward Gray had become less harsh than it had been when he'd first arrived.

"Oh come on, I'm great at scaring people." And he shimmered into an illusion of a Sarlian pirate with bulging muscles and a metal helmet with bone horns curving from it. He snarled and his teeth were pointed.

"Well," Trillium said, "I guess together the two of you should be all right." She stood and moved to the doorway. "Let me see how the packing is going."

"Nem doesn't need our help anyway," Burne said after Trillium had left. "I'm pretty sure she could kick both our asses."

"Even mine?" the pirate growled.

Burne smiled. "Woodbine teaches them all self-defense."

The pirate vanished back into a smiling Gray. "Well, all right then. Nem can protect us."

By the end of the day, they had three packs ready with food and extra clothing and a few coins the two older fairies had saved. They each had a bedroll and a blanket tied to the bottom of their pack, and Burne had an additional tarp they could use in case of rain. Woods Rest was only two days away, three at most. But the bulging packs seemed to hold enough to get the travelers to Nor Bay.

Burne made a pot of stew for the whole group for dinner and they ate as usual around the courtyard fire. Everyone knew Nem was leaving, and all the children tried to sit beside her or in some cases, on her. Trillium stayed close beside Woodbine, holding her hand. Nem had been with them the longest.

Somehow the dinner felt final to Burne, too, as if it was the end of his time at the Haven and this would be the last meal he'd share at this fire. Would he be back? Of course he'd escort Nem back if things didn't work out with Kitty. And if Nem stayed with her mother, he would return to see how else he might help. Now that Alyss had left, the other children talked more about their mothers. Trillium and Woodbine had been discussing how they might send word around the continent to find them. They all had a lot left to do.

So why did he have a hunch he'd never be back? Burne sat there until the embers burned to ash before going to bed.

Early the next morning, Burne, Gray, and Nem set out for Woods Rest. They each carried a pack, and Nem had wound her long braid into a bun on the back of her head. And they were all barefoot, although Burne had again tucked his shoes into his pack. He kept expecting to need them when he reentered human spaces, but so far he hadn't.

They headed northeast this time. The others let Burne walk first as if he had navigating experience that they lacked. He'd traversed the forest to Woodglen numerous times but he'd never been this way. But he didn't want Nem to worry any more than she already was—although she hid it—so he pretended he knew where he was going. He checked the sun's position as it rose and watched for the landmarks Woodbine had told him about. Even with his uncertainty, leaving the Haven today felt so much easier than it had two days ago. He didn't yet feel any fear about what would happen when they reached the road.

For the first hour, the trek was easy and they hiked in silence. Birds chittered in the trees. They passed through shadowed glens where the forest floor was flat and open, and they crossed bushy open areas with rotting logs and creek beds heading through the undergrowth to the sea. The chill of morning wore off as the sun climbed higher and the breezes died, and squirrels appeared, hunting through the pine needles on the ground.

Another hour passed with nothing to observe but more trees. Walking was easy, but he'd done so much of it lately. Even with the steady outdoor activity of life at the Haven, his calves felt sore. Why hadn't they reached the road? They walked at an angle to the road as it cut through the forest—it would take longer to reach the road today than it had when he'd walked straight east to Woodglen. He shouldn't panic because they hadn't reached it yet.

But walking to Woodglen, he'd been familiar with the markers to spy along the way; today, nothing was familiar. And he'd been alone. Now he had Nem counting on him. And Gray was walking behind him and waiting for him to turn confident so they could start kissing again.

"We can't miss the road," he muttered. The forest road cut

through the trees from Woodglen to Woods Rest, so as long as they headed in a somewhat easterly direction, they'd have to run into it.

"What's that?" Gray asked.

Burne turned. "Nothing," he mumbled. His companions seemed fine—Gray came first behind him and farther back, Nem was scanning the forest. For some reason, she had tied her blanket around her neck and wore it like a cape. "All we have to do is keep walking this direction and we'll come to the forest road, and we follow it north. We're not lost."

"No," Gray said, "I'm not lost at all. All I have to do is keep watching your—"

"Do you hear something?" Nem asked.

"My what?" Burne asked Gray.

"Shhh," Nem ordered and Gray closed his mouth. She stopped walking and turned her head. Burne and Gray stopped and waited.

They'd descended into what might be an old stream bed, a wide swath across the forest floor with tall, steep sides they'd had to shimmy down. The depression led away in both directions, slightly uphill to the west and downhill to the east. The high sun illuminated the open space. A few trees had grown quickly in the full light, standing as tall as the older trees above the depression.

Burne closed his eyes and listened.

Overhead, the wind rustled the evergreen boughs and the still-naked branches of an oak tree scraped together. But he didn't hear anything else.

Except he should have. He should have heard birds singing.

He frowned at Gray. Gray shook his head.

"That way," Nem said, pointing. A cloud of dust rose over the top of the ridge where the depression disappeared over the incline. And now he did hear a faint thumping like horses passing on the road and the strangest noise, a snuffling-barking-crying sound all mixed together.

Something flickered at the top end of the depression. An animal was running toward them. And then another of the animals. The thumping grew to a pounding and more animals surged over the top, thundering down toward them. Not horses. They were—

"They're boars," Gray gasped out as a flood of the creatures crested the hilltop.

Burne gaped at the sight. A herd of wild pigs, funneled downhill by the depression, was stampeding toward them. Leaves kicked up under the animals' hooves and the cloud of dust rose as they pounded down the old stream bed, shaking the ground beneath his bare feet. What had started the—

Nem smacked Burne's arm and he shook himself from his stupor. Act, he needed to act. Nem strode to the nearest tree and reached up for a thick branch. She pulled herself up, pack and all, with her blanket hanging behind her. Burne followed, hitching up his pack, and gripped the branch as Nem clambered away from it and worked her way higher, climbing from one branch to another.

Wait, where was Gray?

Burne spun back. Gray stood rooted in the middle of the depression and staring at the thundering herd. The boars were halfway down the incline, squealing as they ran.

Power surged through Burne as he dropped his pack and darted across to Gray. He dragged Gray into motion and pulled him to the base of the tree. Gray's eyes were wide and lost. Burne placed Gray's hands on the branch.

"Climb, Gray!" he said and reached for his waist to lift him.

Gray gripped the branch but he missed Burne's lift. His arms tensed but he barely moved. Burne pulled Gray's pack off to make climbing easier.

"Harder this time." Burne gripped Gray's body and hefted him up. Gray shook his head awake and lifted his arms as the roar of the animals heightened. He caught the upward motion and pulled himself up into the tree, getting his legs up and reaching for the next branch up. Burne steadied Gray's body as Gray held on and stood. Gray stretched his leg over the higher branch. He wasn't going to fall.

Burne darted around the tree. The lowest branch on this side was too thin to support him. He dug his foot in against a knot in the bark and held onto the base of the thin branch, stepping up against the trunk. His fingers found another knot and he boosted himself higher to reach the next branch. This one was strong. As soon as his fingers were around it, he pulled himself up with one arm. He hugged the trunk against his body with his other arm and got a leg over the branch. The position was awkward but he hung on. Dust filled his nostrils and a boar plowed past beneath him. Then a sea of boars surged by.

The rough trunk in his arms vibrated in time with the pounding beats of hooves, and the dirty haze rising from below tickled his nostrils. He held tighter and sneezed before pressing his cheek into the scraping bark. Boars flooded past several hands below his perch as the herd parted to flow around the tree. The animals were huge, with bristly hairs on their gray skin and long snouts, snorting and braying as they thudded into each other.

Burne twisted his neck to peer uphill. The back end of the pack was coming. He coughed and forced himself to swallow the dryness from his mouth. What would startle a herd of boars? Hopefully nothing worse appeared at the top of the hill in their wake.

Gray's foot pressed into the tree near Burne's head. Gray hugged the trunk like Burne did, sitting on a thick branch and with his legs wrapped around the trunk like he didn't trust the branch not to break. His face was turned away. Higher up, Nem sat sideways, leaning against the trunk with one arm around it and swinging her legs. She lifted her free hand in a wave.

Burne exhaled and leaned his forehead on the trunk. The strength ebbed out of him so he shook slightly, but not like he did when he panicked. They were safe. He'd gotten Gray out of the pigs' path in time. Hopefully Nem would be so excited about her new mother she'd never think to tell Trillium and Woodbine they'd almost been trampled by wild pigs not two hours after leaving the Haven.

The end of the herd passed beneath the branches with a few stragglers loping along after it. Silence returned as the cloud of dust and boars moved down the channel, disappearing into the trees. Gray sneezed. Burne swallowed again and held onto the trunk until the last boar had disappeared.

He loosened his stranglehold on the tree and inspected the ground beneath them. The low bushes and plants where the boars had passed were mauled into pulp with the branches stripped bare. Tattered remains of last fall's leaves scattered over hard-packed dirt. A grayish shape clung to the side of the channel. Burne's mood sank—it was his blanket. The packs they'd abandoned on the ground were gone.

Burne cursed quietly. But they were unharmed and that was more important than losing their packs. And Nem had hers. He maneuvered his leg off the branch until he could drop to the ground.

Burne kept his arms out as Gray climbed slowly down from the tree. Gray's face was ashen and his hands shook as he reached for handholds. When he sat on the lowest branch, Burne lifted him down. Gray swayed like he might collapse. Burne kept an arm around his shoulders, holding tight, and Gray's body trembled under Burne's fingers. Nem peered down from her high perch, and when she saw Burne staring up at her, she made her way down. She descended easily on her own so Burne turned to Gray.

Burne squeezed Gray's shoulder. "Hey."

"Black stars," Gray whispered.

"You okay?"

"I would've died if you hadn't been here."

Burne couldn't deny that. "We all made it up safely."

Nem dropped lightly to the ground, landing in a crouch. She stood, arranged her cape blanket, and leaned on the tree trunk, surveying the forest.

Gray stared unfocused. "I'm bad at everything. I can't sense anything around me in the forest, I'm bad at communicating with animals, I can't even climb trees properly. I'm the worst fairy ever."

Burne put his other arm around Gray and pulled him in to hug all of him. He smelled sweaty with fear and dust coated his hair. "You did fine. Even Hyacinth couldn't have stopped that bunch."

"She'd have known they were coming, though," Gray said into Burne's neck. "She'd have been out of their path and watching them parade past."

"You'll get better with practice," Burne said. "You said Hyacinth is teaching you. You're just getting a late start."

Gray sank slightly, pressing into Burne's chest. "I'm so embarrassed. You'll think . . ."

Burne could think only to kiss Gray's temple. He held him close another moment before reluctantly releasing him. "Come on, we'd better get going."

Burne retrieved the dirty blanket and shook it, releasing a cloud of dust. Further down the stream bed lay one of the packs. He plodded down to get it. Bits and pieces of their food were strewn beyond it, trampled into the dirt along with scraps of the bedroll and tarp. The pack had shredded open but his shoes were wedged down in the bottom. His blanket must've been thrown to the side from the start to have survived the hooves. Gray's pack was nowhere in sight.

Burne folded the blanket, tucked it into the dilapidated pack, and slipped the straps over his shoulders. Gray and Nem watched him from beside the tree they'd climbed. He trudged back to where they stood and turned northeast.

He didn't bother to check the sun after that. It didn't matter—they'd keep pushing forward until they hit the road. They didn't stop for lunch. After the boar incident, Burne had no appetite, and when he asked the others if they wanted to stop, Nem said she was fine. Gray simply shook his head.

They reached the forest road by late afternoon. Walking on the cleared, flat surface of the road was easier than the forest, but the soles of Burne's feet ached. Even a season of fairy life hadn't prepared his bare feet for this much walking. Nem walked briskly with her eyes alert and said nothing about being uncomfortable, and Gray trudged after them silently, which was unusual for him. How were his feet? He'd been barefoot when Burne first met him but he had shoes in his bedroom. If he wore them in the village, maybe his bare soles weren't used to this much walking, either. He hadn't said two words since they'd left the site of the boar stampede.

The road remained deserted. Where had the men from two days ago gone? What if they'd gone to Woods Rest and were heading back? If he heard them coming, should he face them or lead the others off the road and try to hide? Could Gray hide them in his current state? He seemed confident about his illusions but he must be tired after all the walking and climbing the tree. Anyway, it was better not to daydream about bad things happening, if it didn't help him plan a course of action.

After a few minutes on the road, they reached a leaguepost marking the distance. The carved stone was clean and straight, not like the markers Burne remembered near Woodglen. Maybe the new Council of Villages had erected this one. The shops and park in Woodglen had been spruced up since last spring. With the king gone, maybe the new leaders were undertaking projects like improving the sparse, dilapidated markers that had long designated distances on the forest road. This one showed they had over two leagues left to walk to Woods Rest.

A stiff breeze lifted Burne's hair. He glanced up. How had the sky clouded over so quickly? Between the interlaced branches, gray clouds loomed over them, darkening even as Burne watched. Thunder rumbled to the west.

"Black skies," Burne muttered, stopping. His shoulders sagged in exhaustion and his feet ached on the hard dirt. "We should find shelter," he said aloud. On either side, the trees loomed in the gathering darkness. It had grown so dark inside the forest that he squinted to see under the trees. A drop of rain tapped on the side of his nose.

Nem peered up into the branches of a thick pine tree but a tree wouldn't do in a thunderstorm. If he even had the strength left to climb.

"How about that thicket," he said, pointing at a bush with thick, waxy leaves a few paces into the trees.

Nem darted off the road as the rain drops increased. She pulled off her cape and clutched it to her chest. Burne indicated for Gray to go after her and followed behind him. With only the new leaves of spring, the trees sheltered them from the rain, but they wouldn't for long.

A clap of thunder echoed through the forest as Nem knelt beside the thicket. She crawled into the leafy branches, hugging her pack and blanket in front of her. Burne nudged Gray to follow and crept in last. The branches caught in his curls and scraped his cheeks but they were widely spaced enough for a person to fit through. The leaves screened out the forest completely, leaving him in dim darkness. Hopefully they'd block the rain when it came down hard.

No cozy clearing filled the center of the thicket like in storybooks, just a tangle of branches. Nem sat upright and worked herself around to face him and Gray. She carefully wrapped her blanket around her shoulders. Gray tried to find a seat, leaning back off his knees and getting stuck, then finding a clear place, leaning back into a poking branch, and jolting forward. Burne couldn't reach over to help him through the branches. He crawled alongside Gray and twisted his body until his butt reached the ground. Rain pattered on the leaves overhead but nothing dripped through yet.

In the semidarkness, Nem opened her pack on her lap and rummaged inside it. Gray settled with an exhale. Burne tried to scootch closer but the branches snagged him. He leaned so he could see Gray's face. After all this, was Gray sorry he'd come?

Nem pulled out a bundled kerchief. She untied the knot and handed Burne and Gray each a handful of dried apple slices.

Burne bit into one and ripped off a piece. It was mildly sweet and overly chewy but right then, it was the best thing he'd ever eaten. Nem sipped from her water gourd and passed it to Burne.

Burne took a sip. "Are you doing okay?" he asked her.

"*I'm* fine," Nem said, her eyes darting to Gray and back. He sat hunched over, slowly chewing an apple slice.

Thunder boomed and a gust of wind rattled the branches. The rain drummed steadily on the thicket but their refuge remained dry.

"I think we should sleep here," Burne said. "We'd have to stop for the night even without the storm. We can make it to Woods Rest tomorrow."

Nem nestled her pack to the ground and piled her blanket beside it. She dug around in the pack again and came out with a loaf of bread.

They ate in silence for a while, listening to the rain. It reached a peak, with thunder rolling through the forest and flashes of lightning piercing the thicket's leaves. But the rain penetrated only with a drip here and there. Burne licked the sticky residue of an apple ring off his fingers and tasted dirt.

At last the storm moved off. The darkness grew denser, as if behind all the clouds, the sun had set. The wind moaned through the trees, releasing drips of rainwater and bursts of moist cool air through the thicket, but the rolls of thunder had ceased. They could return to the forest to sleep in an open space, but the ground would be wet. And more storms might come through in the night. Besides, Burne was so tired he wasn't sure he could crawl out of the branches. And he was dirty enough that sleeping on the dirt and dead leaves and branches didn't seem to matter. He might find a pool of rainwater to scrub his face clean but the effort to search for it was too much.

Gray sniffed and slowly pushed his hair off his face. "Thanks for sharing, Nem. Food always helps." His face was devoid of his smile and his eyes dull. He appeared miserable but a more upright kind of miserable than when they'd first crawled into the bush.

"You can have the bedroll," Nem said.

"We'll be fine," Burne said. "We've got one blanket still." He worked the dirty blanket out of the torn pack.

"Why didn't you heat it?" Nem said.

Burne squinted at her.

Nem held up the edge of her blanket, although the darkness obscured it. "They have the solar chips, same as the winter clothing. Didn't you know?"

Burne exhaled, cursing to himself. Nem hadn't been wearing her blanket like a cape for no reason. She'd been gathering the heat of the sun. "I forgot."

"Well," she said, and if Burne didn't know better, he might have thought she was holding back a smile, "I guess the two of you will have to huddle for warmth. Goodnight." And with that, she shifted away from him and began spreading her bedroll under the branches.

Burne met Gray's eyes in the dark.

"At least something about this day doesn't suck," Gray said.

It took them a full ten minutes of shifting between branches until they were lying on the ground. Burne paused a moment to relax his muscles. His body was dirty and tired but the rain had brought alive the scents of the forest, releasing them from the bark and the moss, and they overpowered the dirt and sweat. The spring growth pushed up through the soil, adding to the forest smell. Burne yawned, stretching his back and then his legs. Gray was near him. A peace stole through him, the feeling of being near Gray and of making Nem's journey with her. He was so glad to be here with them.

Gray sniffled again, and happiness ebbed. Gray was uncomfortable. And he didn't have to be here. But he hadn't said anything about turning back. Would he resent Burne for leading him on this trip? No, that thought was worrying for nothing. Gray didn't blame him for the pigs or the storm. And Burne would do what he could to make him less uncomfortable. And tomorrow they'd find Nem's mother. She'd be wonderful and once Nem had settled in with her, he and Gray would be done with their duties for the moment and free to go off together. They'd be clean and warm and dry, and Burne could hold him, not rushing this time. Maybe if he went slower and held him longer it would be okay and he wouldn't get so overcome with it. If they could just be alone together.

Burne could barely see, but he groped beside himself until he found Gray, an arm beside a hip. He wiggled across the dirt until his chest came up against the solid heat of Gray's body. "This okay?" he whispered. In answer, Gray rolled to fit his back snugly into Burne's chest.

With his free arm, Burne spread the blanket over them. He caught the far end in his toes and stretched it down to cover their legs. He reached his lower arm up and nudged it under Gray's head as a pillow, and tucked his other arm under the blanket and pulled Gray against his chest.

Through the smells of dirt and rain and the mushroomy fragrance of the forest floor, Burne inhaled Gray's scent. He sighed out the whole day and held Gray tighter, burying his nose in Gray's hair. Without the pressure of expecting this moment to lead to more—to kissing, then tumbling—he could simply enjoy lying with Gray. In his arms, Gray relaxed, too, and his fingers slipped up under Burne's hand and between Burne's fingers, curving their fists together. Gray pulled Burne's hand to his chest.

Patters of rain dripped above them, and somewhere distant an owl called. Burne almost didn't want to fall asleep so he could revel in holding Gray, but he couldn't stop sleep from taking him.

Chapter 9

AT LAST, AS THE THICK trees ended and fields spread before them, they neared Woods Rest. The road ahead meandered through the lush green of spring wheat waving gently, and farther back, dirty white sheep grazed on grass behind a fence. The scent of new hay carried on the breeze. The late morning sun broke through a mass of clouds high in the sky and warmed Burne's face. His whole body ached from the journey but the clear morning made his mood light.

"Stop," Nem said and came around to face Burne and Gray. "You two look terrible."

Burne ran his hand through his hair for the hundredth time that morning and another twig fell out. Their clothes were dirty and torn in a few places. But Burne had woken to Gray's smile and they'd lain staring at each other until Nem started to move, and "terrible" was not a word that made any sense at all where Gray's looks were concerned. Maybe *he* looked bad, but—

"If I'm going to meet my mother with you two, I don't want you looking like you crawled out from under a thicket."

Burne couldn't tell if Nem was making a joke, but he lifted his chin and straightened. "Have at it," he said.

Nem began brushing him off and stood on her toes to comb a few more twigs from the top of his head, and once she'd finished with him, she moved on to Gray. It was encouraging she wanted to impress Kitty. Her own straight hair was combed and neat in a braid down her back.

They ate the rest of the dried apples as they continued along the road. A farmer with a hoe over his shoulder trudged past them whistling and waved hello, and soon after they reached the outer cottages of Woods Rest. Burne had visited Woods Rest as a child but he didn't remember much.

The cottages became denser, one beside another with only the kitchen gardens between them and softly clucking chickens darting among the plants. More villagers were about, walking home with packages or carrying baskets into the village. Hammer blows on iron rang out from the eastern side of the buildings ahead. A row of budding fruit trees led to a wide space and they entered the village square. Folks lingered on the porch of a general store and children ran in the garden beside the modest grange hall. A few other shops had doors propped open. Only the pub was closed up and quiet.

Ladi's directions led them across the square and a short way down a lane. The house was easy to spot with its stone walls instead of the usual boards. A row of budding spring flowers lined a walk up to a wide front porch. A child wailed inside. And suddenly, Burne understood Nem's connection with the people who lived in the house. Something clicked into place in a way it hadn't before. It wasn't only Nem's mother who lived here. Kitty lived with other children who'd been held captive by the former fairy queen the way Nem had. They'd been the youngest ones and had not yet been smuggled out to the Haven when Princess Rose rescued them last spring.

Nem might have met these children before. Would she remember them? What would that be like? Burne glanced at Nem but her face was impassive as she faced the front of the house.

"Hyacinth would approve," Gray said, indicating a bud of blue hyacinth unfolding into the sun beside a few spring squills.

A woman stepped out the door with the wailing child on her hip. She faced them on the porch, clearly waiting for them to approach. The child's wails died away as, distracted, he gaped at the wide outdoors, blinking. When his gaze reached them he waved his chubby arms. Two more young children slipped out the door, along with a large tabby cat who wound through all the legs before sauntering to the end of the porch and flopping over in a patch of sunshine.

"Ready?" Burne asked quietly, and Nem stretched taller and exhaled. They started forward. The woman's eyes flicked between the three of them and her arms tightened on the child. She spoke a word to the other children and they scurried back inside. Did he and Gray appear menacing? Nem certainly didn't. Maybe the woman had seen Gray's and Nem's green eyes and realized they were fairies. Given her history with fairies, that might scare her.

"Ladi sent us," Burne called as soon as he was close enough. The woman's stance relaxed a smidge. "We're here to see Kitty."

"Kitty's out."

Burne checked Nem one last time. She still faced straight ahead. Burne took her hand and squeezed. "This is Anemone," he said. "She may be Kitty's daughter."

The woman jerked back so fast she almost dropped the child. She opened her mouth but couldn't speak for a moment. Finally she uttered, "I'm Maryanne. You'd better come in."

Inside the house was a mess. On the floor of the sitting room, button-eyed dolls made of cornhusks and bundled rags lay in the middle of a tea party, with broken-handled porcelain tea cups fancy enough for the castle. A half-made splint basket took up most of a sofa. Across the hallway, crates of potatoes covered half of a dining table. Maryanne put the child down on a blanket on the sitting room floor. He rolled around, apparently not yet able to stand. Four children appeared at the end of the hallway, but Maryanne went to them and herded them back into the kitchen and out a back door. Nem watched them go.

Maryanne returned and motioned them into the sitting room and onto chairs, pushing aside a sewing project. She sat on the floor and held up a doll for the child, who gurgled and reached for it. Nem studied the floorboards and held her hands in her lap.

Trillium had helped Nem practice what to say, but they'd imagined Kitty being in the room. Since Nem didn't move to speak, Burne cleared his throat. "I'm Burne, and this is Nem and Gray. Nem grew up in the fairy caverns as one of the former fairy queen's servants. Some fairies smuggled her out eight winters ago and told the queen she had passed on. They rescued the children one by one, but they kept it secret so the queen wouldn't find out."

Maryanne had frozen with her lips parted. "Where have they been?" she whispered.

"They've been living in a shelter in the forest. Now with the queen gone, they're trying to find their mothers. Gray lives in Woodglen and he knows Ladi, and when he met the children, he recognized Alyss as her child. Ladi thinks Nem might be Kitty's daughter. She's sixteen."

Burne regarded Nem and she smiled awkwardly. Maryanne had forgotten her child and he fussed. She gave him her hand to play with. She shook her head slowly and opened her mouth, but said nothing.

"Do you think it's true?" Nem said timidly.

Something shifted in Maryanne, as if some mothering instinct kicked in, and her voice sounded kinder than it had so far. "You favor her. You have the same face and hair."

Nem wet her lips. "The children who live here. The tallest one—is that Cedar?"

Maryanne startled and her eyes narrowed. "We don't use those names. He's Amare now."

"I'm sorry." Nem stared at her lap.

Gray scowled and Burne reached for his hand and squeezed to keep him silent. Maryanne's antagonism wasn't ideal, but arguing with her in front of Nem wouldn't help. And Nem would tell them if she wanted to leave.

But Maryanne exhaled. "No, I'm sorry I spoke to you that way.

You didn't know about the names and this must be strange for you. I just don't want anything to hurt them again." She peered at Gray. "I've met only two fairies in my life and they were both liars."

"I'm a lot of things," Gray said, "but not that."

"Do you . . . have children?" she asked.

"I do not," Gray said, holding her gaze, "and I've never seduced a human."

Burne's face flamed hot.

"Um, a human woman," Gray added, touching his hair. He dropped his gaze and fought a grin trying to spread across his face.

Burne fidgeted with the hem of his shirt and Nem actually peeked over at them.

"You said Ladi's found her daughter?" Maryanne asked.

"Yes. Alyss," Burne said, smoothing out his shirt and folding his hands. Maryanne hadn't even noticed his awkwardness. "We brought her to Woodglen three days ago."

Maryanne's eyes shone. "I can't wait to meet her. So how do you know Ladi?"

"She's friends with my sister," Gray said. "Hyacinth runs the flower shop in Woodglen."

"The flower shop in Woodglen is run by *fairies*?"

"She's far better with flowers than any human's likely to be," Gray said, and Burne grabbed his hand and squeezed again. He wasn't enthused with Maryanne's attitude either, but she had her own history with fairies that none of them understood. And her attack hadn't been aimed at Nem, at least.

Maryanne shook her head and turned back to Nem. "Kitty will be . . . so happy to meet you," she said. "She'll be shocked. We all thought you were . . . gone. But she's not here. She went to visit her mother in Cliffside and she hasn't come back."

Burne shifted at her tone. "Is that unexpected?"

"She meant to go for a quarter-moon and it's been three. I've twice sent letters with travelers going north and gotten no response, and I haven't been able to find either of those travelers to ask in person if they saw her. Jane and Liza are visiting Knotty Knob and left me with the five of them"—she tilted her head toward the back of the house—"so I can't leave the house easily. I went by the grange this morning to see if anyone had been out toward Cliffside. But the grange was in chaos because all the peacekeepers have fallen ill all at once."

"What?" Burne said as Gray came to attention.

"The peacekeepers all ate some stew or something, and—"

"It can't be a coincidence," Gray said.

"The peacekeepers in Woodglen all fell ill," Burne told Maryanne, "after eating together."

"Could it be from the food?" Maryanne suggested. "Maybe a spoiled ingredient used both here and in Woodglen?"

"If it were food poisoning, it would pass quickly. The Woodglen peacekeepers remained sick a day later."

The child started to slump on the floor. Maryanne picked him up and rested him against her shoulder. "Now I'm alarmed. Strangers passed through a few days ago, which wouldn't be alarming but two of them had horses, which is odd for how they were dressed. And they stirred up trouble at the pub and gave Wells a black eye. We were just glad they were gone in the morning and didn't wonder where they'd gone to."

"What if you can't find the two messengers," Nem said quietly, "because they never returned from Cliffside?"

No one spoke as her words sank in. Had something happened in Cliffside? Nem was on the brink of meeting her mother, and now Kitty had vanished in Cliffside amid these odd circumstances. They couldn't sit in Woods Rest and wait to see what happened. She might never return.

"Someone has to go to Cliffside," Gray said, echoing Burne's thoughts. Gray kept his gaze averted from Burne.

They'd seen Cap and his crew on the road three days ago, heading north from Woodglen. And the strangers brawling in the Woods Rest pub sounded like the men Burne had met in the King's

Guard. If those men were converging on Cliffside, they had to be up to something nefarious. The thought of facing them—of heading straight into their clutches—tied Burne's stomach in a knot, and his hands trembled. But Nem clutched her hands in her lap, her eyes wide and glassy. She deserved to find her mother and to find her safely. And Gray—

It wasn't a noble reason to want to go to Cliffside. But Burne wanted Gray to look at him and see someone brave and confident, not someone who'd shirk a task because he was scared of bullies. Maybe if he went to Cliffside and faced the men there, he would finally be brave enough. His eyes met Gray's.

"I'll go," Burne said.

"I'll go with you," Gray replied, and the fear in Burne's chest eased a little. One side of Gray's lips curved up and he mouthed some words.

What was he saying? You. . . You need me?

You need me to keep you warm.

Burne heated on the spot.

"That's settled then," Maryanne said.

"I'm going too." Nem was blinking rapidly and watching Burne.

All three of the adults protested.

But Nem's face was set. "I'm going. Those two need me or they'll never make it in one piece."

Burne couldn't disagree.

Chapter 10

Maryanne insisted they spend the night in Woods Rest before starting out for Cliffside. They spent the afternoon preparing to continue their journey and finding the local grange leader, so they wouldn't have had much time to travel before sunset in any case.

They told the grange leader about the ill peacekeepers in Woodglen and the ex-guardsmen traveling through and he agreed something seemed odd. Gray questioned him about the peacekeepers' symptoms and suggested they might have been poisoned. He arranged to send a message to Hyacinth to alert her and the rest of Woodglen that something was amiss, and the grange leader said he would speak with the herbalist in Woods Rest.

Maryanne stitched up Burne's pack, filled both packs with food, and added an extra blanket. She warned them someone had been harassing travelers north of Woods Rest. Apparently, Wells the tinsmith had lost all his coins. He'd almost lost the horse the farrier had just shod, which he had taken out for a quick ride and planned to return before its owner reappeared. But he'd risked mounting it and riding away. The bandit hadn't shot after him, thankfully.

Maryanne had invited Wells for dinner when she heard about his ordeal. Her housemates were away so she'd been glad of the company and she felt sorry for him since he'd lost a half-moon's wages to the bandit. Plus, she'd had a stew on the stove that was his favorite, and the boys loved goofing around with him, and—

Gray had cocked his head to one side as Maryanne told this

story until she reached the part where Wells was a bachelor. Gray subtly lifted his eyebrows at Burne and Burne had to stifle a snort. He forced himself to attend and smile as Maryanne rambled on about Wells's many attributes. Why hadn't Wells offered to go to Cliffside and find Kitty, if he was such a catch?

"Maybe he's not a catch," Gray said later as they lay in their beds. The house had an awful lot of beds crammed into the upstairs rooms, but it had an awful lot of occupants to use them. Maryanne slept in one room with the five children who were present. Her missing housemates, Jane and Liza, slept in the other room with their children, but since they were away, Maryanne gave Burne and Gray their beds, and Nem asked to stay with them.

"Not a catch? What do you mean?" Burne asked from the lower bunk. He wished he could see through the mattress to where Gray lay in the semidarkness above him.

"Maybe Wells the tinsmith is just a good tumble."

"Gray!"

"What? Nem's old enough to talk about tumbling. She knows all about it." He leaned off his bunk toward Nem, lying in the bottom bunk against the opposite wall. Burne could barely make out Gray's silhouette in the starlight through the windows. "You do, don't you?"

Nem snorted in response.

"Fairies teach children that stuff," Gray said, settling back where Burne could no longer see him. "They make sure the girls understand about taking bitter herbs to stop pregnancy. And they teach lessons that've been used since Queen Delphinium made them up centuries ago. Like about the difference between lust and love, and how not to mix them up—so no one gets confused, you know?"

Gray leaned over the edge of the bunk again, but this time he twisted far enough to regard Burne.

"So nobody's feelings are hurt because one person is in love and the other just wants to tumble."

Burne swallowed, trying to see Gray's eyes. Which one was Gray—someone who was in love or someone who just wanted to tumble?

And which one was he, for that matter?

Clearly they both wanted to tumble. But was there more?

"Trillium taught us all that stuff," Nem said, and Gray disappeared again. "And she made us pretend to be couples flirting with each other and practice saying no."

"Saying no?" Burne asked, confused.

"For when the other person wants to and you don't."

Burne remembered the maids coming on to him in the castle pantry and how he'd mumbled that he was busy or needed to get back to the kitchen. Maybe he could've just told them no.

"No one taught you all this?" Nem asked.

Burne watched the bunk overhead. "My father tried to tell me the basics but it was so embarrassing, I barely listened. He'd taught me to swim when I was four and he taught me to read, so I think he figured he could manage love lessons. But I was only twelve and I hadn't yet thought about romance. And even when I started to be interested, if anyone showed interest in me, I'd avoid them. I was just too shy and I didn't know what to do. But it sounds like the fairies teach young people a lot more than my da did anyway."

"I can tell you," Nem said.

Burne turned on his side to face her. He felt a little weird about getting lessons in love and tumbling from a girl sixteen winters old, but he kind of wanted to hear what she had to say.

"Trillium said the most important thing is to be honest with yourself about what you feel, and to be honest with the other person, so no one is confused or misled and so both persons' needs are met. And also, to be honest about what you want. Some people want to find their life-mate and settle down or start a family, and other people just want to enjoy being with another person but they're not ready to commit to a life-bond, or maybe they're not interested in that ever. That's okay, as long as the other person understands."

Was he ready to commit to a life-bond? It seemed a bit extreme when he'd only just learned to kiss. But maybe Nem didn't mean bonding with the first person you met. Maybe she meant in general, what did you want in life? Immediately, a cottage popped into his mind, with children scampering about and Gray smiling up from the table as Burne carried over a pie from the oven. He blushed just from thinking it. Gray couldn't possibly be thinking the same things—even if Gray liked him and wanted to get to know him the way he'd said, he probably didn't imagine them sharing a life together.

But he wanted to be with Gray even if Gray wasn't thinking of life-bonds and children. What if he *knew* Gray was the opposite extreme from him, and that Gray wanted someone only for a tumble and didn't want to share a home with him or stay with him forever? Would he end their relationship before it grew, knowing Gray would never be able to meet his needs? He didn't think he would. He still wanted the man. And how could he even know what Gray wanted without asking him outright? Did Gray even know what Gray wanted?

Skies, this was confusing.

"But what if you're confused about what you feel?" Burne asked.

"You ask yourself a few questions." Nem lifted her hands out from the blanket to tick off her fingers. "How do I feel when I see them? Do I daydream about us kissing, or talking, or both? Do I only ever want to be alone with them, or do I want them to meet my friends?" She made eye contact with Burne. "If it's all physical and all you want to do is kiss and tumble, it's lust. Which is fine, as long as the other person feels the same. But if you want to talk and stuff, it's more."

Burne swallowed. "Okay."

"And then," Nem continued, settling back against her pillow, "whether it's just tumbling or more, you should agree on if you're going to see only each other, or if you're casual courting and being with other people, too."

Skies, handling one partner was hard enough. Burne couldn't imagine managing two at the same time. Did Gray want that?

"Uh, how do you know which you want?" Burne asked.

Nem turned to him again. "Do you want to be with anyone else? And how would you feel if you saw them with someone else?" Her eyes flicked up toward Gray before she lay back.

Gray stayed silent up on his bunk. Burne's mind wandered back over all their interactions, trying to remember what he'd been thinking and feeling. Had he wanted Gray to meet his mother? Gray had been excited to introduce Burne to Hyacinth, so maybe that meant Gray felt more than lust for him? And Gray had said he wasn't courting anyone else at the moment, but that didn't mean he wouldn't.

Nem yawned and pulled the blankets up to her chin. "Any more questions?"

"No," Burne said quietly. He had enough to think about. "Get some sleep."

"Goodnight Burne. Goodnight Gray."

" 'Night Nem," Gray said, and her name ended with the sound of a yawn.

Burne lay on the bottom bunk and stared upward with Nem's words cycling through his mind. Love or lust? A cottage with children or a tumble in the forest? Or both? Maybe he wanted both.

Gradually Nem's words gave way to his worries about going to Cliffside. They'd probably find more ill peacekeepers in the coastal town, but what else? He didn't want to go. But he didn't want to *not* go, either. He didn't want to be afraid to go was the thing. And he wanted to help Nem meet her mother and to impress Gray.

The moon crossed over the sky outside the bedroom window, gleaming onto the frayed rug as Burne rolled over one more time and finally drifted to sleep.

The next morning Maryanne offered them oatmeal. With the bustle of all the children, who wanted to sit by them and ask questions, they didn't set off until several hours past sunrise. They walked through the center of the wakening village and headed north on the road. The sky was light behind a pall of gray clouds. Hopefully they wouldn't get rained on again.

They walked slowly. No one commented on it but Burne suspected they were matching Gray's pace. By the time they reached the place where the road plunged back into the forest proper, they all wanted to stop for lunch even though it meant they'd never make it to Cliffside in one day.

"It's not likely we would have made it today anyway," Gray said, lowering the pack to the ground. He and Burne were taking turns with it. They'd both offered to carry Nem's but she'd declined. Maybe she didn't trust them not to destroy it. "Maybe you two could walk to Cliffside in one day," Gray continued, "with your toughened soles, but not me. I've gotten used to wearing human shoes on the village roads."

"Do your feet hurt much?" Burne asked as they sat on some low boulders at the edge of the fields under the trees.

"Not much," Gray said, digging into the pack.

"Gray." Nem's tone was chastising.

Burne scanned between them.

Gray lifted his eyebrows at Nem, his eyes widened in surprise, and she smirked.

"Well then," he said. His feet shimmered a moment and bandages appeared. "Maryanne put some sort of salve on them and tied them up. They feel much better than yesterday."

Burne stared with his lips parted.

"Don't look at me that way."

"Why did you hide it?" He regarded Nem. "Is he hiding anything else?"

"Not that I can see," she said, and she dug a kerchief from her pack and unwrapped a hand pie. She bit into it. "Cheese and broccoli," she announced, and took a bigger bite.

Burne felt torn between anger that Gray had kept his blistering feet a secret and a desire to sweep him up and carry him the whole way to Cliffside.

"Here." Gray held out another hand pie he'd taken from their pack. "I'm sorry I didn't say anything. I didn't want you to think I couldn't keep up. And I didn't know Nem could see through my illusions."

"It's okay," Burne said, although the words came out sounding grumpy and not okay.

They ate quietly. The forest twittered and rustled with birds and chipmunks and other small creatures and the day warmed even without the sun shining down. The road ahead was straight for a bit before it disappeared around a bend.

Burne swallowed his last bite of hand pie. "Promise you'll say something if you need to take a break from walking."

"I will."

"Does that count?" Burne asked Nem.

"Not really. He needs to swear on something."

Gray rolled his eyes. "I swear on every uncomfortable prickly thing I stepped on yesterday I will tell you if I need to stop walking."

"Okay." Burne snatched their pack and fastened it shut before putting it on. At least Gray wouldn't have the extra weight of the pack.

"It's a lucky thing Maryanne packed food," Burne said as they entered the gloomy trees, "since we lost all our coins yesterday."

"Those hand pies were superb," Gray said.

"I know. It was hard not to eat them all at once."

"We *could* eat them all."

"No we can't. We need them for dinner tonight and for tomorrow."

Gray grinned. "We don't actually need coins to acquire food," he said. "Not real coins anyway." He opened his hand in front of Burne. A stack of coins rested there.

They looked so real. "Let me see one," Burne said, reaching, but even as he felt a coin in his fingers, the image and the hard edge of metal disappeared.

"They can't leave my hand. I can change my appearance to make it look like coins are resting on my hand, but they can't exist on their own—not without a lot more magic."

"So how would we pay for something with them? They'd disappear when you handed them to a shopkeeper."

Gray shrugged. "I thought I could pretend to drop one into those coin jars they always have on the counter in shops and make a little chinking noise as I did it."

The coins reappeared in his hand. This time the stack started growing.

"But we'd be cheating the shopkeeper."

"I'd only do it in an emergency," Gray said, affronted.

"We'd have to pay them back."

"You sound like Hyacinth." The stack of coins was ridiculously tall, swaying as Gray walked, until it toppled over and the falling coins disappeared. Gray put his hands together in a bowl and filled it with more coins.

"Sorry. I just hate to cheat—"

"No, I like that about you."

Beside Gray, Nem rolled her eyes.

"Watch this," Gray said. He took the handful of coins he'd amassed and lifted it up and dumped it over his head. The coins rolled down his hair before falling off him and disappearing. This time, a chinking noise sounded as they moved.

"That looks weird," Nem said.

"Well it's not like I've ever seen anyone pour a bowl of coins over their head. I have to work on it to make it look normal. The sound works though, right?"

"Can you put them on something else if you're touching it?"

Burne asked. "Like could you put them onto a shop counter and keep your hand on the counter and stretch out the illusion to the coins?"

"Why? Change your mind about cheating shopkeepers?"

"No!"

Gray grinned. "If I concentrate, I can do it. Here, watch." He pulled the empty kerchief left over from his hand pie out of his pocket and held it on both sides, focusing. The center of the kerchief wavered a bit as he created an illusion of the kerchief over the real thing, and the center filled with the illusion coins, one after another. The kerchief bottom sagged lower as if it were actually filling with coins. The coins kept coming, covering Gray's hands and climbing up his arms. He pretended to be alarmed, making such a silly face that even Nem laughed.

A man stepped out of the woods.

Burne jumped, and Gray dropped the kerchief. All the coins vanished. Nem stood motionless.

The man faced them in the center of the road, blocking their path. He wore a dirty leather vest and boots, and gray stubble covered his chin.

"I'll take those coins," he said in a gruff voice.

"They're not real," Gray said. "They were an illusion."

"That's one I've never heard before," the bandit said. He reached inside his vest and drew out a dagger.

"No, really, the coins were an illusion," Gray said. "See?" He held out his hand and the coins appeared, one by one, then disappeared.

"I see them. Hand them over," the bandit said, and his free hand pulled down a sack from over his shoulder. He shook the sack open. Something heavy jangled in the bottom of it, like someone's brass candlesticks.

"But they're not really here," Gray said. He held both hands up vertically, and coins flashed in and out of existence, balanced on his fingertips.

"I don't know where you're hiding them, but put them in the sack. No one's coming to save you. I know them peacekeepers are all laid up in bed."

The bandit waited in the middle of the road. They had him outnumbered three to one, but he had a weapon and probably had experience using it. Could they take him down without anyone being hurt? How? If Gray could distract him, maybe—

Gray drew his arm back and flung a handful of coins into the forest. The coins seemed to leave his hand and sail toward the trees before winking out of existence, and the bandit turned after them, squinting. He took a step toward the trees, searching over the ground.

Gray pushed Burne the other way, gripping his arm and dragging him past the bandit and into a run. Somehow Nem was already in front of them, sprinting down the forest track. Burne dug his soles into the dirt and chased after her until he was the one pulling Gray. He glanced back.

The bandit had moved into the trees and crouched on the ground, hunting for the coins. They kept running, around a bend and away from him. After a minute, they slowed to a jog, but they kept going until they were so out of breath they had to slow to a walk. Nem clutched her side as she staggered along, panting.

"He was a terrible bandit," she said.

Gray stopped and bent over. Burne tugged on his arm to keep him walking, in case the bandit gave up his search and came after them.

"I don't know if we're much better," Burne said. "We knew he was out here, harassing travelers, and we walked right into it."

"Did you see how he was holding his dagger?" Nem asked. "That's not how Woodbine taught us at all. To maximize the force when you strike."

"Skies, Woodbine," Gray said with a long exhale. "She teaches combat now?"

"Self-defense!" Nem said, incredulous.

Apparently Burne had missed dagger lessons. Or maybe Woodbine had known he wouldn't want to touch one and given the lesson on a day when he was elsewhere.

"Anyway, we got away without fighting," she said, straightening and shifting her pack.

They had—thanks to Gray. Whereas Burne had been planning to leap onto the bandit and try to disarm him. Burne shivered. The confrontation was over now and they'd gotten away. All they'd lost was one of Maryanne's kerchiefs.

The rest of the afternoon passed without incident. They met one cart carrying a load of rutabagas toward Woods Rest and warned the driver about the bandit. He grinned, flexing his brawny arms, and dared the bandit to try to steal his rutabagas. Burne couldn't tell if he was kidding.

Gray didn't complain about his blisters. But every time Burne noticed the bandages, he wished he could carry Gray on his back. Or in his arms.

They arrived at the forest crossroads as darkness fell. The crossroads served as an outpost in the forest, but it had only a few cottages and an inn. A new building was half-built and a lopsided sign announced it would be a general store. The innkeeper was jovial and didn't seem to mind dusty travelers who declined to eat in her dining room. When Burne told her they'd encountered the bandit and had no coins (Gray grinned as Burne said the misleading words, and Burne's face heated), she gave them half a loaf of bread and offered they could sleep in the stables behind the inn.

"Just give a shout when you walk in," she said, "case any of the young folks are up in the hayloft."

"The hayloft?" Why would—

Gray was grinning.

"You know how the youngsters get," the innkeeper went on. "Specially 'round here where there's nothing to do but house chores and busywork. Seems like every time I stable a horse, Darren and

Jonas come scrambling down the ladder. I should tell them, just stay up there and be quiet and wait for me to leave."

Skies, they'd be sleeping in the local teens' love nest. Hopefully their need of a free bed wouldn't interfere too badly with what sounded like an enthusiastic affair.

"So where are you headed?" the innkeeper asked.

"Cliffside."

Her face grew grim. "Lots of men have been heading that way the past moon," she said. "But not like you lot. More like the fighting type like we used to see before the revolution. The last batch caused a skirmish in the dining room and hightailed it out of here without paying their bill. And good riddance. Last thing we need's a bunch of men playing like the King's Guard and waving their daggers around."

Burne shivered at the mention of the King's Guard.

"Not to mention the threats."

"What threats?"

The innkeeper waved her hand. "Just a lot of posturing, saying they're going to remove the peacekeepers and bring back the old Guard."

Burne and Gray exchanged a glance.

"Has anyone come from Cliffside?" Burne asked.

"Sometimes they come back through. I've been closing up the dining room early to avoid the trouble."

"But has anyone else come from Cliffside aside from the fighting men? Like anyone who lives there?"

The woman chewed her lip. "Now that you mention it, seems like I haven't seen anyone come by from Cliffside in a while, not even the quarter-moon delivery wagons. And the one lady who came through three quarter-moons ago—"

Nem's head jerked up and she inhaled sharply, her lips parted.

"—she never returned."

Chapter 11

THEY NEEDED TO REACH CLIFFSIDE and make sure Kitty was safe. The innkeeper at the crossroads assured them they could walk it in less than a day. The road to the coast was flat and fairly well maintained.

The next morning dawned cloudy again. Nem eyed Burne as he came out the stable door, no doubt assessing his appearance and making sure he was fit to meet her mother. Sleeping in a hayloft wasn't ideal for being presentable the next morning, but Burne had taken care to brush the stray bits of hay out of his hair and clothes when he'd crawled from the nest his body had made in the hay. And then Gray had come over and said, "You have one more bit," and reached to comb his fingers through the top where Burne's mother had left the longer curls. Gray did it so slowly Burne had plenty of time to breathe in the smell of his skin, darker than the sweet smell of hay, and to sense his heat warming the cool morning air drifting in the open window of the stable. And Burne had imagined pulling Gray down into the hay to kiss him.

But even if Burne was sure he was ready, Nem had been waiting outside. And they needed to get to Cliffside before any more peacekeepers were incapacitated, assuming the ones in Cliffside hadn't already been. So he'd followed Gray down the ladder and out of the barn.

They washed up at the inn's pump and split another hand pie for breakfast. A short while later, they started off. The distance to the coast was only three leagues so they expected to reach Cliffside around noon.

The road east from the crossroads was less traveled than the main forest road. The trees grew closer in, with barely enough room to fit a wagon between them, and the center of the track was thick with weeds. Burne walked in one rut and Gray walked in the other, and Nem trailed along behind them, keeping her thoughts to herself as usual.

"This road is creepy," Gray said.

"Maybe." There *was* something eerie about the road but Burne had been trying to ignore it.

"It's too quiet. The birdsong is muffled and the trees seem menacing."

"Isn't that irreverent, coming from a fairy?"

"Well, I'm sure they're nice trees," Gray said. "But look how they lean toward the road."

"That's where the sunlight is. Or would be, if there were any today." Thick gray clouds filled the sky between the two palisades of trees lining the track.

"And look how densely they're growing."

"There's more pine trees here than there were on the main road. The pine trees appear denser than the others because of their needles."

Gray huffed.

"It is creepy," Burne conceded, "but I bet it's not as creepy as the western road." The road heading west from the crossroads outpost had been completely overgrown, with vines hanging down from branches that covered the way like a tunnel of bones, and a fallen tree trunk blocking half the track not a hundred paces in.

"Well that's true," Gray said. "But no one should go that way anyway, because that's where the dragons live."

Dragons? There weren't really—

"Someone's coming," Nem said behind them.

They halted. A quiet thumping sound came from the road behind them.

"Woods," Burne said, and they stumbled over the grass and broken limbs into the trees. The thumps grew to a pounding as the rider neared. Gray was out of reach—Burne flung himself to the ground, hoping the trees would hide them and the rider wouldn't be looking their way.

The horse thundered past.

The road quieted in its wake. Burne pushed himself up. He picked a pine needle out of his bangs. Gray and Nem sat up beside him. The pine forest cast deep, cool shadows, and a carpet of sweet pine needles covered the bare forest floor. The light glared out on the open road.

"We seem to be walking right into something," Gray said.

"We don't have a choice."

"Couldn't we sneak through the forest and come in from another direction?"

Nem stared at him, her lips tight.

"There's not time," Burne said. "If we get there soon, we might be able to stop them from hurting the peacekeepers in Cliffside. If they haven't already. But they've already sabotaged the ones in Woodglen and Woods Rest and maybe other villages—their plans are moving forward. Whatever is going on in Cliffside, it's coming to a climax, I can—" Burne frowned at Gray. "Why are you laughing?"

Gray bit his lip but couldn't stop the smile twisting his features.

Nem shook her head and, as usual, rolled her eyes. "You said 'coming' and 'climax' in the same sentence. Gray can't handle it."

"Stars, it's like you're twelve winters old," Burne said, trying to act annoyed when he wanted to smile and itched to reach for Gray.

"I agree with Burne," Nem said. "Something's com— Something's about to happen, and it's probably something we need to prevent."

Gray stopped smiling. "I just hate walking into it like this. I'm more of a sneaking type."

Burne sighed. He didn't like their chances, given the men who'd been converging on Cliffside. "I hate it too, but going through the woods would take all day. Unless you want to sneak in and I'll go on the road with Nem?"

Gray shook his head and reached for Burne's hand. "Absolutely not."

"We could sit here a moment and eat?" Burne said. But no one was hungry.

When no more riders came along the road for a few minutes, they crept to the edge of the trees and climbed out.

They walked in silence, listening for any sounds of approach. The air changed as the hours passed, with the high cloudy sky becoming more hazy as hot sunshine fought to radiate through a fog over the trees. The forest transitioned to entirely pines and the track they walked on crushed lightly under their steps and had occasional patches of fine white sand. The new leagueposts erected by the Council of Villages apparently hadn't made it this far because Burne hadn't seen a marker in a while. Hopefully the old posts had fallen into the grass and they were nearing Cliffside and not just walking very slowly.

They rounded a bend. Something stood in the road ahead. Burne stopped so fast Nem walked into him.

Wooden boards formed a gate across the road, and a tiny hut stood beside it. Something moved inside the hut and two men with daggers on their belts stepped out. They were guarding the road.

Burne turned to Gray and found him gone, completely gone. He scanned the nearest bushes but a butterfly caught his gaze, fluttering yellow beside him and at eye level. Below it was Gray's body, all shimmering in dark greens like the trees and the dirt brown of the road. Hopefully his camouflage was adequate enough the guards wouldn't notice him from a distance.

Nem wedged herself beside Burne on the track. "They've seen us," she said quietly.

Burne swallowed. They had to go forward. If they ran away, the guards would chase them and it would be worse than whatever would happen if they approached. He couldn't make out the men's features from this distance. What if they recognized him from the King's Guard? The new leadership in Woodglen might not care that he'd deserted the Guard, but his old comrades certainly would.

Gray's hand slipped into Burne's and squeezed. Then Gray let go and the butterfly drifted away into the trees. One of the men turned his head to follow the fluttering and Burne lurched into motion, drawing the man's attention back to himself.

Burne and Nem approached the guard station. They stopped ten paces away.

"What's your business in Cliffside?" one of the men asked. Burne didn't recall his face.

"Her mother lives in Cliffside," Burne said, taking Nem's hand and licking his parched lips. "I'm bringing her home."

"Where's her home?"

"Cliffside?" Burne said, willing himself to stay calm.

"Yeah, but which house?"

Skies, Burne had no idea what Cliffside looked like.

"I've not been there yet," Nem said. "My mother came three quarter-moons ago to arrange it and I was to follow if she didn't return."

The men exchanged a look. "All right, go on past."

"Kitty didn't mention a town gate," Burne said as they stepped past the men, and his pulse sped up as he spoke, but he might learn something if he pretended to be ignorant. "Is it new?"

"Yeah. We've had reports of bandits on the road. Lord Amberfeld set up the barricade to keep the town safe."

"Oh, that's smart," Burne said, smiling, and the guards waved them on and stepped back into their hut.

Burne and Nem continued on the road. They'd come through

the gate easily enough but his shoulders hunched with tension. What was going on here? He stole glances toward the wood on the side where Gray had disappeared but nothing moved in the shadows.

The sun blazed behind the white sky cover. It must be afternoon by now. In spite of the mild spring temperature and the cool spots of shade, Burne's back sweated under the pack. A breeze stirred the trees and he caught whiffs of tangy sea air amid the pine scent.

The track grew so sandy that Burne didn't see how a wagon could navigate it without getting a wheel stuck. The side of a building appeared under the boughs ahead and his heel struck a cobblestone under the sand. The hard, sandy street continued into the village. A narrow track led into the forest on the right, and another on the left, where the front of a cottage hid among the trees.

They walked along the gritty cobblestones into a cluster of quiet buildings tucked under the sweeping branches of pine trees. The lane widened between the two rows of wooden buildings to form a small village square. Behind the buildings on the right, the pines climbed up a hillside. Between the buildings on the left, the trees partially concealed more cottages. At the far end of the street, the track narrowed back to one wagon width and disappeared again into trees.

A creaking board drew Burne's gaze to his left. An older man slumped in a rocking chair on the shady porch of the center building, tilting slowly back and forth. The jars and bags on shelves in the windows suggested a general store. The man watched them silently. Was he a Cliffside resident? Hopefully Nem's presence would reassure him Burne wasn't another ruffian come to join the other guards. Not that anyone watching him would think him tough, but—

"You lost?" the man asked, rocking slowly. He was maybe fifty winters, with hair already gray. He didn't smile, but the way he slouched in his chair was non-threatening. He wore dirty overalls.

Burne glanced around the space again. Across from the store

was a building with a carved sign reading Grange, and beside that was obviously the pub, given the haphazard chairs out front and mugs scattered on the porch. The sign at the pub read Baldric's. Cliffside—assuming this was all of it—was almost as small as the outpost at the crossroads, but even the crossroads had more bustle. The rocking chair creaked in the stillness.

"We're looking for a woman," Burne said, turning back to the man. "She came from Woods Rest to visit her mother."

The chair creaked loudly as the man leaned forward and stood. He climbed down the porch steps. "What's her name?"

"Kitty."

"And who are you?"

Burne indicated Nem. "Nem is her . . . family, and I escorted her here. We were worried when she didn't return from her visit."

The man squinted at them a moment. "This way," he said. He shuffled across the lane toward the pub. Burne exchanged a glance with Nem and followed.

The man led them toward the left corner of the building, where he stopped to make a quick survey of the village before stepping out of sight. Around the corner, he hobbled toward the thick trees at the back of the building.

When they stopped beside him, he pointed back into the trees. He had dirt under his fingernails. "There's a trail straight behind that boulder. It'll take you right up to Linota's house. It's steep going but the . . . other visitors don't use it."

Burne thanked him and they left him by the pub wall and walked into the trees. Behind the large rock, a narrow trail began between two trunks and meandered out of sight up the hill. Burne glanced back. The man had disappeared from the back area of the pub. Burne exchanged a glance with Nem and started to climb.

"Creepy," Gray said behind them.

Burne startled and Nem squeaked.

"Sorry, I should've fluttered around your heads a bit first. This place has me unnerved."

"Then let's be quiet," Nem said.

They hiked on in silence. The trail began to climb more steeply, heading to the right around an outcrop of rock and twisting to cross the top, only to meet another rock face and twist again. Soon they were all panting but everyone kept quietly on. A breeze stole into the forest, bringing the salty scent of the ocean, and the trail climbed out from the trees and rocks and onto wind-swept grass. The branches parted to reveal a large house across the lawn. Behind it, the lawn stopped abruptly as if it dropped off, and the gray sea spread to the horizon.

Nem jerked to a stop in the stiff breeze, staring out at the water with her lips parted. Burne halted beside her, but Gray stepped forward, surveying the yard. The view had startled Nem. She had lived her whole life in the fairy caverns and the woods. She had never seen the ocean. It must look startling and remarkable to someone who'd never seen it, much less swum in it their whole life like he had.

White sheets swayed on lines beside the house, and gulls wheeled in the cloudy sky, their calls faint in the blustering wind. The house was painted blue with white trim and was the biggest house Burne had ever seen—two stories with several windows along the side, and it stretched out toward the cliff on the far side plus an extra section came off to the left of a large stone chimney. A few steps led up to a small door. The house's front door must face away from them.

A woman stepped out from the flapping sheets, watching them.

"You ready?" Burne asked, and Nem exhaled, straightening.

The three of them moved forward until they were near enough to speak over the wind.

"Kitty?" Burne asked.

The woman nodded once. Her eyes darted between them, and Burne suspected she had noticed Gray and Nem's telltale green eyes although her face stayed passive and her posture stiff. Kitty was tall and slim, with straight hair like Nem's but pulled back tightly. Her hands were folded together in front of her apron.

"We've come from Woods Rest. Maryanne told us where to find you." He put his arm around Nem. "This is Anemone. Her mother was . . . a human."

Kitty's hands let go of each other as she caught her balance. Her empty hands trembled.

"I'm sorry to surprise you like this," Burne continued. "We heard things in Cliffside have been strange, and we didn't trust a message to get through."

Kitty clenched her fingers into fists. "Why don't you come inside."

She tore her gaze away from Nem and led them to the back door. It opened into a large kitchen. A yeasty smell filled the room and made Burne's mouth water. A fire glowed in a large hearth and a loaf of bread cooled on the table. After the rushing wind, the house seemed silent.

"Come in the parlor," Kitty said quietly and led them down the hall.

The parlor faced out toward the front of the house and the cliff over the sea. They sat awkwardly on the sofa with Nem in the middle, and Kitty took a chair opposite.

She studied Nem until she caught herself staring and looked away. "My daughter died," she said.

"None of the stolen children died," Burne said. "The fairies took them away from the caverns as they grew older and hid them from the queen." He put his arm around Nem again. "Nem is sixteen. Ladi thought you might be her mother."

"Ladi knows?" Kitty's eyes welled up with tears.

"She just found out. She's found her daughter, Alyss."

Kitty gazed helplessly at the ceiling, then the walls, and Burne didn't know how to help her. Gray must have had no idea either because he was uncharacteristically silent. Kitty blinked and tears washed down her cheeks.

Nem leaned in. "I don't have to stay if you don't want me here."

Kitty focused on Nem. "Anemone," she said, as if just remembering the name from decades ago. "I want you to stay. I'm just so overwhelmed. They said you were dead."

Nem offered her hand and Kitty slowly took it. "They were hiding us. After the revolution, the fairies who took care of us didn't know how to find you. Until Burne and Gray came, and Gray knew Ladi."

Kitty held onto Nem's hand across the space as she contemplated the men. "Thank you."

Burne touched Nem's shoulder. "Would you like us to wait outside?"

Nem met his gaze and dipped her head.

"It's warm in the kitchen," Kitty said.

Burne and Gray stood and left the women in the parlor. They walked quietly back down the hallway into the room where they'd entered the house. Burne relaxed his shoulders. Nem was fine. She'd be fine.

He scanned the kitchen. It was large, but the house was large, too, as if many people stayed here. The kitchen had a cast iron stove in addition to the sprawling stone hearth. A smaller, enclosed brick oven was beside the open hearth. The entire kitchen floor was made of large, smooth stones. Did Kitty's mother live here all alone? Why did she have such a large house? Beside the hearth, a second doorway led into a back hallway.

Gray picked up the loaf of bread.

"Gray!" Burne hissed. "Put that down."

Gray held it up to his nose. "I'm just taking in the aroma."

Burne waited, glaring at him. From down the hallway came the low murmur of Kitty and Nem speaking.

Gray gazed back with wide eyes over the loaf. "She won't mind if we have a slice. She's just found her long lost daughter, for skies' sake."

Burne shook his head.

Gray put the loaf back onto the towel on the table. "But I'm hungry," he said so pathetically Burne almost laughed.

"Lucky for you we have hand pies."

"The hand pies!" Gray let out an exaggerated sigh.

Burne took off the pack and lowered it onto a chair. He dug past the blanket, with Gray hovering beside him.

"You two certainly aren't guards."

"Aaah!" Gray jumped at the sound of the voice, stumbling into Burne, who caught him.

A small woman leaned on a cane in the doorway to the back hallway. "Are you thieves?"

"No!" Gray said, affronted.

"You weren't thinking of stealing the bread my girl worked so hard to make?"

"No," Gray said again, but the word twisted with a bit of a whine. "We have our own hand pies."

"Your what?"

"Hand pies," Gray said loudly.

"Hand pies, eh? Who are you, then?" She folded her wrinkled hands on top of her cane and waited.

Burne stepped around Gray. "I'm Burne and this is Gray. We came from Woods Rest to find Kitty."

"And who are *you*?" Gray asked.

"I'm Linota, Kitty's mother. Who else would I be?" She shook her head.

"I thought her mother was bedridden," Gray said.

"Why would you think that?" Linota started forward, and Burne pulled out a chair at the table. She lowered herself into it.

"Because Kitty came for a short visit and stayed longer?"

"She stayed because they won't let her leave," Linota said. "You must've passed the guards' barricade on the way in."

"They said it was for safety," Burne said. He pulled out a chair for Gray and walked around the table to sit opposite Linota.

"And you believed that?" she said, peering from Burne to Gray.

Her eyes stopped on Gray, who'd swung his chair around and sat sideways with one leg tucked up beneath him. She inhaled sharply and shrank back.

He lifted his hands up, open before him. "Yes, I'm a fairy. No, I've never impregnated anyone, fairy or human."

"Well," Linota said, relaxing back into her seat, "that I can believe."

Gray's brow furrowed and he shook his head.

"Tell us about the guards," Burne said. "Something's not right here but we can't figure out what."

Linota leaned forward, done with teasing Gray. "No one knows what the guards are up to but everyone suspects Amberfeld's behind it. He's the old lord up at the manor on the cliff. Bastard." She eyed the bread. "Kitty won't mind if we have a bit," she said, and reached to rip off one end. The sweet and earthy scent wafted across the table.

Gray actually whined.

"Get out your hand pie," Linota said. "I'll trade you."

Burne handed the whole pack to Gray so he could focus on talking to Linota. "Tell us what you know."

"Lord Amberfeld's always been a bastard," she said, "and he didn't much like the people taking control of the village last spring. The village council's had to reprimand him several times since the revolution. The past few moons he's been quiet, but men started arriving—all the same type. Ex-guards and rude and nasty. Three quarter-moons ago they set up that barricade—right as Kitty arrived to visit. The peacekeepers organized to confront them, but before they could, they all fell ill."

"All of them?"

She wagged her head. "Yep. Then a quarter-moon later, they wouldn't let Kitty leave. They kept saying the road isn't safe with bandits robbing people and whatnot. And others started catching the illness—half the village is in bed with it."

"Half the village?" Burne said. Beside Burne, Gray stopped to stare with the hand pie halfway unwrapped in his hands.

"All the peacekeepers and anyone who might be able to ride for help or sneak through the woods. And the village elders are too worried to say anything without the peacekeepers to back them up, and with Amberfeld's guards all about. They've got guns somewhere, too, I've heard." She tore her bread in half and handed half to Gray.

"We could sneak out," Gray said, breaking the hand pie in half for Linota.

"There's no time," Burne said. "It would take days to get back to Woods Rest, and all the peacekeepers there are ill, too."

"What's that?" Linota said.

"The peacekeepers in Woodglen and Woods Rest are all ill, too," Burne told her. "It can't be a coincidence. Something's about to happen and we need to find out what it is. Where do all the men stay?"

"They've got a camp up at the manor."

Burne imagined walking up to the guard camp and shivered at the scenario. It was like asking to be pummeled. And what would he even do when he found the men? Approach them and ask why they were gathering in Cliffside?

"But," Linota continued, "they spend every night in Baldric's pub."

Even better—approach them while they were all drunk.

"Ric's about had it with them. And no one else wants to be in there—or no one did before they all took ill—so it's ruining business all around. You two had better be careful how you approach them—they might see you as a threat."

"No one knows I'm here," Gray said, grinning. Maybe he was warming up to Linota now that she'd shared the bread with him. "I sneaked past the guards."

"How'd you do that?" she said. "Cast a love spell on them?"

"Yuck, no! I used an illusion."

"Let's see."

Gray grinned and disappeared. The yellow butterfly perched on his last bite of hand pie, and the chair where he sat appeared warped and off-kilter. He came right back. "It was better on the road because I could look like trees and things in the background. It's hard to disguise myself as a kitchen."

But Linota was smiling, her head to one side. "You really can do it," she said, and slowly shook her head. "I halfway thought I imagined it, the memories. I haven't seen any fairies or tricks like that since I was a girl."

Gray leaned in. "But you liked fairy tricks when you were young, eh?"

"You make it sound smutty," Linota said. But she blushed.

"You didn't see Kitty's beau?" Burne asked.

Linota shook her head. "She kept him secret."

"What happened with Kitty?" Burne asked. It wasn't his business, but it was Nem's story, too, and he wanted to understand. "I know about her losing her child. How did she end up in Woods Rest?"

Linota frowned. "I wish she hadn't stayed away. She should have come home—I could've helped her. She—" Linota sighed heavily. "I think the spell took a long time to wear off. Later she told me she went all the way to Sar Bay hunting for her child, and she tried searching in the woods and was just about out of her mind. She lost many seasons wandering up and down the kingdom. When she wandered into Woods Rest, Ladi saw her and took her home. Once Ladi told her what had happened, she came back to herself a bit. She came to see me, but she didn't want to live here. I think she found comfort with Ladi in Woods Rest."

Kitty's story was terrible, made worse knowing Nem had been kept underground and treated like a servant for so many winters. "Well, they're together now," Burne said. "I know it can't make up for everything they've lost, but at least they've found each other."

"What now?"

"They're together," Burne said more loudly.

Linota squinted at him. "Who's together?"

"Kitty? And Anemone?" Burne said.

"Stars," Gray said. "We didn't tell you. We went to Woods Rest to bring Kitty's daughter home, and Maryanne said Kitty had come here and—"

"You what?" Linota's whole face was crinkled in confusion.

"Kitty's daughter is alive," Burne said. "She was hidden in the woods to keep her safe, and when we figured out who her mother was, we brought her home."

Linota sat up. "She's alive? Why didn't you tell me!"

Voices sounded in the hallway, and a moment later, Kitty and Nem walked into the kitchen. Kitty smiled at her mother, and Nem smiled at Burne, and no one spoke.

"She looks just like you at that age!" Linota blurted out.

And then the three women were talking and hugging. Burne quietly ripped a piece off the remaining loaf of bread. Gray grinned at him across the table.

Everyone gathered at the table and they told Linota about their trip through the forest as Kitty chopped vegetables and boiled lentils for a quick meal. Burne was glad to eat but more than anything he wanted to be somewhere quiet with Gray. Or to be alone and quiet, but being with Gray would be much better. He could barely focus on the voices around him. Gray was laughing at Linota's remarks, but when he caught Burne watching him, he found Burne's hand under the table and wrapped it in his.

The moment the dinner was eaten and Nem yawned, Kitty decided they should all retire. It had been an eventful day, she said.

And, Nem added, they all needed time to sit quietly and "process"—that was another one of Trillium's lessons for maintaining inner calm and being healthy. At this point, Burne probably needed a hundred of Trillium's processing sessions.

The light was fading from the windows as Kitty led Burne and

Gray into the back hallway off the kitchen. She passed the first doorway and continued toward the end of the hall.

"Nem said you wouldn't mind sharing a room," Kitty said, and Burne was glad she was leading the way so she wouldn't see him blush. He darted a glance back. Behind him, Gray winked. And trailing along behind Gray, Nem actually grinned.

This couldn't get any more awkward.

Kitty opened the door at the end of the hallway. "The sheets should be clean but it might take a moment to heat up in here. My mother's in the first room, but you probably noticed her hearing's not good, so don't worry about waking her with your talking."

"Don't worry," Nem said as Burne hurried past Kitty into the room, "they won't worry about waking her with their . . . *talking*."

Thank the skies, the room had two beds.

"You let me know if you need anything," Kitty said.

Gray thanked her and closed the door behind her as she stepped out.

The large room had two beds side by side, with a hearth set between a pair of large windows. A pile of logs and kindling was laid in the hearth with a stack of wood beside it. Burne was too tired to think of starting a fire. He sank onto one of the beds.

Pinkish light shone in the windows. They faced out over the lawn toward a wall of trees at the top of the ridge they'd climbed up earlier that day. The western sky over the boughs glowed pink but the trees were dark in the coming twilight.

After a moment of Gray fussing in the corner, a golden glow filled the room and the windows darkened.

Gray set the glass chimney back on the lamp he'd lit on the dresser. He undid the curtain ties and covered the windows. "There," he said. "Now it's all cozy." He fell onto the opposite bed and rolled onto his back. Burne lay back too. With his feet on the floor, lying flat stretched his stomach in a mildly-painful-yet-pleasant way.

"We made it," Gray said.

Burne didn't reply.

"We eluded wild pigs and bandits and guards and didn't even lose Nem once."

Burne sighed. "At least Nem is safe."

"Or as safe as anyone in Cliffside. How are we going to figure out what's going on? I could pretend to be Lord Amberfeld—"

"Do you know what he looks like?" Hope filled Burne's chest.

"No. I could try to find out though."

"There isn't time," Burne said. "There's only one way to uncover their plan." He turned his head to face Gray, and Gray gazed back. "I have to go to the pub and find the men. I can pretend I came to join them."

"Won't they wonder why you showed up with a young girl, though?"

"I'm trying to remember what I told them. I think I said I was escorting her to her mother. If I *had* been coming to find the guards, I might not have blurted it out to the men at the gate."

"I can go with you—"

"No. They don't know you're here. It's better if we keep it that way. And they don't know you, and they'd never believe a random fairy would be interested in their rebellion or whatever they're planning. I was in the King's Guard with them. I'll pretend I heard about them gathering here and wanted to join them."

Saying it aloud made his chest skitter in fear but he had no time to think twice about it. All the physically strong people in Cliffside had been incapacitated with the mysterious illness. No one else in the town could help. And what was the worst the men could do? They'd tormented him when they'd been in the Guard together, but they'd never harmed him badly. Not physically, anyway. He could suffer more embarrassment if it meant finding out what they were up to. And maybe whatever they were planning wouldn't be so bad—maybe the men were propping up a crotchety old manor lord yearning for the old days, and no real harm was meant.

Although deep down, Burne knew that wouldn't be true.

"Maybe Lord Amberfeld will show up tomorrow," Gray said. "If I could see him once, I could probably create a fair illusion."

A few locks of hair had fallen across Gray's forehead. The lamplight glinted in his green eyes.

Burne sighed again, wishing they could curl up together and fall asleep. "We can't wait. I have to go tonight."

Chapter 12

YOU HAVE TO GO TONIGHT?" Kitty said. She stopped folding the sheet and dropped it back into the laundry basket.

"The men who've been gathering in Cliffside can't wait much longer for whatever they have planned," Burne said. "Everyone who might stop them is sick in bed. They'll have to act soon or the peacekeepers will start getting over their illness."

"Unless they plan to kill all the peacekeepers," Gray muttered, staring at the kitchen's stone floor. He hadn't smiled once since Burne had decided to approach the men at the pub that night.

"That's even more reason to act quickly. Maybe I can figure out what they've done to make everyone ill so we can help them get better."

Kitty frowned. "Do you need anything?"

Burne ran his hand through his hair. "Uh, could you lend me coins to buy a drink? We had an . . . incident on the way here and lost most of our things."

"Nem had a full pack," Kitty said, her brow wrinkling as she turned toward the counter.

"Yeah well, we should've let Nem carry the coins," Gray said.

Kitty lifted the stump of bread out of the basket on the counter and moved aside the linen beneath it. The bottom of the basket was filled with coins. She held the basket out to Burne. "Take whatever you need."

"Have you been to the pub?" Burne asked.

"No. We've been 'under siege' since I got here so I've stayed close to home. But you can trust Baldric who runs the place. He comes by with news. He tries to keep the men in line when they've been drinking."

"We met a man on the porch of the general store when we arrived," Gray said.

Burne looked up in surprise. He hadn't seen any sign of Gray when they'd entered the village center.

"Gray hair, dirty overalls," Gray continued. "Who's he?"

Kitty pursed her lips. "Everyone around here wears dirty overalls."

"Here, watch," Gray said, and his face changed. He grew older, like the man they'd seen when they'd arrived in Cliffside.

Kitty inhaled, her eyes wide. "Nigel. The head gardener. You resemble him."

Gray turned back into Gray. "Hopefully he's not out having a pint. I'll need a disguise if I have to go into the pub after Burne."

"Don't," Burne said. "It doesn't matter what they do to me. Don't get involved." Facing his old tormentors was bad enough. They could call him names and poke and slap him, or pour ale down his pants, or steal his shoes and make him piss on them—if he wore his shoes, which he probably should to avoid giving the men something unusual to notice about him and pick on him for. They could do any stupid thing they wanted and he would pretend he was upset about it, but he wouldn't care. But he didn't want Gray to witness it, or to risk Gray getting hurt.

Gray glowered at him.

"Good luck and be safe," Kitty said, and she leaned in and hugged him. Through the sick feeling in his gut came a hint of warm comfort. "Whatever happens, you get home before morning. I'll make sticky buns for breakfast."

Kitty lit a lantern for them to carry down the hill. They left her folding the laundry and stepped into the night.

"Sticky buns?" Gray said as the back door closed behind them. The stars were bright overhead now that sunset was well past.

The ocean crashed at the base of the cliff on the far side of the house, and the air was crisp. Burne had donned his shoes and they pinched.

As they walked away from the house, the wind off the water hit them in the back. The moon had risen over the water. A reddish cast dimmed its light.

Burne held the lantern out to light the ground before them. "What about it? Don't fairies have sticky buns?"

"Oh, I've had them, many times."

He was ridiculous. And if he'd just keep talking and saying vaguely suggestive things, it would help Burne forget how nervous he was. "Stars, you're absurd."

"What are human 'sticky buns'?" Gray asked.

"They're like dinner rolls but with more sugar in the dough, and they have a layer of icing on top."

"I like icing."

"Not like cake icing. More like gooey stuff with nuts in it."

"Mmm, nuts and gooey stuff. Even better."

"But I don't see how Kitty's sticky buns can be better than my ma's."

"Well, now you've ruined it."

They started down the path into the woods. They stayed quiet, focused on keeping to the path and not stumbling. Burne didn't care if it took all night to get down to the village, but only a few minutes had passed when a distant shout sounded, followed by a whoop. They stopped in the trees and he blew out the lantern flame. The woods went inky dark.

Gray touched his arm. "You don't have to do this."

"I can't do nothing. I don't want to live with myself if I'm a coward."

"You keep calling yourself that. But you keep doing brave things."

"But I'm scared every time. No matter how many times I make myself do something, I never stop being scared."

"Being scared doesn't make you a coward. I think it's the opposite. It's not brave to do something you're not scared of."

Burne frowned as the words churned around in his head. He was a coward. He always had been, and the other men had spotted it the moment he walked into camp the first day of guard training. They'd known he was the one they could pick on.

And yet . . . what had he done that made him a coward?

The shapes of trees glistened in the light of the strange moon, and he could make out the lines of Gray's face, an arm's length away.

"But why am I always scared?"

Gray shrugged one shoulder. "Maybe it just means you care about things. Not everyone does."

"I want to try again," Burne whispered, not sure if Gray would understand.

But Gray stepped forward and slid his arms around Burne, pulling him close.

"But I'm scared it won't work again," Burne said into Gray's hair.

Gray rubbed his back.

"And if I try and I panic and stop, I'll let you down."

"You won't," Gray murmured, hugging him tight. Burne hugged back with his free arm. He let himself stand there with Gray for a moment, soaking in the comfort of having Gray in his arms, before pulling back.

"Let's get this over with," he said, and his attention returned to the sounds of revelry filtering through the trees.

At the opening of the path, Burne stashed the lantern behind the boulder. A door at the back of the pub was closed. They crept along the side of the building until they reached a window. Orange light shone out, and through the wavy glass, Burne glimpsed people seated at a big table. Were any of them men he'd known before? The rumble of talking came through, pierced by a shout, but the words were muffled.

He didn't dare put his face up to the window to inspect them more closely for fear they'd spot him peeking in. He couldn't ruin his chance to approach them the way he planned to. But even without looking, he knew Cap and Stone and the other men from the King's Guard would be inside.

"I can watch from here," Gray said.

"They might see you."

Gray turned into a shrubbery.

"Right." Burne ran his hand over his hair. "Just don't think you have to help, even if they pick on me. I know what they'll do, and it doesn't matter, not if I can get answers from them."

"Do you know what you're going to say?" Gray's voice drifted out of his branches.

"Sort of. I'm trying to summon my inner jerk so I can blend in."

"I don't know if you have one to summon."

Burne grimaced. "Here goes."

He left Gray and walked to the front of the pub. The town was again deserted—no villagers in the square or lights in the other buildings. No horses were tied outside the pub. The men must've walked here from wherever they were staying. Without stopping to think, Burne pulled open the door and stepped in.

The room was filled with a group of laughing men. Several tables had been pulled together to make one long table down the center. Mugs of ale littered the table, and at the far end, lounging back in his chair, sat Cap. Burne scanned the others. At Cap's right-hand side as always was Stone. Lanterns with orange-tinted glass hung around the room, and a stooped man with white hair watched Burne from the bar at the back.

The man on Cap's left noticed Burne and smacked Cap's chest, and one by one the other men spotted him by the door as the room quieted.

Burne inhaled deeply through his nose and stood tall. He rolled his shoulders back and kept his chin up. None of them knew where he'd been all season. He could've been hunting Gray's make-believe dragons for all they knew.

Cap shifted forward in his seat, staring, and stood. His eyebrows lifted. "Yell?"

Burne grinned.

"It's stinkin' Yell, everybody!" He pushed his chair back and stumbled out from the table. "Blazin' crap, man, where the skies you been?" Cap smiled as he bounded toward the door. His voice sounded welcoming. That probably wouldn't last, but Burne could play along.

"I been around."

Cap reached him and slapped him on the shoulder. "You deserted the Guard, man! I wouldn't of thought you had it in you. Yellow-Bellied Burne, disobeying his orders."

"I didn't mean to desert." Burne smirked.

"Right." Cap snorted. Stone and a few of the others had gathered behind Cap. Stone scowled at Burne, but the others only watched him and Cap interact with mild interest. Some of them looked familiar.

"I didn't. I went into the trees to piss—"

"Long piss," Stone muttered.

"—and the fairies got me."

"The fairies?" Stone scrunched his face in disbelief, which made him bare his teeth like a dog.

"Wait, this'll be good," Cap said, smacking Burne's chest. The hit didn't cause Burne to stumble back as it would have last season. It must be because of all the heavy lifting he'd done at the Haven. "You got captured by *fairies*?"

"They used their magic," Burne said. "I didn't even hear them coming. They knocked me out and I woke in one of their caverns."

"And you couldn't get out?" Stone said with narrowed eyes.

"Typical Yell," someone else said. "Caught by a bunch of fairies."

"But they don't even use guns."

"Yell couldn't fight off unarmed fairies."

"I didn't want to," Burne said, and he grinned again. "They were blazin' hot."

Everyone stopped talking.

He resisted the urge to turn his face down or run his hand over his hair. "Have you *seen* any fairies?"

"That one with the flower shop is pretty hot," someone said, and Burne thanked the skies Gray wasn't there to hear it.

"They're all long legs, and what they can do with their fingers . . ." Burne smirked as if remembering. A real memory of Gray's fingers sprang up and he pushed it back. He couldn't get distracted. "They don't even need their spells, but when they do use them . . ." He shook his head. "And all that tree climbing—they can bend like a willow sapling."

"Yell wants to bang fairies," someone sneered, but the joke fell flat.

"Well, *yeah*," Burne said. "And they like humans. They just wanted to tumble me all the time. Uh, the men and the women. I think the women might have been breeding me. It was one long orgy." He snickered. It wasn't hard, given how ridiculous his story had gotten. He'd better rein it in or they'd start to suspect he was lying.

"Skies tits," Cap said, staring at Burne and bobbing his head. "We need to give you a new nickname. Yell the fairy stud." He turned to the back of the room. "Ric! Get me a drink for my old friend Stud!"

Cap dragged Burne over to the table, and several of the men grinned his way or slapped him on the back. Only Stone glared at him.

Stud. If only they knew how absurd Cap's new nickname was, when Burne had utterly failed at his first attempt to tumble someone. But he couldn't think of that now—he'd lose his charade of confidence. He'd had wild orgies in the woods with dozens of fairies. And he'd liked it. A scene filled his mind with naked arms and legs flailing about in some bushes, and he grinned at how silly it was.

Cap pushed Burne toward the chair Stone had been sitting in, but Burne offered it to Stone and moved to Cap's other side. This was going well. He didn't need to piss off Stone any more than he already had by appearing in Cliffside.

Stone sat slowly in the chair and leaned back while Cap bounced beside him. Burne sat too. Pretending to be cocky and confident was easier when he was standing. He'd probably topple over if he tried to lean back on two legs the way Stone was doing. How would he act if he'd actually been tumbling fairies since last spring? He slouched down a bit and tried to act bored.

A cold breeze drifted across the table. Cap and Stone checked the door. Nigel the gardener stepped in. Or was it? Was that really Nigel, or was it Gray?

He certainly resembled the old man who'd met them in the village when they arrived. And why would Gray have come inside? Clearly nothing had gone wrong since Burne was sitting at the table with the men. So it must be Nigel—which meant Gray wouldn't have a disguise to use if he did need to come inside, unless he wanted to show up disguised as Linota.

Nigel trudged into the room. He made a wide circle to avoid the center table and slid onto a seat at the bar.

"So how did you escape?" Stone asked Burne across the table.

Burne pulled his attention back to the circle around him. "They stopped guarding me." Everyone waited for him to continue. He had to say something better. "I mean, they untied me after the first few days. I think they got tired of doing all the work."

That earned a few guffaws.

"But like I said, I didn't want to leave. They fed me and . . . serviced me, and they make this elderberry wine. It's as strong as Sarlian vodka. I think I was drunk half the time."

"Remember that time we had the vodka?" someone asked.

Burne had never actually had vodka. Or elderberry wine, for

that matter. And he certainly didn't remember having it with the guards, but the others were chortling.

Cap turned to him. "This guy brought us vodka. We thought it was like ale."

"The guy from the castle? With the whiskey?" someone asked.

"Naw, it was that dude Aaron used to tumble."

"The one with the cheese?"

"He traded southern goods—" Stone began.

Cap barged in, excited. "And this one time—this one time he somehow got a case of Sarlian vodka. And he was so gone on Aaron, he brought him a bottle. And we drank the whole thing while Aaron was out back bangin' the dude."

"Aaron was so mad we didn't save him any!" someone said.

"And then we were all pukin' out back an hour later."

"Oh man, those were the days."

Their voices trailed off. "Tell us more about the fairies," Stone said, and everyone turned back to Burne.

"You ever do two at once?" someone said, chuckling.

"Or more?"

Burne gave a slow, lazy shrug. "Probably. It all blended together after a while."

"So why'd you leave?"

Burne frowned. "Tumbling gets dull after a while if you do enough of it. I started wondering what you all were up to."

"He missed us!" Cap exclaimed. "Stud wondered what his boys were up to."

"I heard someone murdered the king," Burne said, and he tried to appear concerned. "I didn't know if I should come back to Woodglen or if they'd be after the King's Guard. So I stayed in the woods a while longer."

"You don't know what happened?" Cap asked.

"I heard rumors from the fairies but I never knew if what they were saying was true. You can't trust them. When I left the woods, I had my hair long so no one would recognize me. But I didn't dare ask anyone about the King's Guard. So I lay low and picked up bits and pieces, and I heard the guards were gathering in Cliffside."

"Where'd you hear that?" Stone said, his gaze steady.

Burne pulled out the first name he could think of. "Alistair's, maybe?" He vaguely remembered men in the Guard talking about nights in Alistair's Pub.

"No one goes to Alistair's anymore," Stone said, "not since he's bonded."

A mug of ale was set down before Burne, saving him from needing to reply. He leaned back to find Baldric hovering beside him. He reached for his pocket but Cap stopped him.

"I got it," he said, handing Baldric a coin. "Took you long enough."

Baldric exhaled and took the coin. Over at the bar, Nigel sat against the wall, staring into a mug.

Cap leaned in as Baldric returned to the bar. "We used to drink for free but Amberfeld doesn't want us causing trouble. If he wants to pay us to drink, fine with me. Drink up, man."

Stone watched him across the table. Burne wanted to keep his mind sharp but he didn't see a way around it. He picked up the mug and chugged the ale.

"So what really happened to the king?" he asked.

"Stinkin' peasants," Cap said. "They got the fairies to help them—"

"I'm surprised you didn't hear about it," Stone said, but Cap continued right over him.

"—and they lured the whole King's Guard out of the castle and surrounded them. Half the men surrendered on the spot, and the rest they cast a spell on. The whole Guard collapsed."

"Black skies," Burne whispered, widening his eyes.

"They had all the firepower, and the king was trapped in the castle. And the stinkin' princess showed up at the castle gate and pretended she needed help. She was all, 'The fairies kidnapped me and I barely escaped.' So of course they let her in. Talk about tumbling the fairies—they must be magic. Remember how mousy she was?"

"Princess Rose?"

"All that fairy tumbling made Yell a stud, and it gave the princess enough spine to pull one over on her father. She rallied all the ladies in waiting and took him down. Shot him in the head."

Burne didn't have to pretend shock. "Princess Rose? Shot her father?"

"Well someone did. Maybe it was the fairy. She was there, though."

Around the table, the men were losing interest in Cap's story and talking low among themselves. The room was warm in the glow of the lanterns, with a sour smell of old ale and sweat. Burne leaned back in his seat and drank—he'd drained the mug without realizing it. Stone tipped his own mug up and finished it.

"But she didn't take the throne?" Burne said, leaning forward. He had to keep Cap talking.

"Smart girl. She'd have been next. She let the villagers take over and disappeared with her fairy man."

Baldric appeared with a tray of mugs.

"This round's on Nigel," he said, "to thank you for not trampling the garden today." He began passing around the mugs.

Cap took one and lifted it toward the man at the bar. "Sorry 'bout that. We didn't see it in the dark. Won't happen again." Nigel dipped his head in acknowledgment.

Burne sat up and swigged from the second mug of ale. He kept forgetting to act cocky. But did it matter? Stone didn't trust him, but the rest of the guys didn't seem to mind he was there. And Cap . . . Cap was his new best friend. He regaled Burne with memories of the King's Guard before Burne joined it and laughed over the pranks they'd played on him after he'd arrived. Maybe Cap didn't realize how much Burne had hated those times—maybe he thought their pranks had been harmless. The memories were all so fuzzy, as if they no longer mattered.

Talk to Stone, Burne told himself. He didn't like his suspicion that Stone was studying him, hunting for cracks in his story.

"I was so jealous of you," he blurted out. "You fit in so well in the Guard. You were so good at everything." It was halfway the truth. He'd hated Stone, but he had envied him, too.

Stone shrugged. "I liked being in the Guard."

"He was gonna be a lieutenant," Cap said, "just like me. Movin' up the ranks."

"Until the peasants ruined it." Stone downed the rest of his ale.

What were the right words to say this time? Burne wanted to shut down, to finish his ale and go home to bed. To eat sticky buns in the morning. But he had to help the villagers. He couldn't mess up. He had to keep talking. "You should've been a lieutenant," Burne said. "You wouldn't have surrendered to a bunch of villagers and fairies."

"You hated it though," Stone said, staring hard.

"I didn't like being picked on," Burne said. "I wanted to be part of your crew."

"Remember when we stole your uniform?" Cap said. His arms slid onto the table as he laughed. "I can still see you on the field, marching around naked like a baby!"

Stone smiled, his eyes bleary. "We were mean."

"I was new," Burne said. "I figured you'd pick on me. I figured if I could get through it I'd be one of you."

"But you never fought back. You wouldn't let us fight you."

"Was that what you wanted?"

Another tray of ale appeared. Burne passed Stone a mug and took one for himself as Baldric loaded up the empties.

"There was an order, a ranking," Stone said, holding up a hand. He jabbed it into the air above his head. "Cap," he said, lowering it. "Me, Gabe, Rye." He kept moving his hand lower and lower, naming men. Cap watched Stone's hand as if it were a mesmerizing creature.

"I was the bottom," Burne said.

"No," Stone said. He shook his head, as if his thoughts were a few moments behind where they'd usually be and he had to locate them before speaking. "You would've been the bottom rank if we could have proved you were the weakest. But instead you weren't anywhere. You wouldn't fight us so we couldn't put you last. So we kept picking on you."

"Do you still want to fight me?" Burne asked. He'd stand half a chance now. And if fighting Stone was all it took to get on their good side . . . He jerked his head at the door.

"Now?" Stone said, wobbling forward as he leaned in.

"Skies tits, Yell," Cap slurred.

"We'll have to watch for peacekeepers," Burne said. "I don't want to land in jail out here."

Cap shook his head. "No peacekeepers left. They're all out of commission."

"Huh?"

Cap smirked. "Snakeroot," he said.

Burne tilted his head as he reached for a third mug of ale. Or was this four? Snakeroot was toxic. These Cliffsiders had strong ale.

"I'll fight you if that's what it takes," Burne said, before taking a swig. "All I ever wanted was to fit in. I wanted to find my place."

By now, they were all slumped on the table—Cap, Stone, and all the men. Black stars, he was going to have a hangover. But it was worth it. He'd broken through to them.

Cap shook Stone's arm. Stone lifted his head and peered at Burne with bleary, reddened eyes.

"Tomorrow," Stone said. "You want a place with us? Be here at sunset and help us take the town."

Burne pressed his head in his hands. He didn't understand. "Sunset," he repeated.

Cap shook Burne's arm, as if trying to keep him awake, but Cap was the one whose eyelids sagged. He rallied enough to blurt out, "They figured out about the peacekeepers in Woodglen and Woods Rest. We can't wait. Amberfeld says tomorrow."

"We've got a cannon," Stone said, his head falling onto his arms. "We'll blow down the village if they don't give up."

"Gonna be good," Cap said, and he sprawled onto the table too.

Burne's head dropped, falling forward, and he caught himself and forced his eyes open. Half the men were passed out and the rest gazed at nothing or slumped silently in their chairs. A hand landed on his back, then another. Baldric hoisted him up by his shirt, kicked his chair away, and steered him toward the door. Burne tried to twist free but the hold was firm.

Burne stumbled out of the pub door, catching himself to stand on the porch.

Why was Baldric tossing him out? The others were just as drunk. Maybe they were next. Good luck with that, dragging Cap and Stone out half conscious. Odd because they'd always drunk ale, but maybe the past seasons they hadn't as much. He hadn't, never had been a drinker, but still, a few pints of ale shouldn't make him so—

He swayed toward the edge of the porch and caught at a post, hanging on as he lowered himself to sit on the floorboards. His shoes skimmed the ground and he hugged the post. On all sides, the buildings of Cliffside tilted and swayed.

"Thanks for getting him home," Baldric said above him. "I don't want Kitty after me if he topples off the cliff."

Burne held his head. Where was Kitty? What cliff?

A hand gripped under his armpit and hauled him up to stand on the ground beside the porch. Nigel was beside him. Skies, but he smelled good, comforting and warm. He pulled Burne's arm around his shoulders and began to walk.

"Thanks for all the drinks," Burne mumbled as he staggered along beside Nigel. "Must've cost a bit."

"I put it on my tab," Nigel said. He half-dragged Burne around the corner and pulled him slowly along the side of the building. White moonlight shone through the trees. The red moon had risen white.

"Strong stuff," Burne muttered.

"The Baldric special brew," Nigel said. "Designed to knock out bothersome customers."

What was Nigel saying? Why would Baldric want his customers to pass out?

They stopped at the end of the trail up into the trees. Nigel hefted Burne up against his side. "This is going to be fun," he said.

Burne's face fell against Nigel's neck and he inhaled. Nigel smelled like Gray. That's what was so nice about him. He sounded like Gray, too.

Wait, where was Gray? Burne struggled out of Nigel's grip and examined the bushes all along the side of the pub. Gray had turned into a shrubbery. But so many shrubs lined the pub, lit by the bright moonlight. Which one was Gray?

"Gray?" he called.

"Right here." An arm slipped around him and pulled him back toward the trees. Nigel was gone and it was Gray by his side.

Burne held onto Gray and put his face back into the crook of his neck. "I'm so glad you're here," Burne said. "I didn't get pummeled."

Gray's hand rubbed his back. "You were amazing," he said. "Either that or you really do like those guys."

"I think they liked me."

"Mm-hm."

"They're not so bad. I think they just want to fit in, too."

"Come on, Burne," Gray said, and started up the path.

Leaves and pine needles brushed at Burne's face and he kept stumbling over roots. In places the path was barely wide enough for one person and Gray would turn them sideways, leading the way and lifting Burne along behind him. Burne tried to control his steps but the moonlit trees spun around him. Gray was panting in the quiet night.

After several minutes of effort, the branches opened to the night sky at a place where the path rounded a rock face. Gray stopped and leaned Burne against the rock. "I need a rest," he said and leaned beside him, staring at the sky.

A few stars burned brightly enough to shine through the moon's light. A hint of the ocean reached them on the breeze.

"Sorry I'm so drunk," Burne said. He let his eyes drift closed.

Gray took his hand.

Burne forced his eyes open and studied Gray's profile a step away. He could kiss Gray. He wouldn't panic. It wouldn't be like the time in Gray's room. He wasn't frightened now.

He leaned in but his shoulder bumped Gray's shoulder. Gray turned and Burne slipped forward and fell.

Gray caught him as he righted himself.

"What are you doing?" Gray asked, helping him up.

"Trying to kiss you."

Gray patted his cheek. "Try it again when you're not plastered, sweetheart. Let's go."

Chapter 13

THE SUNLIGHT SEEPING THROUGH BURNE'S eyelids was like daggers into his head. He pulled a pillow over his face, and all his muscles ached with the movement. At least the house was quiet. If he listened, he could make out the muffled crashes of the ocean waves below the cliff.

How much had he drunk last night? He'd been in the pub with Cap and Stone, and they'd been glad to see him. He hadn't gotten beat up or even mildly abused, as far as he remembered. But had he gathered any useful information by talking to them? Had he said anything stupid? How had he gotten home?

And what had happened to Gray?

He pushed aside the pillow. He was alone in the room. The other bed was covered neatly as it had been last night, as if no one had slept in it. Somehow, Burne couldn't picture Gray being the type to pull up the bedcovers so neatly each morning.

What if Burne had been snoring so loudly in his drunken stupor that Gray went to sleep somewhere else? Skies knew what he had acted like while he was drunk.

A mug stood on the table beside the bed.

Burne propped himself up against the headboard. The room stayed level, but the motion churned his stomach and a wave of nausea washed over him. He closed his eyes until it passed and picked up the mug. A murky green liquid swirled inside it. He sniffed it—it smelled herby and minty, and his stomach calmed at the very smell. Clearly it was here for him. Burne took a sip. Then he drained the whole mug.

The pains in his head dulled. He still couldn't remember the past night, though.

He pulled back the covers. His shirt was on the floor and his trousers in a heap beside it. A shoe poked out from beneath his clothing. He was wearing his undershorts, and a pair of wool socks he'd never seen before. He combed his fingers through his hair and rubbed his face. Slowly he stood, got dressed, and padded in the socks down the hall to the kitchen.

As he opened the door, a smell of yeast and burnt sugar wafted up his nose. Kitty looked up from the counter, where she had her hands in a pile of dough. Gray was mixing something in a pot on the stove.

"Morning, Stud," Gray said, smiling.

Stud. The new nickname Cap had given him. Burne closed his eyes. "I think I said some things—"

"About how much you like tumbling fairies?" Gray smiled wider.

Kitty rolled her dough into a ball, placed it in a bowl, and covered it with a linen cloth. She moved to sit at the table and began knitting.

"Where's Nem?" Burne asked.

"She's with Linota," Gray said, studying the liquid in the pot.

A tapping at the window drew Burne's attention. A seagull perched on the window ledge, its beady eye peering into the room. Burne rubbed his eyes again.

"You drink your mug of magical healing herbs?" Gray asked.

Burne nodded. "What was it?"

"Fairy recipe."

"I thought you didn't know any fairy potions."

Gray smirked. "I know the one to cure hangovers."

"About last night," Burne said, leaning on the counter beside

Gray, "I can't remember anything. I don't know what the guards are planning."

"You remember arriving at the pub, I assume?"

"Yes. I left you outside being a shrubbery, and Cap and Stone were there, and I told them I'd been kidnapped by fairies—"

"*Serviced* by fairies, I believe you said."

"You heard that?"

Gray couldn't stop grinning this morning. "Fairies who got you drunk on elderberry wine and liked to tumble you two at once."

Burne closed his eyes and rubbed the back of his neck. "I wanted to impress the men. I tried to say things they would say."

Gray raised the hand that wasn't stirring the pot. "I'm not judging," he said. "I myself have been drunk on elderberry wine—and the rest of it—many times."

Burne didn't want to think about Gray's rollicking past, so unlike his own. "I remember all that, but then Baldric brought me an ale and it gets fuzzy. I can't remember anything about how I got home."

"So you don't remember dragging me onto the pathway beside the pub and forcing me to kiss you?"

Burne's face blazed. "Oh, no! I'm sorr—"

"Or how, as soon as we were in the trees, you pushed me against the massive trunk of a cedar tree and put your hand in my trousers?"

"Skies, Gray. I never should have drunk so—"

"Or how halfway up the trail, you leaned against the rocks and pushed me to my knees and dropped your pants and made me—"

"Okay, that's enough Gray," Kitty said.

Gray cringed. "I forgot you were there."

"You're traumatizing the poor boy." Kitty stood and went to the small oven beside the hearth. She picked up the oven mitts. She opened the door and took out a pan filled completely with golden buns, one risen into the next, and an aromatic cloud of buttery baked goods filled the kitchen. Burne's stomach couldn't decide if it still felt sick or wanted a bun.

Tap tap tap. The seagull at the window tilted its head, staring in with both eyes. It stepped from one foot to the other.

"Gray's teasing you, Burne," Kitty said. "I waited up. You were perfectly sheveled when you stumbled in the door."

"I was what?"

Gray smirked. "That's not a word."

Kitty pressed her lips together. "You were *not dis*-sheveled. Your clothing was intact and you were too far gone to undo a button, much less pull down your pants and what have you."

"Maybe I helped," Gray said. "Maybe I buttoned him up afterward."

Kitty narrowed her eyes at Gray and leaned on the counter. "I didn't want to say it but I'm fairly certain *you* didn't have any . . . relief on the way home."

"What's that mean?" Gray said.

Kitty threw up her hands wearing the oven mitts. "You had an obvious erection—not that I would look, but I came downstairs to make sure you were all right and you were stumbling in the door carrying Burne, and it was hard to miss. You didn't seem in danger so I went back upstairs."

Burne squeezed his eyes shut and hid his face in his hands. Even Gray stayed silent. Skies, Nem's mother seeing that was bad enough. At least Linota hadn't been hanging about the kitchen.

The seagull tapped on the glass. Gray and Kitty ignored it. What was up with the bird?

Kitty put a plate upside-down over the buns and deftly flipped the whole pan. She lowered the plate to the counter and worked off the pan and the buns dropped out, with a gooey brown topping oozing down their sides.

"Stars above, Kitty," Gray said, staring. "Those are the best-looking sticky buns I've ever seen."

"And that's saying something," Burne said.

Kitty pursed her lips at them. She dropped the oven mitts on the counter and gingerly pulled off one of the edge buns, leaving a steaming, doughy opening to the bunch. She strode to the window where the seagull pranced. As she pushed the glass open, the bird lifted off, flapping backward to hover near. Kitty held out the bun, and the gull snatched it.

"Thank you, Beaks!" Gray called.

The bird flapped twice, lifting up and tucking in its legs. The wind caught it and it soared away.

"Help yourself," Kitty said, gesturing at the plate of buns, and she left the room.

A moment of silence followed. Burne stared at the empty window. Gray whisked the liquid in his pot.

"I'm not sure my stomach's ready to eat a sticky bun yet," Burne said. "Do you want one?"

"I'll wait." Gray held the pot handle as he stirred its contents faster. "Those are Linota's woolly socks by the way."

"How did they get on me?"

"Your feet kept sticking out from the bedclothes and they were cold this morning and I didn't want to make noise making a fire and your socks were so thin so I mentioned it and Linota gave them to me. And I put them on you."

For some reason, *that* made Burne blush. "They're nice and warm."

"Mm-hm." Gray flipped the hair out of his face and considered Burne. "Would you have been disappointed? I mean, if we had . . . done anything on the walk home?"

"I'd have been disappointed I didn't remember it."

Gray smiled into the pot. After a moment, his smile faded. "Unfortunately, we have a lot of work to do and half the morning is passed."

"I really can't remember anything."

"I can. I couldn't take watching from the window so I went in. They spilled it all, Burne. You were perfect."

"So that was you? Disguised as Nigel? But how did you know about them trampling the garden?"

"Ric mentioned it."

"So what did we learn?"

"They're planning to 'take over' Cliffside for Lord Amberfeld at sunset tonight. I'm not sure what they intend to do with it but it seems to be some sort of counterrevolution to put Amberfeld back in power. They told you to be in town if you want to help. And they said they have a cannon. I'm assuming they've got guns somewhere, too."

"Skies." It was just his luck he'd return from a season of hiding from the guards and walk right into a battle.

"So I figure we need to destroy all their guns. Without firepower, it's just them against the town, and even without the peacekeepers and the others who've been poisoned, there are more villagers in Cliffside than there are men in Amberfeld's band." Gray lifted the pot from the stove, stirring like mad.

"What are you making?" Burne asked.

Gray's smile lit his whole face. "This," he said, "is the antidote for snakeroot poisoning—which last night you discovered is the mysterious illness plaguing the peacekeepers."

He put the pot onto one of Kitty's mitts on the counter and began to sprinkle in flaky bits of herb from a bowl. A strange blue smoke rose off the liquid and the whole batch of it turned deep blue.

"Perfect," Gray said, lowering the bowl of herbs.

"Is that a fairy potion?" Burne said.

"Mm-hm."

"How did you know how to make it?"

"I didn't. But I knew Hyacinth would."

"You reached her this far away?"

"No. After I put you to bed, I went to the beach and found Beaks. He was having trouble sleeping because— Well, that's irrelevant. I asked him to fly to Woodglen and find Hyacinth and tell her the poison was snakeroot."

"You could talk to him?"

Gray's answering smile infected Burne with happiness—seeing Gray so happy and proud of himself made Burne want to hug him. "I sat quietly and focused, thinking I really needed help, and Beaks showed up. And the moment I thought of Hyacinth, he knew her, of course. My sister knows every bird on the entire eastern coast. He was dying to have a reason to go visit her. And I didn't know how much I'd be able to communicate, so I just pictured snakeroot as hard as I could.

"He flew off and I sat there on the beach and waited the rest of the night. He got back right at dawn. He'd had to wake her but that's what she gets for sleeping with her windows wide open. She must've worried I wouldn't be able to figure out a detailed response, 'cause she wrote the whole recipe out and rolled it up and tied it to Beaks's leg." Gray pointed at a scrap of bark curled on the counter, with numbers and words scratched into it.

Burne studied the blue liquid. "Will it cure them by this evening?"

"Maybe? But we'd better not count on it. I mean, now that Hyacinth knows the poison was snakeroot, she'll fix up Woodglen's peacekeepers. So even if Amberfeld's little rebellion succeeds here, it won't be able to spread. And eventually the other towns will send help and his dinky band of rebels will be overwhelmed."

"But we still need to protect the people in Cliffside tonight."

"Right. That's up to us," Gray said.

"So we need to find their firepower."

"Yes."

"Any idea how?"

Gray sighed. "I think you're going to have to join the guards sooner than this evening."

Chapter 14

Burne was going to walk straight into the guards' camp. In spite of how well his first effort had gone, the thought of a second attempt jangled his nerves. At least Gray would be nearby. He stole a glance at Gray as they descended the front porch steps onto a wide lawn over the ocean. The salty ocean breeze hit them, ruffling their hair. Gray's eyes had dark circles like bruises under them and his hair stuck out at messy angles but he was still handsome. Gray caught him staring and took his hand.

They followed the paving stones across the grass and started down the hill on a double track wide enough for a wagon. In places, bare rock showed through the grass and dirt. A few chickens pecked in the grass at the edge of the trees, and more nestled into the pine needles in the shadows. Burne's shoes rubbed at the back of his heels and squeezed his toes. As soon as this mess was over, he was going back to the fairy habit of walking barefoot.

They'd dawdled at the house long enough to eat sticky buns and tell the others their plans. Kitty and Nem took charge of the antidote to the snakeroot poison. Kitty had stayed out of sight since the day the guards had refused to let her leave Cliffside, but she remembered the paths through the woods from her childhood. She could bring the cure to the homes of those who needed it without getting caught.

An orchard covered the lower slope of the sunny hillside. They passed between boughs of white buds and boughs of pink buds ready to burst open. The wind was milder today and the air had a sweet spring grass smell. Far out in the blue water, tiny whitecaps tipped the waves. Overhead was a clear blue sky.

"Linota said this used to be a boarding house," Gray said, inclining his head back at the rambling house as they walked down the rocky track. "She was up early and sat talking with me in the kitchen. That's why the house has so many rooms. But visitors to Cliffside have dwindled in the past season so she hasn't had any business."

"I wonder why."

"According to Linota, people used to come to Cliffside to avoid the king and his guardsmen. The village was so tiny and remote and unproductive the king didn't bother much with it. Lord Amberfeld collected taxes but he had only a handful of guards who mostly stayed around his manor and left the villagers alone. And there's a narrow road along the coast from Cliffside all the way to Nor Bay, so people from the north could get here without using the main forest road. Cliffside was like a king-free vacation hotspot. Plus I had a hunch Linota wasn't telling me things."

"Like what?"

"Like Linota was the head of a smuggling ring of tax-free imports being brought in through a landing at the bottom of the cliffs near her house."

"You are so full of it."

"I'm not! She practically admitted it."

Burne shook his head but smiled. Anything was possible. And Linota with her fiery attitude did seem up to smuggling to avoid the former king's unfair taxes.

"But now," Gray continued, as the path headed into the pine trees and sloped more steeply downhill, "people can travel wherever they want without running into guards, and the import taxes are fair, plus the tax income goes directly to the villages and not to a useless king. So Cliffside has dwindled back into the tiny backwater town it used to be."

"And now it's crawling with guards."

"Ironic, right?"

"You shouldn't be out here with me," Burne said. "Who knows when we'll encounter them." The trees were thick alongside the path to the house, which zigzagged down the hill, but at the bottom they'd come out on the main road east of the village center and closer to Amberfeld's manor. And besides, Burne's plan was to *try* to find the guards. He couldn't have Gray with him when he did it.

"I have a plan for that," Gray said, and he took Burne's arm with his other hand and leaned against him, clinging to his hand and squeezing his arm.

Burne gazed down into the giant, doe-like brown eyes of a lovelorn young woman. He didn't even flinch, he was so accustomed to Gray's sudden illusions.

The woman batted her eyelashes. "You were so amazing in bed last night," she said in a falsetto. "I can't wait to see what you're like when you're sober."

"Don't hold your breath," Burne said. "I'm probably way better when I'm drunk."

"I'll be the judge of that," she said and gave a silly giggle. She kept hanging on Burne's arm.

"Should, uh, should you look like a man?"

"I thought of that," Gray said in his normal voice, although he kept his illusion of the village girl, "but the guards poisoned all the young people in Cliffside. So if they see a new young man, they might get suspicious or feel threatened. I figured little ol' Berthenia would be less of a threat. Will they not believe you showing up with a woman?"

"Last night they seemed to believe I had an orgy with the entire fairy village that lasted a dozen moons, so we should be okay."

Gray squeezed his arm. "Stars, I wouldn't have moved to Woodglen if I'd known I was missing that." He grinned up at Burne, and Burne's heart flopped over.

"So let me get this straight," Burne said, trying to focus. "I left the pub, and I didn't want to return to Nem's grandmother's house drunk, so I . . . ?"

"Well, you don't remember it well."

"That's convenient."

"Baldric threw you out of the pub and Nigel offered to get you home, but you were so inebriated and disagreeable he gave up on you and left you in the road. And you vaguely remember stumbling along the road and Berthenia finding you and offering to help you. And you awoke in her bed this morning."

"Okay."

"Naked. And she wanted you to—"

Burne squeezed Gray's hand to stop him. "You're bringing back my headache. Just give me the basics."

"You can't remember what the men told you last night but you think they said something's about to happen and you want to be part of it."

"And I need to find where they've stashed their guns?"

"And a cannon. If we can find and destroy their firepower, it will give the villagers a chance to fight back tonight when Amberfeld declares himself grand ruler of Cliffside."

"And they didn't give any hint of where they are?"

"No. But we know the men are camped up by Amberfeld's manor, and it makes sense to hide them up that way."

Gray's hold on Burne's arm loosened as the trees thinned. The track down the hill from the house came out on the road running west to east, with a broad cleared area on the far side. The village buildings were hidden among the pines to their left but Linota had sketched a map—they were coming out between the village center and the coast. They turned to the right and continued along the road. A few hundred paces ahead, the road appeared to end at the edge of the land, and the blue ocean sparkled beyond a cluster of trees.

The open fields across the road from Linota's property stretched from the clifftops to a solid line of pine trees at the edge of the forest. Tilled plots filled the fields and a few people worked in the rows, hunched over weeding around tiny green plants or working their way along with hoes, dropping seeds into furrows before tamping them flat. A gentle breeze blew and the sunlight felt hotter. Someone called across the gardens, and Burne squinted to see Nigel directing one of the gardeners, all of whom seemed like youngsters.

They neared the end of the road where it curved left to head north along the clifftops. The crashes of waves echoed up the rocks. The ocean breeze was stronger and gulls wheeled above the water. Maybe Beaks was up there bragging about the sticky bun he'd had for breakfast.

As Burne and Gray headed along the road, Nigel spotted them. Burne waved.

"I hope he's a drinker," Gray said, "so he doesn't notice the extra twenty ales on his tab from last night."

"I'm glad Baldric let you buy them. After what Linota said, I wasn't sure how drunk the men would be, but getting them drunk really got them talking."

"I wanted to get them drunker," Gray said, "and when Baldric mentioned his special brew, I offered to treat them to a round. I guess you don't remember. Baldric brewed a batch of extra-strong ale, hoping to give it to the men to speed up their evenings. He told me he tried it once already and it worked amazingly. They zipped through being rowdy and got sluggish and left without destroying anything."

"Well I'm glad they talked before they passed out last night."

At the far end of the gardens, the trees filled in alongside the road and the road wended into them, moving away from the edge of the cliff. The thick needles muffled the sounds of the ocean and cast the road in cool shade. Birds flitted among the branches.

Though his memories were hazy, Burne knew everything had gone smoothly last night. He'd pretended to be confident and Cap had treated him completely differently than he had back in Burne's days in the King's Guard. Even Stone had come around after they'd talked.

Burne's insides twinged in guilt at the idea of deceiving the men and pretending to be their friend when he was only spending time with them to hunt for information. They were plotting something and endangering the people of Cliffside. Rationally, he knew they needed to be stopped before they hurt anyone badly. But when they found out he had tricked them after they'd been nice to him, it would make them regret being nice. They'd be sorry they'd trusted him, and maybe they'd never trust anyone new again or they'd become worse bullies. He hated to contribute to making them worse people.

It wasn't worth thinking about all this, though, because he didn't have a choice. Innocent people were at risk—including Nem and her newfound family—and who knew what Lord Amberfeld had planned? Maybe only Cliffside was at risk, but that wasn't necessarily the case. Maybe the people of Sylvania were strong enough to resist a new attempt at autocracy, but they'd been free of the king only one turn of the seasons. Maybe they wouldn't resist a new leader who seized power. Maybe rebellious guards were stationed in other towns, and Amberfeld's revolt would spiral out of control if it wasn't stopped at its outset.

So he would continue trying to thwart Cap and Stone and their gang. So far, he and Gray were succeeding. Everything had gone well at the pub last night, better than he had ever imagined it could. So why was he even more terrified now, facing the men a second time? Facing them in the daylight when they weren't drunk might actually be more dangerous. Maybe he wouldn't be able to trick them a second time—maybe Stone would see through his lies. Maybe he wouldn't be able to get them talking about their plans for tonight at sunset.

Maybe he had a lot of legitimate reasons to be afraid. And maybe fear *didn't* ever go away. What had Gray said? Doing something you weren't scared of wasn't brave. If doing things you *were* afraid of made you brave, Burne had become the bravest person on the continent in the past quarter-moon.

Did Cap and Stone ever feel afraid? Back in the King's Guard, they had been excited to follow orders and to practice shooting targets, and they'd always talked as if they were eager to fight in a real battle. So being in the Guard hadn't made them brave. But maybe other things intimidated them—like maybe Stone would be petrified to sleep out in the woods alone or to cook dinner for a household of ten. Maybe everyone was scared of different things.

They passed through the short stretch of forest and came out again on the edge of the cliffs. On their left, patches of trees broke up a grassy area stretching far back from the road. In the distance, the corner of a large, pale stone building was visible behind a stand of trees. It had to be Amberfeld's manor.

Burne had never seen one of the manor halls, but he'd heard they were large and ostentatious, mimicking the grandeur of the castle. Under the king, the kingdom had been divided into provinces with one manor lord in each. The lords had been tasked with collecting taxes for the king, but everyone knew they collected extra for themselves. How else could they have maintained their extravagant homes? While most villagers farmed or fished, a few had worked for the manors as maids and gardeners and other roles, earning their taxes back as wages.

When the kingdom ended, the new Council of Villages decided not to displace the lords. But they no longer received tax incomes and laws restricted them from amassing weapons or organizing fighters. If the Cliffside peacekeepers hadn't been ill the past quarter-moons, they'd have had plenty of reasons to take action against Amberfeld.

Burne and Gray, still disguised by an illusion of a village girl, neared a cluster of pine trees standing south of the manor. Under the boughs were a dozen canvas tents. The manor hall came into view beyond the trees. It was three stories tall, L-shaped, and had multiple stone chimneys and a round, turreted tower nestled in the corner. Windows lined each floor along with small, columned balconies, and a stone terrace stretched onto the grass on the near side. For such a grand house, it didn't have an obvious front entrance—but maybe the builders had tried to imitate the castle, which had multiple gates and no main entrance.

"Wondered where you ended up."

Burne's fingers clenched in Gray's hand but he didn't flinch as he turned toward the voice. Under the trees amid the tents, Stone leaned on a trunk in the shadows, watching them. Burne's instincts screamed at him to duck his head or shrink away from Stone. He had to find the attitude he'd adopted at the pub last night. He had to be a cocky bastard again.

Gray tugged on his hand. Burne again looked down into the adoring brown eyes of the village girl.

"Thanks for last night," she said.

What would Stone do in this situation? Burne pulled the village girl in roughly and kissed her the way he imagined the cocky Burne would. She clung to his shirt front even after he broke away, until he pushed her hands off and stepped away from her. As he stalked under the trees, he didn't let himself glance back.

Stone watched her leave. "Where'd you find her?"

Burne shrugged and ignored the awkward feeling as he spoke the false words. "After Ric tossed me out—I don't really remember. I woke up in her bed with her all ready to go again."

Stone raised his eyebrows and waited.

"She said it was good. This morning was, anyway."

"What's her name? I don't remember seeing her around the village."

"Bertha? Bethany? Something like that."

"Huh."

Burne finally let himself peer after Gray. "Berthenia" was drifting along the road south of where they stood, all the way down where it disappeared into the woods. Burne grinned at Stone. "You lot have probably terrified all the village girls into hiding."

"We haven't been messing with anyone. Amberfeld's orders."

"But guards have a reputation. A season ago you would have."

The words came out sounding like a challenge. Burne could have kicked himself. He didn't need to anger Stone.

"Would you?" Stone asked.

"Would I what?"

"Mess with her? Does Burne the Stud do things like that?"

How far should he take his act? Would Stone call him out on any claims he made? He wasn't about to go rooting out the damsels of Cliffside and terrifying them to prove himself to Stone.

Burne frowned. This act wasn't about being a jerk. It was about believing in himself. He could be confident without behaving like these guys had in the past. Gray floated through his mind, teasing him and smiling.

"I guess I like it better when they want me," Burne said, lifting his chin higher than felt normal. "If they don't want me, someone else will. I don't need to go scaring a bunch of women to prove anything."

So much for not sounding challenging.

Stone flexed his jaw, considering. "Maybe I'll get lucky too and some Cliffside maid will fancy me," he said flatly.

"You ever had someone? For more than a night, I mean."

Stone relaxed against the tree he leaned on, but his fists clenched tight and his face remained serious. "When I was younger. But she found someone else."

Burne didn't trust himself to say the right thing.

"No matter," Stone continued. "I'd be a dirty farmer if I'd bonded with her. I'd rather be a guard than a farmer. Although I'll be glad to see somewhere other than Cliffside."

"Pretty dull here?"

"If it weren't for Baldric's, I'd jump off the cliff. He's got some strong ale at least."

"I thought my head would split open this morning."

"Was that before or after Bertha had one last tumble?"

Burne panicked for a beat. "She had some hangover cure ready for me. No idea what it was, but it worked." He grinned. "I guess she wanted me to participate a little more."

Stone pushed off from the tree. "Wish we had some of that cure here. This lot are going to be a mess." He walked among the tents, pulling open the flaps and calling the men's names. Burne took Stone's place, leaning on the tree trunk and trying to pretend he didn't care about anything. It was so easy to accidentally slip into his usual anxious, eager-to-please self. Being the confident, arrogant Burne took effort.

As Cap and a few others emerged from their tents, they stumbled toward a fire pit farther back in the trees. Burne sauntered after them and took a seat. Stone poked at the fire until it revived and swung the pot hanging above it over the flames.

"Tea," Cap mumbled, and Burne remembered his first morning with Gray. Cap wasn't nearly as cute as Gray had been, but he was less obnoxious than usual when he was half asleep.

"It's coming," Stone said.

When the tea was poured, the men started to wake up. Cap was even more excited to see Burne than he had been at the pub, sliding up next to him and grinning. And when Stone told the crew where Burne had (supposedly) spent the night, Cap called for a tea toast in his honor. There was more back-slapping and calling Burne "Stud."

"So," Burne said when they quieted down, "I remember you said something about tonight, but it's all kind of vague."

"Tonight's the big night, man!" Cap crowed.

Stone was still watching Burne. Burne waited instead of asking another question.

Cap pointed at men around the firepit and a few of the men chugged their tea and stood. "You'd best be off," he told them. "Don't want to keep the lord and master waiting." When he spoke of Amberfeld, his voice grew derisive.

"Or the sausages."

"Want us to bring you some?"

Cap shook his head. "We've got to take care of something. We'll come by after." One man remained seated with Cap and Stone, but Cap addressed him. "You go, too. Stud can help us." The crowd of men trudged out across the field toward the grand house.

"You don't like Amberfeld?" Burne asked.

Stone kept poking at the fire. Cap frowned. "It's been nice to have a job again—a real one. But once we're paid for this gig, I don't know if we'll stick around."

"We won't," Stone muttered.

"Some of them might." Cap indicated the departing men. "Amberfeld's gonna need help."

Were Cap and Stone participating in Amberfeld's rebellion for the income? How much could Amberfeld be paying them that made this job worth more than a job around Woodglen? But this was more exciting than what was available in Woodglen. And it gave them a chance to be in charge.

"Do you miss being in the King's Guard?" Burne asked.

Cap frowned again. "It was nice being a part of things." He sounded wistful and he frowned. But then he grinned. "It was fun when you got there."

"Why didn't you join the peacekeepers?" Burne asked.

"They wouldn't have us. They wouldn't take anyone who kept fighting for the king for two beats after the lot of them surrendered. They said we wouldn't make proper peacekeepers."

"Wouldn't have been the same anyway," Stone said.

"Why not?" Burne asked. "What are the new peacekeepers like?"

Cap scrunched up his face like he'd tasted something foul. "They don't have any leadership. It's like everyone's the same and there's a bunch of rules but no one to enforce them."

That didn't sound right at all, but mostly Burne was trying to keep Cap talking. "You liked being a leader," Burne said. "There's not much point in being a peacekeeper if you can't move up the ranks."

"Exactly. Being in charge shows you made it. You worked for it and beat everyone else."

"You're the leader now, right? What are we doing today?"

"We need to check . . . something." Cap and Stone glanced at each other and away. "You can help," Cap said, "but we have to blindfold you."

Unease prickled all over Burne. Blindfold? This sounded like one of their pranks. They could lose him in the woods or walk him off the edge of the cliff.

"Why? What are we doing?"

"We have to get something," Cap said, "but it's in a secret location. No one knows, not even Joey." He jutted his chin in the direction the other men had gone. "We'd have blindfolded him, too."

Cap gazed earnestly at Burne. He really wanted Burne to do this—or to fall for his prank. But if Burne refused, they could tell him to get lost. Their new camaraderie might turn sour. He need-ed information—helping the villagers was more important than avoiding one of Cap's pranks. He had to play along. He nodded slowly.

Gray had said he wouldn't go far. Gray would be nearby. Burne didn't dare survey the trees for a sign of him, but maybe he was listening even now, although Burne had begged him not to risk getting too close.

"All right!" Cap said, and Burne's stomach clenched at his en-thusiasm. Cap swigged the remains of his tea and dropped the tin cup beside the firepit. "I hate to do it, man," he said as they stood and walked toward the road. "Only Stone and I know the way to where we're going—none of the others know where it is. We've got to follow protocol."

"I understand," Burne said, although it made no sense. Why bring him to the secret location when he'd only just arrived? Why not bring the other man instead of him? But if he could learn something by going with them, he had to risk it.

They stopped at the road, and Cap and Stone both turned to him. Their features were so familiar even though he'd spent only a half-moon or so in the Guard with them, and a whole turn of the seasons had passed since then. They'd both let their hair grow out from the shaved military hair cut they'd worn in the Guard but it was still neatly trimmed and their faces were clean shaven. Stone never smiled but he wasn't as menacing as he'd always seemed before. And Cap's eyes sparkled as he bounced on his toes and moved closer. They were simultaneously the bullies who'd treated him like dirt and two insecure men who didn't much like their lives. They'd been trained to fight and kill, but they didn't seem like killers. He'd have to trust they weren't about to push him off the cliff.

He exhaled as Cap moved toward him. Cap fixed a kerchief over Burne's eyes. Burne tried to appear calm as his view went dark.

"It's a short walk," Cap said, and took Burne's arm. When he tugged, Burne followed, trying not to stumble.

For twenty paces, the sandy road slid beneath his shoes. Burne breathed in deeply to stay calm. He counted their paces and listened to take in as much information as he could—the morning wind blowing out toward the sea and the cries of gulls meant the cliff was on his right side, which made sense since they had headed north on the road. The sun on his shoulders meant they'd moved out from the forest's shadow. After ten more paces, his foot squished on grass as they left the road.

They were leading him toward the cliff.

Keep breathing. Don't panic.

Five paces across the grass, Cap stopped him.

"We have to crawl for this part."

Burne imagined them laughing as they watched him crawl across the ground. But Cap had said "we" and as Burne crouched down, Cap's voice stayed beside him.

"Here, hang onto my heel." Awkwardly, Burne extended a hand. Cap placed Burne's fingers onto the back of his shoe before crawling forward. Bushes scratched his face and tugged at his shirt. A branch smacked his forehead.

"Sorry about that," Stone said from behind him. "Cap isn't paying attention." He sounded like he meant it.

The ocean's roar grew louder and the scraping of the bushes stopped. Wind ruffled his hair. The ground under his knees was hard but uneven, like the rolling rock of the clifftop. Burne swallowed. They wouldn't dump him off a cliff.

"Stop here," Cap said in front of him, and Cap's shoe pulled away from his fingers. "You can stand up." Scratchy footsteps padded away. As Burne stood, a hand came under his elbow to steady him. Something clanged, and clicked, and clanged again, followed by a scraping sound like sandpaper on wood.

Stone nudged Burne from behind. "You need to go down a few steps."

Burne edged his foot forward until he found the edge of the step. The rocks were gritty with sand. With his arms out for balance, he made his way down one step at a time, one, two, three steps down, and his fingers bumped into rock alongside him. He pressed them against the rock wall to steady himself. Four, five steps and his next step hit flat ground, slipping a smidge on the sand. The wind had stopped somewhere above him, and his fingers trailed over rock on both sides as he shuffled forward. Stone's footsteps scuffed behind him, slow and patient as Burne edged along the rock. The ocean roar had quieted. The breeze would be tossing his hair if he were about to go over the edge. Instead he heard his breathing and his heart racing.

Cap pulled Burne's arm forward and he followed without tripping. Wherever they were, the rocks were smooth. The warm sun disappeared from his face and behind the blindfold, everything darkened. Cold air washed over him, damp and cool when he inhaled.

Cap dropped his arm. "We need you to help us guard this until sunset."

Cap's footsteps pattered away, and the scraping sound came again. The little light Burne had under the blindfold darkened to nothing and beneath his frantic heartbeat, the vestiges of the sounds of wind and ocean hushed and went out. The clanging sounded again, muffled this time. He held his breath—neither Cap nor Stone moved nearby. They were gone.

Burne yanked the blindfold off but nothing changed. He was in complete darkness. His pulse thundered in his chest. A muffled laugh came from behind him and he spun toward it but lost his balance in the disorienting emptiness. He caught himself and stood frozen, gasping. The laughter stopped.

Chapter 15

BURNE STOOD FROZEN IN THE darkness, panting. He might be passing out or his vision going dark but he couldn't tell because he couldn't see anything to know what was happening. Panic flowed from his chest to his fingertips and he braced himself as his knees wobbled and his heartbeat juddered. He blinked hard. His eyes were open; there was simply nothing to see in the dark.

He forced a deep breath and let it out slowly. He wasn't passing out. With his hand in front of his face, he blinked a few more times—nothing. But his head was clear, he was standing and not swaying, he could breathe and the air was cool on his skin. He wasn't fainting—he was standing in a dark cavern in the rocks. The ghost pressure of the blindfold crossed the bridge of his nose, and each empty blink of his eyes felt pronounced in the nothingness. He held his breath and everything went silent. Nothing was in here with him that might hurt him. Another deep breath and exhale and he listened again. Silence.

They'd brought him to some sort of cavern. The rock was solid under him and still gritty with sand. They'd been laughing as they shut the door—it was a prank, that was all. They would come back this evening and let him out and laugh about how they had tricked him.

But now he was stuck and he needed to get out if he hoped to make any progress on the plan to stop the fighting. He swallowed against the acid taste on his tongue. He remembered Gray's lips against his—Gray disguised as Berthenia the village girl, but it had felt like Gray when Burne kissed him goodbye under the trees. He'd closed his eyes just before their lips touched and known he was kissing Gray, and the smell and feel of Gray beside him had given him strength to approach the guards again.

Burne opened his eyes in the dark, sighing away the memory of Gray. He was trapped in a cavern. But why was there a cavern in the clifftop? It must be for something, storage or hiding. Maybe something in here could help him break out. Probably it was only potatoes and rutabagas though. He inhaled again, smelling the cool air. It should be musty but instead he caught something familiar. Wood. Sawdust. Like a carpenter's shop.

He shoved the blindfold into his pocket and carefully stretched his arms out, waving them up and down and side to side, and finding only empty space. Where had Cap's laughter come from? He had spun toward it, back toward the place where he'd entered the cavern. He took a small step forward. They would have locked the door—the clanging noises must have been the chains of a lock— but it was the first thing to try.

Ten small steps and his fingertips bumped something solid. He ran them down rough boards and along solid crosspieces. No hint of wind or warmth came through, even at the far edges—the door continued behind the rock walls with no crack he could wedge his fingers into. On the right side, cold iron bands connected the door to its hinges. He skated his fingers across to the left and found the latch, but when he lifted it, the door didn't budge. He pushed and shoved with his shoulder but it had no effect. The wood was solid as the rock beneath his feet. He kicked and his shoe thudded against it without moving it even a hair.

Burne turned and leaned back against the door, relaxing in the steady rhythm of his heartbeat. He reviewed everything he'd seen that morning: The men had gone to the manor house, leaving Cap and Stone behind. To take care of something, Cap had said. What? Or had they meant they had to take care of their prank—locking him in the cavern? Cap and Stone must have followed the other men to the manor as soon as they'd left him. They'd laughed as they left—laughed at how he had fallen for their ruse. Burne ran a hand through his hair.

He bit his lip. He hadn't filled with the shame he'd always felt when they'd played pranks on him last spring. This time, he'd suspected they were going to prank him. He had gone along with it in the hopes he'd learn something useful. He felt . . . different. He didn't care about them laughing at him. All he cared about was stopping them from hurting Nem, Kitty, and the other villagers.

Was this merely a prank, though? A thin trickle of fear slipped down the back of his neck. What if they had found him out? Had they spotted a flaw in Gray's illusion of the village girl? Or guessed Burne was spying on them and helping the villagers? Maybe they knew. Or maybe they only suspected and they had contained him here while they investigated.

And if they investigated . . . His chest lurched. Gray—Gray was out there alone. What if they had spotted him spying from the woods and decided to get Burne out of the way before going after Gray? Had he stayed hidden? He had come right into the pub last night instead of staying safely outside like Burne had wanted him to. He'd have followed when they blindfolded Burne, and what if the men had spotted him? Would he try something dangerous to rescue Burne? What if Gray pretended to be Cap or Stone and they caught him, or he showed up at the guard camp disguised as Berthenia again?

What if the prank was actually a trap? They might have found out about Gray and they needed a way to catch him, and using Burne was the sure way to do it. Gray acted confident but he wasn't a fighter. He could hide and sneak but if they caught him, he wouldn't have any way to protect himself. What if they hurt Gray while Burne was trapped here and couldn't help him?

Or maybe—Burne's stomach churned over—maybe they knew he'd arrived in Cliffside with a young woman and wondered how she fit with his story about coming to Cliffside to find them and join their ranks. What if they decided to find Nem and question her? She was tough but she couldn't fend off a whole group of guards. They could hurt her, as well as Kitty and Linota.

All the possibilities swirled in his head. But he couldn't collapse now. He had to get out of here so he could help. He forced his thoughts back to the present.

Burne held his breath and listened again. At first silence met him, but he waited. The dull washing of waves . . . To his left, faintly, the ocean moved against the cliffs. He peered into the darkness. The faintest glow appeared on a shape about ten paces away and half as tall as him. He crept toward it, shuffling his feet, and halfway there his toes bumped an object. He reached down and felt the edges of a crate. His fingers skimmed over its surface and found another beside it. They were long and thin. He gripped the corner of the crate and lifted, and its weight resisted his hand.

What if the crates contained Lord Amberfeld's cache of guns? Burne couldn't be so lucky that Cap and Stone had deposited him right in the midst of what he'd been seeking.

Burne turned again toward the ocean sound. He could definitely see a glow on the top of a stack of crates. And that glow meant light was getting into the cave somehow, even if it was only through the tiniest crack in the rocks. He moved carefully toward the illuminated crates. When his hand touched them he was able to see the hand's movement. The back side of the crates was visible, so the light was entering from the back of the cave near the ocean.

Burne kept creeping toward the end of the cave, nudging his way past crates. When he focused away from the direction he walked in, he saw a light in the side of his vision, but when he tried to see the light source, it vanished the way stars did when you looked right at them. His knee bumped another item—a barrel this time. He began tilting and rolling barrels aside to create a path, step by step until he reached the end of the cave and could touch the rocky walls.

The barest whisper of cold air tickled his face. A sliver of daylight shone in through a thin crack at eye level. He reached toward it, fingertips scraping over rough, cold stone. Bits crumbled under his touch but the opening was tiny. Burne took off his shoe and covered his hand with it. He made a fist and punched at the rock near the crack. A bit more crumbled away and he squinted in the sudden light as a burst of air blew in. The opening was as wide as his hand.

Behind him, the outlines of the cavern reflected the faint light. Rows of barrels and crates lined the rough walls, with a path down the middle where he had stumbled through. With the added light, Burne moved back toward the center. The cavern door remained in shadow and appeared as solid as it had felt.

The crates were nailed shut. He scanned the space again, hoping to find a tool or a loose piece of anything he could use to pry one open, but other than the stored items the space was empty. He stood over a crate, worked his fingers into the crack under the lid, and pulled, then pushed and pulled, slowly prying it up as the nails creaked. The lid gave enough that he could work his fingers further under it to get a better grip and hold down the crate as he pulled. The nails squealed again but he couldn't pull the lid any higher. The lid had opened about the thickness of his hand.

Burne stood up and stretched out his neck and shoulders. He had to be stronger.

When he was a child, he'd never been as strong as the other boys. If his mother sent him with a bucket to the well, he'd struggle to carry the water home. And anything that required force, from chopping wood to tossing a ball across the park, always required more strength than he had. His mother always said not to worry when he fretted. She said he had other talents, but he always felt like a failure.

But one time last spring, he'd gotten angry. The newest guardsmen had been told to move a pile of rocks for a new wall alongside the road, and after they'd spent all morning carrying the boulders way down the road to the determined spot, Cap told them he'd made a mistake and had them carry all the boulders back. The older guards were obviously messing with the newer ones and making them work when they could have been resting. But they couldn't refuse to do the work. So they'd done it. But Burne had grown more and more angry as the afternoon passed until he'd been slinging rocks into his arms like they were cabbages.

It wasn't that he couldn't wield an axe or toss a ball. He just wasn't assertive when his emotions weren't involved.

Burne made himself think about Nem and her new family and all the villagers of Cliffside who'd been stuck with rotten Lord Amberfeld all their lives—who should've driven him away last spring but had let him keep his ostentatious home, and he was repaying them by destroying the peace in their village, poisoning their leaders, and staging a foolish rebellion. He thought about Gray and how the guards might harm him if they caught him sneaking around Cliffside.

Burne yanked off his second shoe and dropped it to the floor with the first. He lifted a foot and wedged his toes into the opening under the crate lid. Balancing, he stepped up onto the crate and wedged his second foot in so he stood with both feet on the edges. He gripped the top of the crate, bent his knees, and let out a cry as he heaved the lid upward. The nails squealed as he wrenched them from the wood. He pulled the lid clear off, dropped it, and hopped down.

He reached into the straw inside and felt smooth metal. Stars, Cap and Stone really had been foolish. Rows of guns packed in straw filled the crate. The men had brought Burne directly to their supply of firepower. Burne shook his head slowly, almost sorry for their mistake.

But he was trapped. He couldn't destroy the guns unless he could get out of the cave.

He pushed aside the straw packing to extract a gun and carried it toward the light. It resembled the one they'd trained him with in the Guard. A sharp metal blade glinted at the end. Burne shuddered. He'd hated those blades from the first sight. The idea of using it to stab someone made him feel sick.

It will be different, the officers had said, when the other person's trying to kill you. But he couldn't imagine it.

He checked first to make sure the gun wasn't loaded. He gingerly wiggled the blade and then wiggled it more firmly to see that it was securely attached. He carried the gun to the back corner where he'd made the small opening in the cave wall. He could load the gun and shoot at the rock, but the men might hear him. And he might end up killing himself if the bullet ricocheted off instead of digging into the rock. He jabbed at the wall instead.

More of the wall collapsed. Dirt and bits of rock crumbled to the floor, and outside, rocks clattered as they bounced down the cliff. After a few minutes of the work, Burne had widened the opening to a few hands' width. Once the loose material had fallen away, he chipped at harder rock. It went more slowly but he kept at it until he was sweating even in the cold shadows of the cavern. Slowly the hole to the outside widened and an ocean breeze stole in.

He had to move faster. It must be getting on to afternoon and he had to finish before Cap and Stone returned. He lifted his arms over his head, bringing the blade in from above and with more force. Stab. A chip of rock fell. Stab. He thought about Nem and Gray again but that wasn't enough anger. He thought about being tormented by the guardsmen but that was over now and besides, it had brought him to Trillium and eventually to Gray and he didn't care about it at all anymore.

He thought about the old king whom the villagers had overthrown. Why had he been in power in the first place? He hadn't done anything for the people. How had he stayed in power for so long when no one had supported him? He'd stayed in power because he'd controlled the guards, and the guards carried guns and would shoot another person without a second thought.

Rose and the villagers had defeated the king with help from the fairies, but what if the fairies and their magic hadn't been available? There'd have been no hope. It was a world where whoever had the most guns held the power. Energy surged through Burne's arms. Stab! Stab! He jabbed with the blade without stopping.

A chunk of rock fell away, widening the opening, and another and another. He kept at it, turning the motion into a mindless repetition as he cursed the old king and his oppressive regime and everyone who had profited off it at the expense of the villagers across the land.

Burne paused, panting. The hole was much wider. He might be able to stick his head out. When he tried, the wind hit him. Down below, waves smashed into the rocks, tossing up a white spray. The cavern was in the side of the cliff. The rocks dropped away steeply below his hole. He couldn't see what the cliff was like above him. The hole wasn't big enough to climb out, and even if he could, he might not have anything to hold onto. But if he could open the hole a little wider, he could toss the guns into the sea.

He withdrew into the cave and bashed against the edges of the opening until he bent the blade and had to get another. He pounded harder with the new one. His arms ached but he wouldn't let up, not when he needed to do this to protect Nem and Gray and everyone else. He felt like a ram butting his horns or a miner in the mountain, chipping ore from the rock. A piece of the wall fell with a crash as it tumbled down the cliff face, and wind blew into the cave in gusts, chilling his sweaty face.

The opening was about as wide as his hips and over a hand's length tall. He tested out the weight of the gun, holding it like a spear over his shoulder and positioning it in the opening. He launched it out with a grunt and hurried to watch it fall. It flew into the air, sailing out over the water as it curved downward before falling and disappearing into the waves with a tiny splash.

He could keep going and widen the opening further but the men might return at any time. Destroying the weapons was more important than escaping. He might not be able to get away but he was going to toss every stupid gun in this cavern into the sea. No one in the village would be hurt tonight, even if it meant he'd face the wrath of the guards when they discovered what he had done.

Burne hauled an armload of guns to the hole and pitched them into the sea one by one. When the first crate was empty, he pried up the lid of another and tossed those. He worked swiftly, energized by the joy of destroying the weapons. Soon he stood over five empty crates. He opened the smaller boxes next and tossed all of it into the sea: pistols, daggers, more blades for the guns, and a few helmets.

When the crates had all been emptied save for a few items, he turned to the barrels. He could read the labels now—gunpowder. He hefted one up, propping it against the wall and his chest to lift it high enough. But the barrel was too wide for the opening.

He reached for one of the daggers he'd held back, sturdy and sharp, and resumed his attack on the cave wall. Seagulls called outside and the crash of the waves beckoned to him. He wouldn't think about how tired his arms felt, not until he'd gotten out of here. If he stopped to rest a moment, he might have to face Cap and Stone and they'd probably be so angry they'd bash his head against the wall before they came up with something worse to do to him.

The opening became as wide as his shoulders and tall enough to fit the barrels through. At the last moment, he remembered to pull the stopper from the hole in the top of the barrel. If the barrel floated, someone might be able to retrieve it. It scraped through the opening and he pushed it out. The barrel knocked off the side of the cliff as it fell. He poked his head out to watch, hoping it wouldn't cause any sparks before it hit the water. It splashed down into the white foam and disappeared a moment, then bobbed up on the surface. The next wave crashed and drove it under again. It surfaced, down and up until it disappeared for good.

Burne threw all the barrels out of the cavern. At last the dark space was clear, with only empty crates and lids scattered on the floor. He panted in the light shining into the blackness, checking the empty crates in case he had missed anything. The few daggers he had saved to use leaned on the wall. Should he keep one in case he needed to defend himself? Should he have saved one of the guns? What would he have done with it—shot the first person in the door? Would he stab Cap and Stone as they rushed at him, to stop them from hurting him? No. He wouldn't be able to use a dagger even then. He took the last of the weapons and flung them into the ocean.

He rested his hands on the solid rock along the bottom edge of the opening. He pushed himself up and out, wiggling his shoulders through. Resting on his belly, he registered the crashing of waves but he couldn't see yet in the dazzling light. He turned from his belly onto his back to face up the cliff. His hands scrabbled across the rock and found a cleft he could cling to as he tugged his body up and seated himself on the opening. He hunched forward and held on to the rocks. Below his bottom, the cliff dropped into the white spray of waves. The water might be deep enough to jump and he was a strong swimmer, but there might be jagged rocks below and the force of the waves would dash him against the cliffs.

He squinted in the blazing sun as the breeze gusted. The terrain around him was not promising, with shear rock curving away on either side. His best chance was to climb up where the rock was knobbier. About ten paces up, the rock ended with a view of the sky—and a seagull stood regarding him.

The seagull tilted its head and squawked as the wind ruffled its feathers.

"Beaks?"

The bird leaned forward, lifted its wings, and gave a mighty push, flapping to take off. The wind caught it and it wheeled away, crying like a coyote as it disappeared behind the clifftop. The calls faded and returned. Beaks soared back into sight. He hovered over the cliff, lifting his wings and dropping his legs until he plunked down on the rock at the same spot where he'd stood before. He folded his wings and hopped a few times, peering over his wing toward the forest.

Gray appeared at the top, panting. When he spotted Burne, he dropped to his knees and peered over the edge.

"Black stars," he gasped. "What happened?"

"There's a door," Burne said, pointing, "but they've locked it."

Gray scrambled away. A few moments later he was back. "I found it, but I don't think I can get in. There's a huge chain and it's solid as granite."

Burne took a deep breath. "I'm going to have to climb."

"Should I find a rope?"

"Is there anything up there to tie it on?"

Gray shook his head. "I could hold it—in case you slip. Maybe it would help."

"Or I'd pull you down with me."

Gray's wide green eyes peered down at him. "It's too dangerous to climb."

"I have to do it," Burne said, trying to keep his voice calm. "The men might be back soon. They'll hurt me if I'm here."

"Okay." Gray sat back, clutching his hands together.

Burne surveyed the rock wall. It wasn't as bad as he'd first thought. It cracked in a few places where he could grip with his fingers, and it sloped slightly forward so he wouldn't be hanging out over the water. He left his shoes in the cave. He'd do better at finding footings with his toes.

He wiped his hands on his shirt and reached up to grab at the rock. Slowly, he lifted himself up from the cavern. Maneuvering his legs out the narrow opening was tricky, but once he'd pulled himself out far enough, he stood on the edge of the opening and rested a moment, leaning forward on the rocks. He reached higher and found another handhold. He risked a glimpse down to find a crack he could wedge his toes in and pulled himself up with one leg dangling. He didn't check on Gray. He didn't want to see him looking frantic.

Where to next? His free hand patted over the rock face but everywhere was smooth. His gripping hand ached. There had to be somewhere. Or he'd have to go down and move to the side and try another route . . . but his free hand found a knob. He gripped it and rested the other hand before he pulled up with the higher hand and searched for a new footing.

All he could see was the rock. Slowly, he climbed up the face of the cliff, his shirt and hair blowing about him.

A voice drifted to him on the wind.

Focus, he told himself. He kept climbing. He was halfway up.

He found another handhold, and another narrow ledge to push his toes against. As he pulled himself the rest of the way, Gray moved back from the edge. Burne's view cleared the top. Gray crouched before him, peering away over his shoulder. A wide expanse of rock stretched out to bushes and beyond that were the treetops. Gray scrambled forward to offer a hand, and as Burne found a final place to hold onto, Gray helped him to the top. Burne crawled away from the edge and sank down to rest, sucking in air as the wind rushed over him.

"Someone's coming." Gray crouched beside him. "The path is behind those bushes."

Burne forced himself to stand and extended a hand to Gray. Gray's hand shook as he took Burne's and stood. His eyes were wide and something about him was different but Burne couldn't figure out what. Burne took a careful step away from the edge, pulling Gray after him.

The rocky area around them spread along the cliff's edge to the north and south. The surface was ridged and uneven, with deep shadows from the stark sunlight. On either side of the cluster of bushes hiding the entrance to the cavern, far back, bits of the road were visible between bushes and trees, and to the south the rock disappeared and trees grew all the way to the cliff's edge. The chimneys of the manor peeked over the top of the bushes and trees.

More voices came on the wind.

"Can you hide us?" Burne asked. He gripped Gray's hand. "Can we look like the sky?"

"It should be easy," Gray said, but his voice sounded desperate. He stared off at the water. Burne dropped Gray's hand. As soon as he did, he could see Gray flickering with bits of sky blue but never disappearing. "I can't hold it." Gray's hands trembled and tears gathered in his eyes.

"We'll go then," Burne said, taking Gray's hand again and leading him across the rock and away from the path to the cave. Seagulls hung in the air, riding the wind and circling above them. Burne angled toward the place where he could see the road to the south. He tried to hurry but the ground was so uneven he had to watch each step. If they could reach cover before the men began hunting for them, they could disappear into the forest. Or if they reached the road, they could run.

Shouting erupted behind them. They dropped hands and clambered faster, leaping from one ridge to the next. They had cleared the nearest bushes and had a straight path to the road. Burne chanced a glimpse back. Figures appeared on the cliff where he had climbed up, pointing after them, and more shouts reached him.

He and Gray struggled over the rocks. They were halfway to the road. The men chasing them would be as slow as they were. But the men weren't chasing them. They were pointing and shouting.

Figures emerged on the roadway ahead. They'd been hidden by the trees and bushes but now they poured into sight, shouting and waving at the men on the cliff. They'd be able to outrun Burne and Gray on the road and cut off their escape. Burne halted, panting.

"Beaks says there's a way down to the water." Gray said.

"Where?"

"A little farther."

How could there be a way down when they were so high up? But the men were moving, some coming right at them across the rock while others headed along the road, and the men behind them were moving forward. Burne followed Gray along the cliff and back toward the water. They stopped at the edge.

Far, far down was a smooth round pool. Outcrops on both sides circled it and shielded it from the crashing surf.

Beaks flapped into the wind, hovering alongside them.

"Jump?" Gray said. "Are you joking?"

Beaks squawked. Behind them, the guards were closing in.

Gray took Burne's hand, his face distressed. "He said there was a way down but he meant a place to jump. He says the pool is deep enough."

Burne took in Gray's sunlit face, stained with tears. He'd rather jump off a thousand cliffs with Gray than fight those men—especially with Gray now in their sights. He gripped Gray's hand.

"I don't know if I can do this," Gray whimpered.

"You can. I'll be with you."

Gray swallowed. "Hold them off, would you?" he said to Beaks, and the bird flapped upward and cried a piercing note. The seagulls wheeling overhead soared together into a cloud of birds and dove. They cleared Burne's head and flapped straight into the oncoming guards.

Burne turned once more to Gray and squeezed his hand as tightly as he could. "Now," he said, and they jumped.

Chapter 16

THEY FELL TOWARD THE WATER. Burne forced himself to watch so he could suck in a deep breath before he went in. He squeezed his eyes shut and clung to Gray's hand as they plummeted into the rippling surface. He plunged deep into the cold, the force of the fall pulling him down as he kicked against it, stopping the descent and struggling toward the surface. The water was frigid and Gray was twisting in his grasp but he held tight and pulled Gray up. Burne broke into the air and gasped, letting go of Gray's hand.

Gray flailed beside him, splashing in his face. Burne reached for him and Gray tried to climb on top of him, dunking him under. Burne shoved him away and escaped his reach. He surfaced and tried again, darting up behind Gray and pinning an arm across his chest. Gray struggled, coughing, but he couldn't escape.

"I've got you," Burne said, treading water, and Gray's motions quieted. He coughed more and took a ragged breath.

Burne kicked toward the nearest wall. Overhead, the rocks towered straight up and disappeared. They could swim over to the outcrop and climb out of the water but they'd be exposed to the men atop the cliff. If they stayed here beneath the cliff, the men wouldn't be able to see them. It seemed safest to hide for now.

Once he'd reached the edge of the water, Burne found a place to hold on to the rock. A little to the left, a narrow ledge sloped down to the water. Burne swam for it, holding Gray's body up behind him. Gray stayed immobile but his chest expanded and contracted beneath Burne's arm.

When Burne reached the ledge, he found Gray's hand and put it on the flat rock. "Can you sit up here?" he asked. Gray licked his lips and nodded, and Burne slowly let go of his hold across Gray's chest. He lifted him up and Gray twisted and sat, coughing again. Burne pushed himself up beside him. Gray shivered and hunched forward, coughing.

Burne slid over to Gray and wrapped his arms around him. The water had chilled Burne, but Gray felt colder.

No sounds came from above. They were hidden, but the cliff and the rock walls also hid the sun. In his soaking clothes and the deep shade, Burne shivered, too. At least they had no breeze. The pool was sheltered from the wind and the violence of the waves.

Burne hugged Gray until his coughing subsided.

"Do you know how to swim?" Burne asked, loosening his hold a little. Gray was still shivering.

Gray shook his head. "I was supposed to learn."

"Yeah?" It seemed smart to keep him talking.

"My friend said she'd teach me—the mermaid."

There he was talking about mermaids again. Maybe he was delirious.

"But you can't swim?"

"No."

"How did you find me up on the cliff?" Burne asked instead.

Gray leaned into him, hiding his face and twisting a fist into Burne's shirt. "I watched from the woods and I saw them blindfolding you. But I couldn't get close with all the open space. I lost you when you went into the bushes. And they came back without you."

"Where did they go?"

"They stood around their camp and went up to the manor. I tried to find a way through the bushes." Gray's voice rose as if he might become hysterical.

"It's okay," Burne said, rubbing his back. "Tell me what happened."

"There was no path. From above I could see it, but not from the front. I searched along the bushes and I crawled into them but I couldn't see anything and I kept getting stuck and I couldn't find you."

"Beaks helped you."

Gray nodded against his chest. "He saw you. He said you were dropping sticks into the sea."

"Guns," Burne said. "They left me in a cave with crates of guns. It was a lot of them—it might have been all of them."

"Really?" Gray said. His voice sounded calmer and he leaned back enough to gaze up at Burne.

"They're gone. I got rid of all of them."

"Did the men hurt you?"

Burne shook his head. "I think they meant to play a prank. Like they used to but—" Burne sighed. "I don't know. The pranks used to seem so mean but this was just silly. Like they wanted to watch me stumble around blindfolded and wanted me to wonder what they'd do. They said I needed to guard something until tonight, and they shut me in the cavern. It was pitch dark so I panicked a little, but I figured out what had happened. Maybe they found out I was spying and planned to hurt me, but it didn't seem like it."

"But why would they leave you *there*?"

"I don't think they realized how foolish it was. I don't think they had any idea I'd be able to get out."

"How did you get out? Did you find a tunnel?"

"No. There was a crack and the rock was thin so I broke through. I got angry and hurled all the guns out. And then I kept going so I could make it big enough for me."

"You broke a hole in rock?" Gray's fist loosened on Burne's shirt, and Gray hugged Burne's waist and nuzzled into his neck. "With your bare hands?"

"No, with the end of a gun. What are you doing?"

Gray was kissing his neck. "Trying to warm us up."

Gray's lips were warm and when he nipped the spot below

Burne's ear, a flash of heat drove the worst of the cold from Burne's body. Maybe kissing was the best way to keep Gray calm and warm . . . but they needed to get out of here. They were hiding on a ledge surrounded by the ocean. They needed to get to safety, and they needed to stay hidden from the men who'd been chasing them—men who might come hunting for them at any moment. And Gray couldn't swim. Burne had to get them out of this situation as soon as possible, and kissing Gray wouldn't make it happen.

But Gray was clinging to him and sucking on his earlobe. Burne gently detached Gray's arm and held him back.

"I like when you kiss me," Burne said, and Gray's face lit up. His green eyes were huge and his dark hair was plastered to his face.

His hair—that was the difference Burne hadn't been able to name. Gray's hair no longer had silvery highlights at the tips. The silver must have been an illusion as Burne had suspected. And now Burne remembered how the silver had shifted to green and back when Burne first saw Gray in the forest—that had been an illusion, too. But why? Burne blushed. Gray had been showing off for him.

Gray lifted his eyebrows. His hair appeared darker, too, as dark as Hyacinth's. But it was wet so maybe that was why. "I like kissing you," Gray replied and tried to lean in, but Burne held him off.

"I just don't think it's the best use of our time right now," Burne said.

"If we're going to die," Gray said, "I'd like to kiss you as much as I can before I go."

"Die? Gray, what are you talking about?"

"Using my last hours in this body to do the best thing I can think of and—"

"We're not going to die." Burne took hold of Gray's arms and held him firmly. "I'm not going to let you die."

"But we're trapped," Gray said. "No one knows we're here except Beaks, and there's no one he can tell unless he flies all the way to Woodglen, and by the time Hyacinth sends help, Cliffside

                    Jane Buehler

could be under siege and we'll probably have perished of thirst or cold or the tide will sweep us away."

Crap, the tide. "Is the tide out now?" Burne asked.

"It's out."

"I'll swim."

"What? No!" Gray pushed past Burne's hold and clung to him.

Burne moved him back again. "I can swim, Gray. I grew up swimming. I can tow you under my arm like I did."

"You're not worried about the waves?"

"We'll have to get away from the cliffs. Once we're farther out it will be calm."

Gray frowned. "You should go without me."

"But—"

Gray took Burne's hand. "You have a better chance without me. You can get help and come back for me."

Burne hesitated. If he left, there'd be no one to protect Gray if anything happened. Not that Gray was helpless, but illusions and an obliging seagull could do only so much. And what if Burne didn't make it? What would happen to Gray then?

But if he did nothing, they'd be stuck. And Gray was right that it would be easier to swim on his own. He had to try. "Can you reach Beaks?" Burne asked. "We need to find out where I can get up the cliffs."

Gray sat up and quieted. A moment later, a gull swooped into the cove. He dropped, flapping, and landed in the water, where he folded his wings and paddled over to them.

"Two sticky buns?" Gray said. "You can have a whole pan if you get us out of this. We need to get up the cliffs." He closed his eyes—imagining a path up the cliffs, Burne guessed.

Gray's eyes opened. "He says there's a way up, and guess where it is?"

Burne shook his head.

"At Linota's house. Because she's a *smuggler*! It's hidden in a cove like this one. He says there's a pointy rock at the entrance."

"So if I swim out far enough to see the top of the cliffs, I can watch for that break in the trees where the gardens were, and the cove at Linota's should be a little farther."

"Oh, he wants sticky buns for his whole flock because of how they drove the guardsmen away."

"Beaks can have a lifetime of sticky buns, assuming one of us survives this to let Kitty know."

"I'm going to save that offer," Gray said, "in case we need his flock to join a battle."

Gray helped Burne tug off his sodden trousers and shirt. The air on his bare skin was agonizing but his clothes wouldn't warm him once he was in the water, and swimming would be easier without the clothing.

"I don't know how long this will take," Burne said. He gestured to the side where the ledge rose up above the water. "Climb up there before I go. That's the highest spot."

Would it be high enough if the tide came in before Burne could return with help?

"If the water rises higher than your seat," Burne added, "don't panic. Mostly your body will float if you stay calm. Find a place to hang onto the rocks to keep yourself up."

Gray's lips parted and his face paled as if he might be sick.

Burne reached out to touch Gray's cheek. "Don't give up—promise?"

"Promise."

Burne lifted his eyebrows.

Gray smiled. "I swear on every grape hyacinth that ever lived I won't give up on you."

Burne kissed him one last time. He'd have the memory of those warm lips on his as he swam through the cold water. Once Gray had climbed up to the higher ledge, Burne jumped in.

A few strokes brought him past Beaks and across the pool. Outside, the waves crashed against the rocks, but in front of him they only rose and fell, and a faint current tugged at him. Hopefully he could head straight out and clear the rocks without any currents grabbing him. He focused back at Gray, perched on the ledge and shivering with Beaks floating below his feet. Burne waved and Gray lifted his hand. Burne had to make it to safety or Gray would perish, too.

Burne swam out into the sea. The wind hit him and the water churned around him. He put his head down and stroked as hard as he could, first one arm and then the other, kicking out toward the open water and surfacing only when he needed to. He made himself keep at it and not stop to see how far he had gone so he'd be sure to clear the dangerous area near the rocks.

When he finally stopped to check, he was a hundred paces out. The water rolled under him harmlessly. The narrow entrance to the cove had drifted to his right—or rather, he had drifted away from it. That was lucky—the current was pulling him southward. Nothing moved at the top of the cliffs except for the gulls circling overhead. What were the men up to?

Burne began a slow, even stroke through the water. His fingers and toes were stiff with cold but moving should warm him. He headed south and also out farther into the sea, checking the clifftop until he could see the pine trees where the road passed through them. After everything that had happened today, he should be tiring, but he felt strong and awake.

The trees broke ahead, and farther south, Linota's house stood on a crest of land with the sun high overhead. He headed straight for the house.

The house slipped out of sight, but Burne kept focused on the rocks below it. One of them looked pointy so he used it as a guide. He was panting and his chest had the ache of exertion, but he was so close he didn't try to pace himself. As he neared, a raucous cry went up and a burst of gulls lit out from the rocks, circling over the water and crying. Behind them, a narrow opening appeared beside the pointy rock. The gulls swooped around him as he neared like they were cheering him on. Beaks must have told them about the sticky buns.

Burne approached the cove straight on, the same way he had left the previous one. The entrance here was wider—wide enough for a rowboat—but the cove itself was tiny, not like the pool where he'd left Gray. On the back side of the cove, a wooden ladder climbed the vertical wall of rock. Burne swam to it and pulled himself up.

The first rung gave out under his weight, and he fell back into the water.

He surfaced, sputtering. The tide was out—that rung must be under water half the time and it had rotted away over the past seasons. The rest of the ladder might be better, but he'd have to climb carefully. Burne reached up for the next rung, and also the side of the ladder. Gripping both, he pulled himself from the water. He found a notch in the rock to prop his toes in and reached for the next rung. It felt solid so he let it carry a little more weight. Carefully, he climbed up the ladder, spreading out his weight and finding holds in the rocks in case the ladder should fail.

At the top of the ladder, a wooden platform covered a flat area in the rocks. Burne crawled onto it and rested a moment. The seagulls had drifted off and all he could hear was the crashing waves. He lifted his head. Steps had been cut into the cliff, tucked behind a boulder and leading higher. Burne pushed himself to his feet and climbed. His shoulders shivered as the breeze hit.

A series of steps and ladders led all the way to the top of the cliff. The wind caught him as he neared the top. Panting with the effort of climbing, he emerged from behind a rock onto the lawn below the house.

The wind blew steadily across the grass. The orchard and the drive were empty. Something moved in the trees but it was only the chickens. When no one appeared, Burne crept out from the rocks and jogged to the house, shivering in his undershorts. The sun was high in the west but its light did little to warm him. He trudged up the porch steps and tried the front door, opening it and entering. Voices from the parlor abruptly stopped.

Kitty stepped out into the front hallway. "Burne!" She came at him but stopped, inspecting him, and turned back to the parlor. "That blanket," she said, pointing.

Nem ducked into the hallway holding a blanket. "Are you all right?" Nem asked.

Burne closed the door as Kitty wrapped the blanket around him. His shivering intensified, jittering him until he could barely speak. Linota, Nigel, and Baldric had clustered into the hallway.

"Gray . . ." Burne started, but he couldn't stop shaking enough to get the words out.

"Come by the fire," Kitty said, and she took his arm and steered him down the hallway to the kitchen. She seated him in front of the hearth and added a log to the glowing embers.

"What happened, Burne?" Nem asked, pulling up a chair beside him. "Where's Gray?"

Burne surveyed the worried faces surrounding him. "In a cove. He's in the water. I have to go back."

"Where is it?" Nigel asked.

"North. We jumped."

"Skies," Kitty muttered, exhaling. She rubbed Burne's back through the blanket.

Burne pictured the cliffs where he and Gray had jumped. "Near the manor," he said. "Between the manor and the place where the woods stretch to the edge of the land. A big cove with a narrow entrance."

"I know it," Nigel said.

"The tide is out."

Nigel and Baldric exchanged a look. "We'll go now. The boats are at the dock but it should be quick once we're sailing."

"He can't swim." Desperation clawed its way up Burne's throat. "We had to jump and he can't swim and he's been there for hours."

"We'll get him, lad," Nigel said. "No sense in you coming—you're half frozen."

"Take blankets with you," Kitty said, leaving Burne and hurrying out with the men.

Nem and Linota moved in closer.

"How far is it to the boats?" Burne asked, huddling in the blanket.

"Not far," Linota said. "There's a trail from here to the dock. Baldric's on the water fishing most every day—he can sail up the coast in a trice."

"What happened?" Nem asked as Kitty rejoined them.

Burne told them about his encounter with Cap and Stone, and everything that had happened after.

"Thank the skies you destroyed all their guns," Kitty said.

"We don't know if that was all of them."

"I can't believe you jumped off the cliff," Nem said.

"Burne," Kitty said, "could you eat some soup?"

"I don't think so."

"They're going to get Gray. He'll be back soon."

"What if they can't find the cove and the tide climbs over the ledge where he's sitting?" Tears were filling Burne's eyes.

"They'll find him."

"Do they know he bought twenty ales on Nigel's tab?" Burne smiled in spite of himself and the tears trickled down his cheeks.

"They laughed when I told them Gray was imitating Nigel. Baldric can't believe it wasn't Nigel in the pub last night."

Outside the windows, the sun crept toward the treetops. Burne stayed by the hearth until all of his skin was warm, but he felt cold inside. One of the women stayed by him, even when villagers came by to talk about the coming evening. Burne couldn't stop watching the break in the trees where the men had taken the trail to the docks. He willed Gray to walk out from the forest but nothing happened.

"Are the peacekeepers better?" he asked.

"I went back round this afternoon," Kitty said. "They're awake but too weak to leave their beds. Gray might've saved their lives."

"What should we do tonight?"

"Amberfeld sent a message to the grange leader telling him to be in the village at sunset. We're all going, everyone who's able. But . . ." She bit her lip. "Elder Edwin doesn't want us to fight. He doesn't want anyone hurt, and he thinks help will come eventually from the other villages. One manor lord can't stage an uprising that takes down the whole continent.

"But others are worried. Maybe similar rebellions are planned in other villages. Maybe no help is coming. What if we keep waiting for help and end up like it was back in the old days? People are scared. They're tired of the ex-guards hanging around the village and disrupting life. They've not been violent but people are intimidated. Some want to fight back—they think there's enough of us to stand up to them. And now that you've destroyed their arsenal, and the peacekeepers are mending, we might have a chance. You've given us a chance, Burne."

"What do you think we should do?"

Kitty shook her head. "I've no idea. There's too many unknowns. You?"

"I never wanted to fight. But I've always thought it's because I'm a coward. But if I'm not, maybe I just don't believe in fighting." He frowned. "But if this uprising leads to Amberfeld running the village and oppressing the people—if this isn't contained, and there's no help coming from the other villages—then maybe it's better to fight." He shook his head. "I don't know Kitty. I don't know what's right."

She rested her hand on his arm. "We'll have to wait and see what happens tonight."

Burne scanned the windows again. "Maybe Gray will be home by then."

Chapter 17

THE SUN BLAZED ORANGE ABOVE the treetops. Gray hadn't returned.

"He's fine," Kitty said for the hundredth time. "If he'd been gone from the cove, Nigel and Baldric would have returned."

"Unless they're hoping to find his body," Burne said, fighting back the panic. What else could be taking so long?

"You can wait here," Kitty said.

"No." Burne turned from the window. Staying here wouldn't help Gray. But Burne might be able to help the villagers with whatever happened tonight.

Linota had found him a set of old work clothes and he'd managed to eat a little. He didn't have shoes to wear as they prepared to leave the house, but he felt more comfortable with his feet bare. Nem was also barefoot.

Kitty took a lantern, which they'd need after the sun set, and led them out the main path. They weren't taking the shortcut through the woods because the main approach to the house was easier for Linota to walk on. As they headed out, Burne glanced back, but the house blocked the end of the trail to the docks.

Twilight had come under the trees but they emerged across the road from the community gardens to a brilliant orange and pink sunset streaked with blue-gray ribbons of cloud. They turned into the sunset as they walked the track through more patches of forest toward the village.

Something boomed, reverberating throughout the woods behind them. All four of them jumped.

"The cannon," Burne said. "I guess they're planning to bring it."

Kitty snorted. "They'll need more than a cannon to take us down." But her face creased with worry.

The road passed through a gap between the trees and Burne's steps padded onto cobblestones. People had gathered in the center of the half-dozen buildings—older folks leaning on canes, men and women older than Kitty, children and young people of ten or so winters . . . but not a single person Burne's age, or anyone with a gun or other weapon. A few of the older people carried long-handled garden tools. And a lot of people had gathered.

The village elder stood on the porch of the grange hall, turning this way and that to speak to the people around him. Kitty went to consult with him and returned.

"Edwin still doesn't want us to fight," she said, "whether or not Amberfeld's men are armed. He still thinks help will come from the other villages once their peacekeepers are healed. He wants us to get through tonight without anyone being hurt."

The faces in the crowd were impassive. No one seemed agitated or ready to start a fight right away, at least. The villagers' response would depend on what Amberfeld's men did.

Creaking noises came from the road to the east and the crowd quieted and turned to watch. Footsteps beat on the ground and someone barked an order. From the darkness under the trees, men appeared. They weren't in uniform but they marched in two lines without talking. Their arms were straight at their sides, not holding guns. Burne inhaled slowly. He didn't recognize anyone yet.

The crowd of villagers parted as the guard arrived, drawing back into tight huddles to avoid them. The cannon appeared in the middle of the company. Men surrounded it, holding up the front and back as two men rolled the large wheels over the hard road—Cap and Stone, sweating and grunting as they did the bulk of the work. Why were they hauling the cannon when they'd been the leaders of the band of men?

Burne's stomach sank as it hit him—they'd been demoted. Amberfeld must've found out that their prank lost all his guns. A mix of emotions churned in Burne's gut—because even though he was glad to be rid of the weapons, he understood what leading the men had meant to his former enemies. He'd taken away what they valued most and they must hate him, even though they'd brought it on themselves.

Burne counted about twenty men—not as many as the number of villagers, but all young and rough looking. Some had blades in their belts. The front of the company passed the center of the town and stopped. Cap and Stone halted the cannon in front of the grange hall. They tugged on the barrel and other men joined them, heaving it around to face the building. Another order rang out and all the men turned forward. Even with the guards unarmed, the villagers who were present were probably too weak and inexperienced at fighting to stand up to this many guards.

But they didn't have to, Burne reminded himself. Whatever happened, the other villages would send help. Maybe Amberfeld's little rebellion would blow a hole in the grange hall with their cannon. No one was inside and a wall could be repaired.

But it had been almost a moon since Cliffside had been under siege and no one in the other villages had realized anything was wrong. Cliffside was too small and self-contained—the residents had no reason to leave regularly so no one outside thought it strange if they didn't hear from anyone in Cliffside for a moon. And the other villages had their own difficulties. What if the rebellion was more than one disgruntled former lord? What if the other lords were in league with Amberfeld and similar uprisings were happening across the continent? Burne tried to remember anything he'd heard in the pub last night, but no memories had survived his drunken state.

Burne found Cap and Stone in the line. They faced forward like the other guards but they would spot him eventually. Had they seen him jump off the cliff with Gray? They hadn't seen him swimming away, as far as he knew—maybe they thought he was dead. What had they been doing all afternoon? His guts twisted: what if they'd found ropes and come down the cliff after he'd gone? What would they do if they found Gray sitting there alone?

Lord Amberfeld stepped out from the back of the group. Unlike the men in their plain leggings and mismatched shirts and coats, Amberfeld wore a long red coat with white trim and rows of brass buttons. His shirt underneath was ruffled and several decorative pins lined his collar. Under his arm, he carried a hat with a feather sweeping off it, and a long blade hung in a sheath at his hip. Hopefully he didn't know how to use it—under the king, the manor lords had had an easy life, leaving the fighting to the King's Guard.

Amberfeld marched across the front of the line and stopped in front of the grange beside the cannon. He jerked his chin down and up, and a few of the men scurried into motion. A pole came out and they slid it into the gaping hole of the metal gun. They were loading the cannon already?

Edwin—the village elder on the porch—stood forward. "What's your business here, Amberfeld?"

"I think it should be obvious," Amberfeld said, not bothering to regard Edwin.

As Burne watched the men at the cannon, he remembered his training. Now that they'd cleaned the bore, they loaded the bag of gunpowder, tamping it down into the bottom of the barrel. The cannonball would be next. But a man stepped forward with a tin cylinder and loaded that into the barrel. Burne's stomach clenched. They were using canister shot? When they fired the cannon, the cylinder would disintegrate, releasing its contents—shot pellets or scraps of nails and other metal—which would spew from the gun and kill anyone in the vicinity. The villagers who were here might not recognize the danger. And with the way they were gathered so closely . . .

Burne started forward.

"I've run this village for decades," Amberfeld continued, scanning over the villagers with narrowed eyes. "It was always mine, and now it is again."

Burne slipped between people in the crowd, moving closer to the cannon, even as the guardsmen closest to it edged away. A few guards held ropes to stop it from rolling back as it fired. Cap stepped forward with a long spike. He inserted it into the venting hole to pierce the bag of gunpowder.

"This is a democracy," Edwin said. "That's treason against the people. We've all witnessed it. You will be detained and taken to Woodglen to face the village council."

Cap stood beside the cannon holding the final piece needed to fire it, the small striker. It went into the vent and was pulled with a string to ignite the powder with friction.

Don't, Burne begged silently. Don't put it in. Once it was in, the cannon could easily fire by accident, even if Cap didn't pull. Burne pictured the flame shooting up the vent, the cloud of smoke as the cannon bucked backward, and the shrapnel bursting out to hit Edwin and everyone around him.

"Who'll stop me?" Amberfeld said.

"We will."

Everyone turned, even the guards at attention.

Three people stood at the corner of the pub. Burne didn't recognize them, but they were about his age and looked strong, and they were carrying guns propped on their shoulders, ready to drop into shooting position.

The crowd drew back, creating an opening between the newcomers—healed peacekeepers, Burne guessed—and the center of the line of guards where Amberfeld stood. Amberfeld staggered back and moved behind his men.

"Fire the cannon, blast it!" he said.

Stone turned to him. "They have guns."

The peacekeepers pointed their weapons but didn't move. "We

don't want to hurt anyone," the one in the center said. "Leave the cannon."

Amberfeld turned on Stone. "They can't shoot all of you at once. Do as you're told."

Cap hadn't moved. Burne could see him sweating, fearful of firing the cannon but unable to ignore a direct order from his leader. His hand reached out toward the vent and slipped the friction piece in. He clung to the string, moving out to hold it taut.

The peacekeepers remained motionless, although the crowd had stepped far back, clearing their way to fire. And then Burne realized why they were hanging back. They weren't actually peacekeepers. And the guns were not actually there at all.

Burne's heartbeat thundered as he stepped from the crowd and moved in front of the cannon. Cap's eyes widened and his chest moved in and out. Stone froze on the other side of the barrel.

"Go ahead and fire it," Burne said, his voice steady.

Cap swallowed.

"It's just me," Burne said. "Yellow-Bellied Burne."

"We didn't want to kill you," Cap said.

"You haven't," Burne said. The last thing he needed was Cap thinking he was some kind of spirit from the great beyond come to exact revenge. If Cap fainted, he'd pull the string and fire the cannon as he fell. "You don't have to kill me now."

"Fire it!" Amberfeld shouted, and Cap flinched.

"I just wanted to be good at something," Cap said.

"I know how you feel. But you are good at something. You don't need to kill people to prove it."

He held Cap's gaze. Slowly, Cap's shaking hand went back toward the cannon. He withdrew the small piece and lowered it to his side.

The cannon was still loaded with the canister and gunpowder. Burne held Cap's gaze as he stepped carefully around the barrel and pushed it downward. Amberfeld was shouting and the guards stood frozen, but Stone helped Burne lower the barrel to the ground, and the canister slid out and onto the cobblestones.

The villagers swarmed forward, reaching for the guardsmen. Some of the guardsmen drew daggers, while others darted into the darkness of the trees. The skirmish nearest Burne lasted mere beats before three villagers pinned the guard's arms and twisted his wrist to force him to drop his blade. A meaty guard with fists raised gaped helplessly at the elders around him, unwilling to hit them, and his chance passed and too many restrained him. All around, confounded guards were surrounded and pinned. Kitty and three other women pounced on Amberfeld and knocked him to the ground, holding tight as he squirmed. Cap stood quietly, staring at the dirt at his feet.

Burne turned to the three peacekeepers at the corner of the pub. Their guns disappeared and their appearance changed, aging the ones on the sides into Baldric and Nigel. Between them, they held up Gray with his arms over their shoulders. His hair was dark black and his face was too pale. With his eyes half open, Gray smiled at Burne and collapsed.

Chapter 18

BURNE SAT ON THE STEPS of the pub, cradling Gray in his arms. Gray had stopped shivering now that the villagers had lit a bonfire in the street, but his face was pale. Baldric came by with mugs of ale but Burne waved him on. If he got drunk again, he wouldn't be able to carry Gray home later if he needed to—although Baldric probably wasn't serving his special extra-strong brew tonight.

Lord Amberfeld and his rebels had been tied up and locked in someone's barn, and Nigel had gone up to the stables at the manor to take a horse so he could ride to Woodglen to see what was to be done with them. Once the guards were secured, someone had started playing a fiddle and now the villagers had a circle dance going on the other side of the village square, and the children ran in a ring around the fire. Linota hung on Nem's arm, introducing her to the other villagers in the crowd.

Gray snuggled into Burne's chest. They'd stood by the fire long enough to dry his shirt, but his trousers remained damp from the ocean. He, Nigel, and Baldric had come straight to the village center from the dock where they'd landed after Gray's rescue.

According to Gray, the rescue had taken hours because the trek from the dock was ten leagues, uphill, with rocky, uneven ground and a track barely wide enough for a child to pass. And also, before that, Amberfeld's guards must have lingered on the clifftop because when they saw the sailboat coming, they'd decided to hurl debris at it, using the empty crates Burne had left in the cavern.

So for a while Baldric couldn't bring the boat near enough, until eventually the men were called away.

Then Baldric had to navigate carefully as he approached. The sailboat wouldn't fit easily into the narrow entrance to the cove, which had narrowed further with the higher water. In the end, Nigel had risked the waves and swum in to retrieve Gray, who'd been up to his waist in the water but sitting where Burne had left him.

Gray hadn't slept since their night in the hayloft at the crossroads, and neither of them had had anything to eat all day. And Gray had spent half the day wet and cold, not to mention frightened. Pulling himself together and using his magic to animate illusions of three separate people had taken the last of his strength. As soon as he'd recovered enough to walk, Burne was taking him straight home and wrapping him in dry blankets and wool socks.

Burne brushed back the locks from Gray's face, and Gray opened his eyes.

"How do you feel?" Burne asked.

Gray mumbled and tried to push his face under Burne's arm.

"What's that?"

"It's warm here."

"It'll be warm at home, too. And dry. And there are wool socks."

"Fairies don't wear socks."

"They do when they've spent all day in the ocean and are likely to fall ill."

"Fairies don't get illnesses. They don't do the stupid human actions that make one ill."

"Like jumping into the ocean in the springtime?"

Gray humph-ed.

"Can you make it home?"

Gray gazed up at him. The firelight danced in his eyes, and a spark of mischief glinted there. "You've been fantasizing about me wearing woolly socks, haven't you?"

"What?"

"You probably had some woolly sock experience when you were a wee lad, and the moment you saw me, you thought, He's the one! I need to see him in nothing but woolly socks."

"You're getting delirious," Burne said, pulling Gray up to a sitting position and depositing him on the floorboards. "We're going home."

Burne stood, scanning the crowd until he spotted Kitty. He waved and pointed toward the path home, and she nodded. He turned back to Gray.

Gray was sitting on the edge of the porch, his legs swinging in time to the fiddle. His eyes turned up to meet Burne's.

"You suddenly seem very awake," Burne said.

Gray smiled and stood.

"Were you pretending to be exhausted?"

"No! I really was exhausted. At first."

Burne shook his head and made his way behind the pub, and Gray followed.

"But it was so nice in your arms I didn't want to leave. Don't be upset."

Burne stopped. "I'm not upset. I was so worried about you all day. I wanted to be sure you were okay, and you seemed so ill."

In the shadows of the pub wall, Gray came close beside him. "I'm sorry. I didn't realize you were so worried."

"You're really okay? You'd tell me if you felt faint again?"

"I'm a little cold now we're away from the fire."

Burne took his hand. "It's warm at home."

But Gray resisted, bringing Burne to a halt.

"You know what would warm me up faster?"

Burne started to laugh. He should insist they go, or toss Gray over his shoulder and carry him home—which he'd probably like—but he couldn't resist the gleam in Gray's eyes. "I have a guess."

"And look where we are," Gray said.

"Behind the pub?"

Gray tugged on his hand. "This is where you dragged me last night and forced me to kiss you!"

"Oh right," Burne said. "But I can't remember it."

"Want me to help you remember?"

Burne ducked his head and smiled. "Yes."

"It was here," Gray said, pulling him toward the building. Gray backed against the wall. "You missed my lips the first time because you were so drunk, and you cursed a bunch—"

"No I didn't."

"Is it coming back to you?"

"I think so," Burne said, pinning Gray to the wall with his hips. He placed his hands on Gray's shoulders. "I said, 'Stars you're beautiful.' And then I leaned in"—he leaned in and continued in a whisper—"and kissed you."

He pressed his lips to Gray's and melted against him, letting their bodies fuse together. Gray kissed him back, inviting him in. They kissed until his hands were on the back of Gray's neck and his lips felt abused. He broke away. Their foreheads leaned together and Gray's arms were snug around his middle.

"I like kissing you," Burne whispered.

"Was it okay?"

He was asking about the anxiety. "So far."

"Do you want to kiss again?"

Burne grinned. "I want to see the place where I put my hand in your trousers."

Gray's lips parted and a smile crawled across his face. He let go of Burne's waist and tugged him toward the woods. Burne stumbled in keeping up with him.

"You'll definitely want to remember that," Gray said as he dragged Burne up the dark path into the trees. "It was really good. I think it was here." He stopped and turned.

"Here?" Burne scrutinized the nearby trees. "I thought I pushed you against the massive trunk of a cedar tree."

"Right. Or maybe it was this little cedar tree right here."

"I don't know if that tree will be strong enough to hold you up, once I have my hands on you." Gray opened his mouth, but Burne stepped over and kissed him again. He pulled Gray into his chest and kept kissing him as he walked him into the trees.

"This one looks good," he murmured. He leaned Gray back against the trunk and slid his hands down Gray's sides and under the edge of his shirt. Gray tilted his head back against the tree and closed his eyes. Burne kissed him just below his ear, then down his neck as his fingers found Gray's trouser buttons and slipped them open, one by one. Gray was hard beneath his knuckles. When he'd undone the buttons, he trailed his fingers over Gray's skin and down inside the hem of his underclothes.

"I was imagining this all day," Gray said.

"Were you," Burne said into his neck, but it wasn't a question. His fingers hovered inside Gray's clothes and he couldn't think straight anymore. He teased the curls of hair he felt with his fingers.

"When I was sitting by that pool. I didn't want to think about how afraid I was so I thought about tumbling you the whole time. I hope you don't mind."

"Not at all." Burne rubbed his cheek against Gray.

"When I started getting tired, I was a little out of it, and I imagined you were lord of the manor instead of Amberfeld and you were pointing your cannon at me and giving me orders—"

Burne smiled. "Like what?"

"Unbutton your pants, guard."

Burne shook his head. "That's so many kinds of wrong."

"You're right, it should be the other way around. I'll be Amberfeld and you can be the guardsman but *you* give *me* orders—"

"Please don't turn into Lord Amberfeld. I don't want my hands in his pants."

"—like you can say, if you want me to fire your cannon, my lord, then drop your—"

Burne reached down and curled his fingers around Gray's erection. Gray's words cut off with a gasp.

Just being near Gray turned him on, but having his fist around Gray's hard shaft sent shivers through his body. He wanted to undo his own trousers and take himself in his other hand. Instead, he shoved Gray's clothing down to give himself more room and began to work Gray back and forth. He rested his free hand against the tree trunk to keep himself steady. His mouth pressed into Gray's neck above his collarbone, and when he bit gently, Gray moaned. Burne left his lips on Gray's skin and focused on his hand.

He slid the soft skin up and down, pressing over the head of the shaft in the way he liked it done. Gray's sharp breaths near his ear told him it was working for Gray too. Once he found a rhythm, he sped it up. With his face against Gray's neck, he could feel as Gray's heartbeat accelerated. He kept going, inhaling the warm scent of Gray's skin and wishing he could see his face. Gray's fingertips were digging into Burne's shoulders, and his breathing became erratic. Burne sucked on his neck, careful to keep his hand moving. When he used his teeth again, Gray gasped and came in his hand.

Burne stroked a few more times until he was sure Gray was done. He waited as Gray panted beside him. Gray's skin gave off heat like a fire. Burne smiled, glad he was no longer chilled.

Gray's hands stole down Burne's shirt front, caressing his chest, and he kissed Burne's cheek. He took Burne's hand and wiped it in his own loose shirt.

"We'd better find that third spot we stopped at," Gray whispered, "before you have to wait too long."

Burne swallowed, excitement and anticipation swirling through him. He was so hard a single touch might undo him, but he watched Gray button his pants and let Gray lead him back to the trail and upward.

Now that he wasn't listening to Gray's ecstatic breathing, the distant sounds of the revelry in the village drifted up the trail. The noises faded the higher they went until Burne wasn't sure if he was hearing the music and laughter or imagining it. White moonlight fell around them, brightening the path, and he held tightly to Gray's hand in front of him, like a lifeline bringing him up from the deep.

The trail arrived at the place where it skirted around a rocky wall, and Gray turned, pulling Burne into his arms.

"You still okay?" Gray asked, gazing up at him.

Burne's tongue didn't seem to work so he nodded.

Gray walked him back toward the rocks. "You want to do this?"

"Yes." Burne was going to burst with wanting it.

"You'll tell me if you want to stop?" Gray asked softly.

"Yes."

Gray leaned him against the rocks. He began kissing him, his fingers working through the buttons of Burne's shirt until it fell open. Gray smoothed his palms over Burne's chest and pressed their bodies together but only for a moment before Gray began kissing his way down Burne's neck. His fingers were on the trouser buttons, deftly opening them. He kneeled slowly, planting kisses on Burne's chest and stomach on his way down. Burne closed his eyes and leaned into the rock, letting it steady him.

Gray tugged Burne's trousers down his hips, baring his front to the cool night. Burne waited, silently begging Gray to touch him. At last, fingers wrapped around his erection, stroking a few times from the base all the way up, and Gray's lips pressed against the tip. His lips parted slowly as his hand kept stroking, as if Burne's body were forcing his lips open, and his tongue swirled over the head of Burne's shaft, and Burne had to hang onto the rock because his knees went weak.

Gray's lips pushed back his foreskin and sucked on him, and while one hand gripped around his penis, the other was stroking its underside, the fingertips brushing against his balls and rubbing up toward the head. Gray was sucking and pulling on him, and Burne moved his hips, thrusting into Gray's mouth. Once Burne was moving, Gray let one hand go and placed it flat on Burne's hip. Gray's hand slid back as Burne drove into him and he resisted as Burne pulled out, sucking him back for another round. Burne thrust faster, losing control, and Gray's fingers dug into the back of his thigh, his nails biting with a sharp thrill, and Burne cried out and climaxed in Gray's embrace.

With a final suck, Gray released him. Gray leaned his forehead on Burne's hip as Burne gasped. The cool night air soothed him, although he couldn't decide if he wanted to button up his pants or pull all his clothes off. He touched Gray's head and Gray gazed up. In the pale light his eyes were dark but his skin shone.

Burne stroked his hair. "It's black like Hyacinth's," he said.

"I'm too tired to fix it."

"I like it."

"You do?" Gray bit his lip, eyes wide, but then he grinned. "Would you like some tattoos to go with it?"

"What? No, I—"

"They could be dirty tattoos."

"What?"

"Of people doing all—"

"Gray, stop. No illusions. I just want you."

"Oh." Gray kept gazing up at him.

Burne tucked Gray's long hair behind his ear and withdrew his hand. He buttoned his trousers. "Let's go home and find those socks," he said and pulled Gray to his feet.

Chapter 19

BURNE WOKE IN BED THE next morning with Gray curled naked beside him.

They'd fallen into bed exhausted when they'd reached the house last night—but not before Burne had peeled all Gray's damp clothes off and stood him in front of the kitchen fire to make sure he was dry, and wrapped him in a crocheted blanket. Linota's wool socks were on their bedroom floor so Burne had pulled those onto Gray's feet before shedding his own clothes and crawling under the covers beside Gray.

Gray must've pushed off the swaddling during the night because his warm legs entwined with Burne's and his bare chest pressed against Burne's torso. Gray's head was tucked below Burne's, his cheek smooth against Burne's heart. Burne watched him breathing in the hint of light coming in around the window curtains. He liked how Gray made him feel strong, like he was a protector. And at the same time, how Gray made him feel safe.

The room was warm and a pop came from the hearth. Burne leaned slowly up to see it. His muscles ached with the effort. Embers glowed on the brick floor behind the fire screen. Kitty must have come in to light the fire while they slept.

Burne carefully extracted himself from Gray's legs and the bedcovers, and slid out of bed into cool air. He rotated his head around, stretching his sore neck and shoulders. He hadn't exactly been in a battle, but his body felt battered. His shoulder especially . . . that was from breaking through the wall of the cave. And his feet were sore from the long journey, and he'd swum along the coast. But through the soreness and stiffness of his whole body, he felt a glowing happiness. He contemplated the lump in the bedcovers that was Gray and had to stop himself from reaching for him.

He padded across the room and crouched beside the hearth, where he added a few logs to the fire and replaced the screen before crawling back into the warmth of the small bed. He slipped an arm over Gray and held him against his chest, exhaling and relaxing into the mattress.

The house was quiet, but now that Burne lay still, voices murmured from the kitchen: Linota's cackle, Nem with a high-pitched squeal, and a calm third voice that must be Kitty. The crashes of the ocean were so faint he might be remembering them from yesterday, when he'd listened to them up close for so many hours. A gull cried outside, and a few cries answered it. Maybe it was Beaks and his flock. Hopefully Kitty was up for spending her whole day making sticky buns.

Gray's fist, tucked between them, shifted. Burne glanced down and found Gray's green eyes watching him.

"Good morning," Burne said.

Gray blinked. "Mm-hmm."

"Do you want me to get you some tea?"

Gray closed his eyes and burrowed against Burne. "No."

Burne held him until he moved again, pushing away and crawling up the bed until his head was on the pillow beside Burne's. He wound his feet—still in the wool socks—back into Burne's legs. Burne tugged the blankets up after him, tucking him back in. For a few heartbeats they lay motionless, gazing at each other.

"You stood in front of a loaded cannon," Gray said.

"You jumped off a cliff into the ocean even though you can't swim."

Gray smiled. "What should we do next?"

"Something that doesn't involve almost dying."

"How do you feel now that you're safe? Has it made you have any . . . stuff inside?"

"Last night when we were sitting in front of the pub, everything was noisy and you were safe and I started feeling jittery. But it wasn't bad. I told myself we were okay and took deep breaths and waited it out, and it faded."

"Do you want to stay here?" Gray asked.

"Yes. Maybe if it gets late enough, Kitty will bring us sticky buns and tea in bed."

Between them, Gray's hand found Burne's and twined their fingers together. His eyes were wide and serious. "I meant in Cliffside."

Burne squeezed his hand. "I want to be wherever you are."

"Me too."

"I want to help Trillium and Woodbine though, as long as they need me."

Gray licked his lips. "What if they came here?" he asked.

"All of them?" Burne imagined all the children—Freesia and Chrys and the others—playing on the clifftops in the sun and helping Nigel in the garden.

"It's nice here," Gray said. "It's quiet. In Woodglen, there's always someone about, and wagons and dust and movement and shouting, but here it's more like the forest. And Nem is here."

"Is Nem going to stay here?"

"I think so. Linota wants Nem and Kitty to stay, and Kitty seems like she's okay with being here now."

"What would you like to do? If we lived in Cliffside?" Burne asked.

"I could learn more about plants. Maybe Woodbine would let me go on her nature walks."

"This would be a wonderful place for the children to live while we searched for their families. If they lived here and we stayed, I could help with them. I liked helping at the Haven. I felt like I was finally good at something."

"You were wonderful with the children. And your soup was okay. For a human, anyway."

"What's that supposed to mean?"

"Fairies make better soup than humans."

"But they probably cheat. They probably put magic in it to make everyone think it tastes better."

"Among other goals." Gray grinned.

"What about Hyacinth?"

Gray's grin faded. "I think . . . I think she'd want me to stay here if I had a reason to. I think she doesn't need me as much as she pretends."

Burne rubbed his thumb over Gray's. "You helped her. I bet she needed you in the beginning. Maybe it's easier now that her business is established and she's got Featherstone bringing in so many customers."

Gray snorted.

"I like it here, too," Burne said.

Gray scootched himself toward Burne a smidge. "We're talking."

"Yeah?"

"That means it's not lust."

"What?"

"It's more than just tumbling between us."

Burne moved in too, so their noses were almost touching. "Yes. Although I'm pretty sure there's some lust involved, too." His eyelids half-closed as he inhaled Gray's warmth.

"Do you remember what else Nem said?" Gray asked. "About love and lust and all?"

Burne remembered, and his chest tightened. "You mean about courting, and about if—"

"I'd be sad if I saw you kissing someone else."

Burne's mind slowly processed the words. "Me? With someone else?"

"I know how it goes," Gray said, and his voice changed to his nonchalant, teasing tone, but now Burne wondered what emotions hid behind it. "Now that you've stopped a rebellion and faced a cannon, you'll be swaggering around the village, and everyone will be falling at your feet, *begging* for your attention, and—"

"I don't want anyone else," Burne said.

"But you might."

Burne shook his head, and his nose brushed Gray's smooth cheek. "I don't think I'm made that way. I think I'm more a cottage person."

"A what?"

"Like a cottage, with the person at the table. The one person." He couldn't get the thoughts into proper words, but Gray's hand tightened on his.

"Me too."

Burne's already full heart swelled even fuller.

"How did everything feel last night?" Gray rubbed the tip of his nose against Burne's.

"Kind of amazing."

"Do you want to do more?"

Burne swallowed and nodded. Down beneath the sheets, he felt himself stirring at the tone of Gray's voice.

"Do you have any questions?"

Without thinking, Burne blurted out the thing he'd been wondering. "When I came in your mouth, did you like it?"

Gray smiled and leaned in to kiss him once. "Yes."

"I didn't want—"

"I like it. But not everyone does. It's okay."

"It is?"

"Mm-hmm."

"It seems rude to spit it out."

"I could stop before it happened," Gray said. He leaned in again. "Where would you like it to go?"

An image flashed in Burne's mind and he got harder immediately. "Here," he said, and he pulled their joined hands up to touch his neck, just below his ear.

Gray's fingers uncurled and settled on his skin, stroking him above Burne's hand. "I can aim for here," he said, "but I might miss sometimes." He grinned again.

Burne wouldn't mind if Gray got it all over his face. The men at guard training had made so many jokes about their penises and ejaculating on things—like it showed they were in charge and like they'd do it even if their partner didn't like it. But talking with Gray about it felt so different. Like it was no big deal and kind of fun.

"Remember when we were in your room?" Burne said.

"Yes?"

"When you tried to take my shirt off and I panicked?"

Gray waited.

Burne paused a moment. "There was this day right when I'd first arrived at training. Cap tricked me. He was in charge of my unit, and he told me I had to change my uniform five minutes before I had to report to the field. And then he took my clothes and left me without any. And I didn't want to be late because I'd get in trouble so I went to training without clothes on."

Gray was rubbing his arm. "I'm sorry they did that."

"All day the other men were whispering about how scrawny and pathetic I was, and by the end, no one wanted anything to do with me. And Cap started calling me 'Yell' because I was a coward. It was short for 'yellow bellied.'"

"How exactly were you a coward in that scenario?" Gray said.

"What?"

"They played a mean prank and you kept your chin up and went to training."

Burne stared at him.

"It sounds like you *weren't* a coward. And I bet that really pissed them off. So they had to come up with something else to propagate their phony little story."

Burne remembered what Stone had said at the pub—they'd wanted to fight him so they could put him at the bottom of their hierarchy. But he'd refused to fight.

"I was scrawny, though," Burne said. "They were right about that."

"Were they?"

Again Burne stared.

"You don't seem scrawny to me," Gray said.

"Not now. But I've been living in the woods for a full season, chopping firewood and carrying water."

"What did you do before you joined the King's Guard?"

"I helped my mother in the castle kitchen."

"Doing what?"

Burne's face heated. He mumbled an answer.

"What?"

"Chopping wood and carrying water." Burne squeezed his eyes shut, smiling.

"I bet you were as strong as you are now. You just weren't confident and they knew it so they picked on you."

"Maybe."

Gray didn't push the issue.

"Gray?"

"Mm?"

"What's a thumb war?"

"A thumb war?"

"You said one time, 'Remind me never to challenge you to a thumb war.'"

"It's a game children play. Here."

Gray shifted and brought his left hand up from beneath him, taking Burne's left hand in his so that their fingers curled together. He placed his right hand flat along the bottom of their joined left hands.

"So normally we'd be sitting at a table," Gray said, "so pretend my hand is a table and we've got our hands resting on it. You have to keep your hand on the table and pin your opponent's thumb. Ready, go."

Gray's thumb nabbed Burne's and held it tightly. Burne struggled against him as Gray smugly counted to three.

"I win," Gray said.

"Of course you do, you cheat."

Gray kissed the tip of his nose. "I bet I win again."

This time Burne was ready, but as he arched his thumb over Gray's, Gray called him out for moving his hand off the "table." They started again. Their thumbs darted out, daring each other to make a move. Burne went for a catch, and Gray slipped out and caught him from above. "One, two, three."

Burne couldn't believe how happy this game made Gray. "Were you always this proficient at thumb wars?" he asked.

"I was the reigning champion of the fairy enclave."

"I don't feel so bad about losing then."

"You really never played thumb wars? I thought it was universal among children."

"I've never even heard of it. Nor imagined anything like it."

"What did you think it was?" Gray said.

"I thought it must involve penises."

"What? No! Why would you think that?"

"Maybe because half of what you say seems to be about tumbling."

"It is not. Maybe it's just you who thinks I'm always talking about tumbling because that's what's on your mind." Gray's grin was mischievous.

Burne narrowed his eyes.

"No, you're right. I'm always talking about tumbling. Speaking of which, I kind of like this idea you've suggested."

"What idea?"

"A 'thumb war' with our penises." Gray tugged on the band of Burne's underpants. "Want to try it?" He leaned in to kiss Burne. "Please?"

Burne smiled and tugged down his underpants, pushing them to the foot of the bed. As he settled, Gray sneaked an arm underneath him and pulled him close.

"I have no idea how this will work," Burne said.

"Me neither. How about . . ." Gray started stroking him under the blankets, and in a brief moment he was hard as the logs on the hearth. Gray found Burne's hand and moved it to the base of Burne's shaft. "How about, you can only hold yourself with your finger and thumb, and you have to keep the rest of your hand pressed against your body."

Burne did as he was told.

Gray came in closer. "No cheating just because we can't see our hands."

"No cheating," Burne repeated. "I swear on every woolly sock and bad human soup in Cliffside."

Gray rubbed his own erection against Burne's. "How about," he said again, slowly, "whoever makes the other come first wins."

Burne was going to lose in a moment if he didn't watch it. Gray's touch on him was taking his breath away. He changed hands so he held himself with the arm trapped below and his top arm was free, and he moved closer to Gray. "Okay."

Gray snuggled closer too. "Ready, go."

Burne pushed his pelvis in and rubbed his whole length up against Gray's, but it felt so good it was as likely to push him over the edge as Gray. He reached across Gray and pulled their bodies together, and this time when he rubbed, their chests and bellies scraped against each other, and his knuckles were tucked against Gray's balls, and—

Fingers dug into Burne's backside.

"Cheater," Burne said breathlessly. Gray's lips were a hair's breadth from his and both of Gray's hands were firmly on Burne's butt.

"You win," Gray said into Burne's mouth and kissed him, pushing his tongue inside.

Burne let go of his erection so he could crush it firmly against Gray's, grinding them together as Gray's chest massaged his nipples and Gray's tongue ravaged his mouth. His hand slid up to Gray's neck, encouraging Gray's kisses. Gray twisted his hips from side to side, his hard shaft rolling over Burne's. Their legs tangled together as Gray tugged him closer, and Gray was mashing their balls together and he bit Burne's lower lip and moaned quietly.

The sound of Gray's climax and the hot liquid spurting on Burne's belly and smearing onto his own erection triggered Burne, and when Gray made one final wiggle with his hips, Burne was thrusting and gasping as he came.

They panted together, their parted lips not quite aligned. Burne let go of Gray's neck and cradled his head on his arm, gathering Gray to him and hugging him tight. Words bubbled up from his heart and the thought of saying them aloud made his heart race so he let them go unsaid. He had plenty of time to tell Gray that he loved him. And besides, Gray probably already knew.

Four Moons Later

BURNE TROTTED DOWN THE STONE steps from the terrace of the manor house. He strode onto the grass and maneuvered between the saplings to cross the lawn toward the road. The guests at the manor were enjoying breakfast in the summer sun of the terrace, but he didn't want to join them. He'd stopped by only to bring his mother a basket of plums. She wanted to make plum tarts for the guests' dessert that night.

Burne's mother had moved to Cliffside to help him run the kitchen at the manor, which was now open to the public as a vacation resort. In the past two moons, the Inn at Cliffside had become known across Sylvania as a destination where guests could escape the hubbub of village life to relax by the sea and eat scrumptious meals prepared by the former king's personal chef. The more adventurous guests could swim in the cove—some visitors even jumped from the clifftop to get to the water instead of climbing down the rope ladder that now hung pinned into the rocks. All the income from the new inn went to the Cliffside grange and its projects.

Of course, Kate would have plenty more plums to use in her cooking next summer, given the dozens of plum trees Hyacinth had planted on the vast expanse of land beside the house. "Imagine having all this open space and sun," Hyacinth had said in disgust on one of her visits, "and planting grass." The orchard now had apple trees, plum trees, apricot trees, and more, and they were all growing at ten times the normal speed of fruit trees.

"Showing off for my sister," Gray muttered each time Burne mentioned how big they were getting in such a brief time.

Burne had also spotted Hyacinth kneeling beside the trees with a shovel, planting bulbs in the ground. No doubt more grape hyacinths. Burne wondered if, come next spring, the entire village would be covered with the little purple flowers.

He turned onto the road, automatically searching along the coast to the south although he knew he couldn't see the boat dock from here. Gray had gone to the dock for swimming practice again that morning, along with all the children. The dock area was safe—it was blocked from the main force of the ocean by a small jetty, and the water remained shallow for a long way out even at high tide. And Baldric would be chaperoning.

And besides, Gray had been fine during all the previous swimming lessons. It turned out Gray actually did know a mermaid. Apparently, Woodglen had been fairly overrun with merpeople while Burne had been hiding in the woods, and Gray had befriended one. She'd swum up the coast a few times and begun teaching him to swim, and soon all the children were attending the lessons. And no one had drowned.

But Burne's nerves still twisted when he thought of Gray in the water.

Burne passed through the shade of the pine trees and proceeded on toward the vegetable gardens. A few of the men were out with Nigel, bent over the rows of leafy chard or stepping through the twisting squash vines. Burne recognized Stone, who caught sight of him and gave a small wave before turning back to his task. Some of the men who'd participated in the failed rebellion—the ones who'd expressed remorse for endangering the villagers—had been offered community service in the village as a way to atone. But Lord Amberfeld and some of the others had refused to apologize and were serving time at an iron mine in the mountains.

On the far side of the garden, Trillium sat on a bench in the shade. As he neared, Burne recognized Cap beside her. Stone had thanked Burne for helping keep them out of prison—it had been Burne's suggestion they perform community service, and he'd personally vouched for Cap and Stone—and they had a cautious friendship. But Cap wouldn't acknowledge Burne, even on days when Burne went out to help in the gardens. Maybe Trillium could help Cap. She spent time with all the men who were doing community service. She held group sessions for them with titles like "Finding fulfillment" and "Living in joy."

When the children from the Haven came to Cliffside, Trillium and Woodbine had come, too. They'd built a treehouse somewhere in the forest behind Linota's house. Gray insisted on calling it the Love Nest and said they'd hidden it from humans, but Trillium told Burne that if he ever needed to find it, he would.

Burne and Gray still lived with Linota—although they'd rearranged the furniture so they had a proper bed for two. Kitty lived there as well, helping with the remaining children in the house. Since they'd started hanging posters in the villages across Sylvania, a few of the children had found their birth mothers. And Nem lived in her own small cottage under the trees.

Past the gardens, Burne followed the curve of the road around to the west. He met Berthenia and greeted her as they passed. It turned out there actually *was* a Berthenia in Cliffside—Baldric had mentioned her name to Gray that first night at the pub—but she looked nothing like Gray's illusion of her. And she was courting Stone. She went by the gardens constantly when he was working and hung around so long Nigel had to send her off, and she haunted the pub and sometimes walked Stone home. Cap teased him about it, but Stone admitted nothing. Burne wasn't sure if he was playing hard to get or was not interested in Berthenia—or possibly was tumbling her and not saying a word.

Burne started up the track to his house. More evidence of Hyacinth's planting surrounded him, with elderberry bushes clustered in the sun by the road and disrupted earth lining the path, probably the result of more hyacinth bulbs. Hyacinth and Ladi visited about once a moon, bringing Alyss to see her friends. Burne knew it meant a lot to Gray to see his sister, although he so often muttered darkly about her. It didn't help that Hyacinth showed up and said things like, "We met the nicest herd of wild boars in the forest on our way here." But deep down, the two of them were close, and she was constantly thrilled for his new pursuits. Gray had been studying with Woodbine and the children, going on forest walks and learning to use barks and herbs and roots to make potions.

Burne emerged onto the windy lawn and climbed the final stretch through the orchard to the house. Beaks was sunning himself on the porch railing. He opened one eye but closed it when he saw Burne. After a few moons of sticky buns, Woodbine had decreed Beaks was on a no-bun diet, since apparently buns weren't terribly healthy for birds. But if it had been Kitty arriving home instead, Beaks would have been at the kitchen window in an instant. He knew Kitty was a sucker when he begged with his beady little eyes.

The house was quiet and smelled delicious. That morning, as soon as Gray had left for the swimming lessons, Burne had made plum jam to surprise him. Hyacinth had said it was Gray's favorite, and they had more ripe plums than they could possibly eat. Burne left his shoes by the door—his mother insisted he wear them at the manor, to keep with its brand of luxury accommodation—and padded down the hallway to the kitchen to check the rows of jars on the counter.

The hearth was cold and the curtains pulled against the bright summer sun. Burne smoothed his fingers over the lids of the jam jars. The wax seals were solid and the jars mildly warm. Except—

One jar was missing.

That was odd. Had Beaks gotten in somehow? Burne wouldn't put it past the bird to carry a jar out to the clifftop and drop it on the rocks, smashing it open to get the contents. He'd have to ask Gray to tell the bird he could have some jam—they couldn't afford to lose the jars that way.

The floorboards creaked outside the kitchen door.

Burne left the kitchen and entered the deserted hallway. "Gray?" he called. Kitty and Nem were up at the manor helping with the housekeeping, and Linota had gone with them—purportedly to visit with Kate, but actually to enjoy some of the breakfast Kate cooked for the visitors.

The house was silent. Burne went down the hall to their room and found it dark. He'd closed the curtains before he left to block the afternoon sun later in the day.

The door clicked shut behind him. Before he could turn, arms slipped around his chest, holding him fast.

"What are you doing?" Burne asked, trying to twist around, but Gray squashed him and held him in place until he gave up. Whatever Gray was up to, it was better just to go along with it.

"Imagine," Gray whispered, his exhale tickling the back of Burne's ear, "you're ten winters old and your passionate fairy spirit yearns to run free through the forest, but you're trapped underground and all anyone wants you to do is work, day after day."

"Gray, what are—"

"Shhhh. I promised I'd tell you about my first time."

"Oh . . ."

"One day you're tasked with sweeping the corridors in the fairy caverns, and it's *so* boring and you drift off into a daydream and discover the most amazing place—The Land of a Thousand Penises."

"The *what*?"

"The Land of a Thousand Penises."

"No, I heard you, but—"

"Shh. It's a magical land where no one has to work."

"Fairies daydream about magical lands?"

"Everyone daydreams about magical lands."

"But why was it called . . . that?"

"Good question. When Little Gray's sweeping neared the broom closet, he decided to take a break from working. But it wouldn't do to stand idle in the corridor so he hid in the closet. And while he was standing in the dark, touching the handle of the broom, he started feeling something else, down in his trousers, and the longer he touched the broom, the more he felt like his penis was turning hard as wood. And he reached down to touch it and guess what?"

"It was hard as wood?" Burne said, trying not to laugh.

"Exactly! And he put aside the broom and started fondling himself, and that's when he began imagining he was all alone in a new land, and the trees and branches were all shaped like broom handles, only then he realized that wasn't what they were. They were erect penises."

"Ah."

"And the bushes along the narrow path had hands growing on them—"

"Ugh—"

"No, they were nice hands, and as Little Gray passed by, they reached for him, pulling him into their embrace and reaching around his front to stroke him, and it felt . . . so . . . good."

Gray held Burne tight but his fingers were undoing the buttons of Burne's trousers. And—Burne had to admit—the thought of being held prisoner by a thicket of gently stroking hands was seeming less crazy by the second.

"But then," Gray continued, and Burne could tell he paused to lick his lips by the air tickling his ear, "someone passed by the closet, talking loudly, and broke the spell. Young Gray found himself back in the broom closet, holding himself and unsure what to do. He still felt unfulfilled. And he remembered the fairies had harvested the plums that day, and the cook had planned to make plum jam. And it had been the cook passing by, heading away from the kitchens. Gray loved plums because their mottled purply color made him think of—"

"No."

"Mm-hmm," Gray said, and his hand that had weaseled into Burne's underpants reached down and cupped his balls.

    Jane Buehler

"That's why plum jam is your favorite?" Burne said as his head started to spin. Gray's fingers were magic.

"Well, it also tastes delicious. Now stop interrupting. You keep ruining the mood, and this is the good part."

"I can't wait." Gray was holding him in front and rubbing up against his backside, and did Gray have any clothes on? Gray nudged Burne's pants down in front.

"The jars of plum jam glistened in the firelight of the deserted kitchen. They looked perfect for what Little Gray had in mind. He crossed the room and snatched one up. It was still warm and the seal was soft, so he dug into it and pulled out the cork and it came out with a pop, and he pushed his trousers down and stuck himself in."

And Burne's erection slid into something warm and sticky and delightful. He cursed and gave himself up to Gray's ministrations.

Gray held Burne across his belly as he moved the jar of jam up and back. His fingers dug into Burne's ribs and his voice was below Burne's ear, right at the spot that drove him wild when Gray touched it. "It was amazing," Gray purred, "better than anything Little Gray had ever imagined. He'd found himself, there in the dark kitchen with his little shaft deep in plum jam."

Gray moved faster and dug his fingers into Burne's stomach and bit the back of his neck, and Burne jerked and spurted into the jam.

Gray held Burne tight as he panted. Burne tried again to turn but Gray held him back. "It's not over," he insisted, and Burne relented. "As Little Gray stood there, drifting through the stars in bliss, the lanterns flickered to life and the horrible cook was standing in the kitchen doorway. Her callous face sneered with glee at the sight and Little Gray dropped the jam jar, which shattered on the kitchen floor, splattering plum jam across the stones. She pointed at his little, smeary wilting erection and burst into cruel laughter. His pathetic adolescent heart shriveled in shame."

Burne wrapped his hands around Gray's arm. "I'm sorry she ruined it," Burne said.

"That's okay. I stole jam from her all the time after that."

"I'll bet, seeing as how you stole it from me, too."

"You don't mind." Gray was nuzzling his neck again.

"I can't believe you wasted that jam," Burne said softly.

Gray leaned in to whisper, "It's only a waste if you don't let me lick it off."

Burne forced Gray's hold to loosen enough that he could turn to face him. He slid his arms around Gray to pull him close.

"You're getting jam on my clothes," Gray whined.

"You should've taken them off before detaining me."

"I was going to, but you arrived before I was ready."

"I'm sure it's not the first time you've made a mess on your clothes." Burne rubbed his nose against Gray's.

"I hope it's not the last time *you* make a mess on my clothes."

"I love you, Gray."

The jar of jam smacked into the floor and rolled away, miraculously unbroken.

"And every summer when I make plum jam," Burne said, "I hope you'll still be here for me to smear it on."

"I will be," Gray whispered. "I love you, too."

A Note from the Author

DEAR READER,

Thank you so much for reading *The Woodland Stranger*. When I finished drafting the previous book, *The Ocean Girl*, Gray's character kept kicking around my head as if he were after his own story. When I wondered whom I might pair him with, I immediately thought of Burne. He'd been mentioned in the first book of the series as "shy and anxious, not fit to be a guard" and seemed like a good foil for Gray's abundant confidence. He also seemed prone to panic attacks, which was something I wanted to write about. (The symptoms of anxiety Burne experiences in the story are based on my own experience of anxiety.)

I'd also been thinking of how I could "rescue" the half-fairy children who'd supposedly died (what was I thinking writing that?!), and when I imagined Burne deserting the King's Guard and finding the children living in the forest, the story seemed to be writing itself. I felt nervous about being a woman and writing a romance between two men, but I decided to draft it and see what happened. Once I had it written I wanted to follow through with publishing it.

I love writing my cozy fantasy love stories, and I'm hoping other book lovers might enjoy reading them. If you did like the story, I would truly appreciate if you'd leave a review online to help other readers with similar interests find the book.

I'm hoping to have the next book in the Sylvania series, *The Fire Apprentice*, out in 2025. It takes us back to Woods Rest to find out what happens to Jane, one of the "widows" reunited with her daughter in *The Forest Bride*. You can subscribe to my email list at https://janebuehler.com for an email when the new book is available. I send only a few emails each year so I won't crowd your inbox. When you subscribe, I'll send a link to bonus material (including Kate's recipe for Easy Plum Jam!). The email list is also one way I give away advance review copies.

The "Connect" page on my website lists all my online platforms and author pages. And you can email me at jane@janebuehler.com. Thanks again for reading!

Sincerely,

Acknowledgments

I'M PERPETUALLY GRATEFUL TO ALL my friends and family, even the ones who don't read romance novels ☺. Through the years I've always had people to turn to and talk to, which is a great thing.

I have two steadfast beta readers, Adrienne M. and Angie M., who always give me such helpful feedback. I couldn't do it without you ladies! Thanks also to Danielle H. for reading a draft and making suggestions, and for giving me the nudge I needed to deal with some scenes. Thanks to Robert G. for being willing to beta read. And thanks to Erel T. for reading something different and helping me with a lot of last-minute fixes.

Christy R., Erin C., and Grace C. are always available when I email with questions like "Which tagline works better?" and "Which ad grabs your attention?" I'm glad you're on my team!

A special thanks to Drew Hubbard at Pride Reads (https://www.pridereads.co.uk) for his sensitive and thoughtful feedback.

And finally, as always I'm grateful to work with Kelly Urgan as my editor (https://www.editegrity.com) and Cory Marie Podielski as my cover designer (https://podielski.com).

About the Author

EMILY JANE BUEHLER WAS ADRIFT for many years before realizing she wanted to work with words. She published two nonfiction books—one on the science and craft of baking bread, the other a memoir of her bicycle trip from New Jersey to Oregon—before venturing into fiction. She now writes cozy fantasy romance: lighthearted stories that focus on a protagonist finding their courage and happiness, as opposed to plots with a lot of fighting and darkness. She also copyedits (mostly science papers) and teaches bread-making classes.

Emily lives in Hillsborough, North Carolina, with a bossy cat named Coco. Her favorite things include letters sent through the mail, made-in-the-USA knee socks, and very dark fair-trade chocolate. She is passionate about living waste free and supporting local businesses.

Emily publishes fiction using her middle name, Jane.

www.ingramcontent.com/pod-product-compliance
Lightning Source LLC
Chambersburg PA
CBHW020756190726
48285CB00006B/2060